To: Mar

Thanks so much
for always supporting
me in my dreams!! :)

T D

War Child

J. D. Wilkins

abbott press

Original cover design by Ben Cuppage

Abbott Press books may be ordered through booksellers or by contacting:

Abbott Press
1663 Liberty Drive
Bloomington, IN 47403
www.abbottpress.com
Phone: 1 (866) 697-5310

ISBN: 978-1-4582-1533-8 (sc)
ISBN: 978-1-4582-1535-2 (hc)
ISBN: 978-1-4582-1534-5 (e)

Library of Congress Control Number: 2015901473

Printed in the United States of America.

Abbott Press rev. date: 07/09/2015

To my biggest fans:

Dan and Emily Holt, who owned the original story, before any editor had ever seen it.

Gwen MacMillan, who read the book so fast I barely had time to leave the house before picking it up again.

My mom, who always supported me and pushed me to follow my dreams.

Amy Cuppage, who became my biggest supporter in 2012 after the world didn't end. And became Amy Wilkins in 2014.

Cassandra Smith, my fellow writer in crime, who inspired me to never give up and never surrender.

Acknowledgments

My thanks to the people who made this dream possible!

Amy Wilkins
Dan and Emily Holt
Cassandra Smith
Melanie Hoski
Kortnie and Derek Thorton
Kylen Ferrett
Mallory Stephen Dreyer
Nicole Baker
Marlene Cartmill
Kyle Dafrosh McBain
Laura Avalos
Gabrial Hounsome
Leya Vanderniet
Caitltn Emptage
Kara Boekee
Nicole Boekee
Richard Apple
Sue Thorton
Susan Trombley
Tasha Cardwell
Gwen Macmillan
Adair Jeffery
Joshua Blake
Jessica Webb
Amy Cuppage
Jamie Robitaille
Audra-Lee-Zeats
Dorothy Stevenson
Diane Cuppage
Joel Smith
Lindsay Barden
Christina Shelswell
Ted and Bonnie Wilkins

Prologue

He would die! He would die for the trail of pain he had caused. My muscles tensed. Our eyes locked. The fog began to rise around us in the wreckage of the battlefield. His piercing eyes tried to penetrate my soul, but he would be disappointed; I would not be manipulated by those eyes anymore. I had sworn to myself that I would win this battle, and win it I would. There was no backing down. Not even death would stop me. There was no "trying," no "doing my best"; there was him, and there was me. And I would *not* lose. This time, on this night, I would do as I had said I would.

I charged hard and fast with no regard for safety. I was exhausted, irritable, and a whole lot of just plain pissed off. His cautious approach would be his downfall. As our swords collided, the clang shattered the dense, foggy silence. As we pressed through the haze, locked in the battle of the ages, our feet maneuvered adroitly around the many dead. Energy waned with each clash of our swords. He swung high, and the blade narrowly missed my head. Wheeling around, I struck at his legs, but his lightning reflexes would not permit such an attack. Back and forth we struck out at each other, yet to no avail. Strength. Desire. Will. Determination. Slipping away. My might was all but spent, yet my body pushed on. It was as though some inner willpower drove me beyond my ability.

We fought as if eternity itself hinged on the outcome. Both of us were pressed to our limit, yet neither backed down. I felt the tip of his sword graze my arm; I knew I was cut, but the pain was a distant enemy. Rage welled within me, and I drove hard at him. He tried to block my blade yet merely changed its trajectory. The flat of the blade slammed off his temple, staggering him. In raw, vicious battle we both fought on, postponing the end. But I smiled to myself; he was just as worn down as I.

My body should have given out long ago, but that force fueled me and drove me forward. The glow of dawn began to seep through the mist, something he had yet to notice. As the blazing sun burst above the valley ridge, he covered his eye. His moment of blindness was my moment of victory. Planting my foot hard into his chest, I sent him flying backward. I could have killed him in that moment, but I was not finished with him. My case had not yet been stated, and before he passed from this life, he had to know!

As his bloody body hit the ground, he lost his grip on his sword, which hurtled away into the fog. Calmly I walked over and looked down at his limp body, his eyes half shut, blood pouring from multiple wounds. I smiled. I pointed my sword at his throat; he would know he had lost, that the death all around us was for nothing.

"Your time has come. The battle is *mine*," I gloated.

As though unaware of his imminent demise, he spoke with composure. "The battle has always been yours, Joshua."

All my rage, all my anger, everything that fueled me, for a single moment was calmed by that simple phrase. But my need for vengeance was too strong.

"Explain." I pressed my sword dangerously close to his throat.

"Joshua." The way he said my name brought a calm within me; even my breathing became steady. "No one can fight your battle except you." His eyes narrowed. "The battle is *yours* to conquer."

"*What* are you talking about?"

"Joshua, you have been letting deception fill your mind. *He* is a liar." His eyes were pained and welled with tears as he spoke. But I would not allow his games. I had seen this before. I'd seen how his kind manipulated those around them. I'd seen the pain they caused.

"*He* has always been my friend. Never has he lied to me. It was he who helped me see what was really true."

A mixture of compassion and fire for the truth laced his words. "*No*, Joshua, he poisoned your mind!"

"You know nothing!" I cursed, nicking the skin of his throat with the tip of my sword.

"You never saw it! You weren't able to, but I was there. I was there every night he filled your mind with hate."

"*You were never there*!" I screamed.

"He is a master of deception, filling your mind with hatred, so when the moment came, he would turn it against me and my kind. You must trust me, Joshua!" he pleaded with me, but I had heard enough. Enough of his silver-tongued lies. I would silence his voice once and for all.

"*My* name is Josh, and *you're* the liar! You had your chance. You had your chance to save me. You had a thousand of them. *But you left me for dead!*" Gaining some composure, I tossed my sword aside and grabbed him by the scruff of his neck. With the strength of pent-up rage, I threw his bleeding frame against the rock face. "If you cared so much, why leave me? Why not take your army and rescue me? Why leave me for dead in such an 'evil' place? You had your chance. You missed your chance. And now you'll die for it."

I raised my fist. Only a moment left before his death, a few seconds and it would all be over. I would finally end the agony. All those years of pain would come to an end right *now*.

Time slowed. The world around seemed to cease to exist. My brain started to whirl, thoughts passing through at a million miles a second.

All those years of pain? Did I even know what that meant anymore? Did I even know ...? It was that moment that shattered my reality. The torment. The flashes. That single moment that changed everything. It felt like reliving my entire life in the snap of a finger.

It came back to me in an instant, right from the beginning. Who knew life would come to this? And who knew that it would all come from that moment?

I let that night fill my mind. I remembered the stillness and security of my backyard. I could feel home becoming more than just a memory, almost like I was back there again. I never knew I could hunger for it this much. I don't think I knew what I had. Thinking back, there was nothing special about that night. Nothing separated it as unique or different. Strange, how moments before everything changes, life is so normal.

Chapter 1

Child of Destiny

The battleground around me faded completely, and I found myself back in my childhood room, kneeling beside my bed, saying my nightly prayers.

"Enough of that." I rather hated the whole prayer deal—kind of dumb if you asked me. But with my prayers said, allowance kept flowing, and that was enough for me.

I jumped between my race car sheets. My eyelids became heavy, and the curtains of the day's show closed. Sleep swept me off to another world, an eleven-year-old world of candy, games, and adventure. Best of all, there were no parents, teachers, or all those sort of rule-making people. This was my world, and no one but I made the rules here.

My sleep was short-lived on that night, though. Something woke me with a snap. I scanned the room. Nothing was there. But I knew I heard something or saw something. I crept slowly across the cold hardwood floor, trying to avoid the creaks with every step. Something drew me to the window. I didn't know what it was, but I could feel the pull. My heartbeat quickened. The palms of my hands got sweatier as I got closer to the window, until finally my nose was pressed against the glass. But I saw nothing out there, just the lawn and the forest on a cold November night. Still, I was sure something had interrupted my dreams.

As I turned to go back to bed, a blinding light flooded the room. Before my eyes could adjust, there was another flash. The light was coming from the forest. I grabbed my flashlight and airsoft gun and ran downstairs. After throwing on my rubber boots, I squeezed out the back door, opening it only a little to prevent the loud squeak it tended to make. As the chill air hit my pajamas, I hesitated. I could see a dim glow coming from the forest behind my house. The woods where we live, just north of New York City, were awesome for daytime adventures. Night was a whole different story. I took one last look at the door behind me, took a deep breath, and made the choice. I knew that if I got caught, it would be my rear end that suffered the consequences, but I had to know.

I took off across the lawn, the flashlight dimly lighting my way. Soon the grass, in desperate need of a cut, turned into forest. It was better not to think about it—about all the things that could eat me, maul me, bite me, kidnap me ...

"Seriously. Stop thinking about it," I whispered to myself.

My feet carried me around trees, under low-hanging branches, and over stumps like it was my day job. I turned off the light when I saw the glowing light ahead. It seemed to dim and brighten like a dying flashlight. I had the uncomfortable sense that the light was alive, as though it was breathing, steady and calm.

I was crawling now, almost reaching a large knoll, where I was certain the glowing creature would be waiting for me. I crept to the top of the hill and peered over the edge. I should have run—I really should have—but my body refused to move. Everything inside was screaming at me to run. But the scene below was too entrancing to merely slip away. It was both horrifying and amazing.

Chapter 2

Sacrifice

There at the bottom of the hill stood a swirling mass of shadows; I could make out maybe fifty creatures. Black as night, their bodies seemed to give off darkness like a fog around them. The first thing I noticed was their eyes, though I tried not to look. But I couldn't help it—I was drawn in. They were not unlike human eyes in shape, but they were glowing red, the most frightening red I'd ever seen. Then there was the sheer size of the things. The smallest was easily the size of a large man, and the biggest had to be eight feet tall. Their black leathery skin was bulging with muscles, and massive, dragon-like wings sticking out of their backs arched above their heads and then flowed all the way to the ground. Each being had a long black tail swinging back and forth like an angry cat's. Their hands looked generally like human hands but with the addition of sharp, knifelike tips at the end of each finger. At least that's what they looked like to me. It was a little hard to tell from that distance, which I would have liked to have been even farther.

In the center of this mass of swirling darkness stood a man—well, mostly a man. He was of average height, with short blond hair and burning yellow eyes, as if someone had lit a campfire in each. He wore white and gold armor but no helmet. In his right hand was a huge sword; I couldn't tell you exact details, but it had a white handle with crystals at all three points. The blade was of metal and sharp. Last, but definitely not least, were the wings. Unlike his creepy dark company, he did not have leathery black dragon wings. No, he had angel wings, like giant eagle's wings but solid white, first coming up above his shoulders and then flowing in perfect form all the way down to the ground. He stood there alone and fearless among such a frightening and large group of what I could only imagine, if Mr. Eagle Wings was an angel, were demons.

As I watched from above, the largest of the group of demons stepped forward. The angel did not flinch, nor did fear cross his proud face. The demon spat at the angel, but a peculiar thing happened. Before the flying wad of spit reached the angel, it boiled and steamed away. The angel smirked at the demon and spoke.

"What comes from your mouth, Lasnek, is pure evil, and I will have none of it upon me."

"What comes out of your mouth is pure foolishness," the demon Lasnek bit back. "Bow before me, Haldel, and I will allow you to walk away with your life." As he spoke, the shimmer of serrated teeth caught my eye.

"I bow to one, and that is all. Do with me what you will." Haldel spoke with complete calm, never once breaking eye contact.

"Fine," Lasnek sneered. "Don't bow. Simply show me where the boy is. Let me take what I have come to claim, and you may live to die another day."

The pack of demons became restless at Lasnek's offer to release their prey.

"Stop speaking. Your words waste my time. You may torture me a thousand years, and kill me a thousand times, yet I will never reveal what I know to the likes of you." Haldel's words held such power that the pack took a step back—all except Lasnek, who moved in closer.

"You will suffer for your insolence!" As Lasnek snapped, his eyes seemed to explode with fire. He leaned back as though a great creature were attempting to crawl through his throat, and when he opened his mouth, a great ball of red flames burst forth, engulfing Haldel.

I gasped at the sight but quickly closed my mouth and ducked lower to the ground. I could just see a few of the pack peering around to see what had made the sound. But they thought nothing more of it and went back to enjoying watching the burning angel.

Haldel's white wings surged open, throwing off the flames. For a moment he stood, wings at their full reach. Again, the pack shifted backward, and even Lasnek took a small step in retreat.

"As I already stated, what comes from your mouth is pure evil, and I will have none of it upon me. I thought at least a small portion of your wisdom would have been retained. I was mistaken. You know, Lasnek, there was once a time I looked up to you." Haldel spoke with a slight shake of the head.

"Funny, you still look up to me, and I still look down upon you, as always," came Lasnek's weak reply.

"Hmm, yes, Lasnek. Once again you prove your ever-reaching intellect," Haldel returned with a roll of the eyes.

"Fine. If you will not speak, then prepare for death, old friend." Lasnek's patience had reached its end. "Prepare to fight, fool."

"I would consider it an honor to be labeled a fool for my master, but tell me, Lasnek, whose fool are you?" Haldel sympathetically shook his head. "If you wish to destroy me, then do so. But I will not waste my time fighting you." Calmly, Haldel lowered his sword and stood back up, empty-handed. With his hands at his side, palms forward, he looked to the skies, opening himself to the slaughter. "Do what you have come to do."

"Have it your way." Lasnek's disappointment was great at the thought of a battle without glory. He raised his great clawed hand in the air, preparing to plunge it down into Haldel's heart. I could feel something bubbling inside of me, something, no matter how hard I tried, I could not suppress. Just as Lasnek released his claw, I leapt to my feet and screamed, "*Noooo*!"

My heart decided this would be a perfect time to stop beating and just relax. All eyes were on the little weaponless boy at the top of the hill. What probably lasted only seconds seemed to go on for hours. Lasnek looked me right in the eye and smiled. Then he spouted something off that just sounded weird.

"He shall stand upon a hill and scream for the one he knows not." Lasnek smiled. "*Get the boy*!"

As Lasnek spoke, Haldel dropped to the ground, grabbed his sword, and rose back up to the fight. There was no calm in him, just sheer control and fury. The sword engulfed itself in white flames.

"*Run, Joshua, run*!" Haldel yelled to me, but my feet were rooted, and this is where I was apparently going to stay. Lasnek leapt the from group headed directly for me. As he did, the group of demons converged on Haldel, but a burst of bright light erupted from him and knocked everyone back. Even Lasnek, who wasn't facing Haldel, lost his footing and collided with a tree, splintering the trunk with his force. My eyes refocused on the battle below. An impossible fight, fifty against one. But Haldel's movements were like smoke twisting and turning in the wind. Not a single part of his body was safe. Everything became a weapon. The lucky ones found their end by the edge of his blade. But others found their faces crushed by his fists. I suddenly wished my parents had desensitized me with violent movies. One after the other, demons fell, cleaved in half, skulls crushed, limbs broken, and all causing my stomach to turn.

Soon I discovered the error of my ways; my mind had been so focused on the battle below that I had not seen Lasnek walk up right beside me. His massive claws wrapped around my tiny body and lifted me off the ground.

"Keep your mouth shut, boy." He really didn't need to say a thing. My mouth, limbs, and heart had yet to find their proper uses. With a snap of his leathery dragon wings, he lifted off into the air. He was shaky and I wasn't sure he was even going to be able to fly, yet we stayed off the ground. With my eyes still focused on the battle, I watched as Haldel held the last standing demon by the neck. He looked up to see us taking off; with a flick of his wrist he broke the last demon's neck and shot into the air. Silent as a bird of prey, he soared toward us. His whole body was glowing, and as he got closer, the night sky began to light up.

"Useless guards!" Lasnek broke my focus. "I'll finish this myself."

With that Lasnek dove hard and fast at the ground, and the wind lashed at my face as we sped downward. Haldel followed suit, behind us. We lurched to a halt as we smashed into the ground. I was tossed aside, finally stopping at the bottom of a large oak. Lasnek rolled to a stop, picked himself off the ground, and dusted himself off as he stood. Then I saw it. The clearing lit up like daytime as Haldel came flying in twice as fast as Lasnek, but he threw his wings out at the last second and slowed to a stop only an inch above the ground, barely even unsettling any dust.

"Give up the boy, Lasnek; you have no idea what you are messing with!" Haldel's calm demeanor was completely gone. Although still controlled, he was menacing.

"I know exactly what I'm messing with, and that is why I was sent." Lasnek smiled arrogantly. "Unlike you, I know what happened two thousand years ago."

"Your knowledge lacks the wisdom to understand." Haldel raised his sword, and the white flames reappeared. "Prepare for the end, Lasnek!"

Lasnek was not afraid but arrogantly raised his hand in front of himself. A red glow emanated from it, and a second later red flames shot straight up and straight down. When they cleared, I saw a weapon meant for evil and pain. It was like a freaky, evil version of the trident from *The Little Mermaid*, but instead of shiny and gold, it was midnight black. And instead of having just three sharp points, it had three sharp points with four little blood-red barbs protruding from the tip of each. Not a weapon meant for death, but a great deal of pain. Along the shaft of the evil trident was some form of writing, in a language I did not understand.

With no warning, Lasnek thrust his trident toward Haldel, but Haldel dodged his strike, narrowly avoiding the lethal barbs. Without a moment to think, Haldel slashed at the trident and knocked it to the ground, then lunged at Lasnek, burying his sword in Lasnek's stomach. Lasnek barely flinched, though; he retaliated with a fist directly to Haldel's face, blasting him backward through the air. Haldel slammed into the trunk of a tree and splintered the opposite side. Slowly he got back to his feet, as Lasnek pulled the sword from his stomach. For a moment he examined it arrogantly, but with a flash the sword turned white-hot and burned his hand. He screamed and dropped the blade.

Haldel took his moment and dove for Lasnek's weapon; he grabbed the trident and struck Lasnek's chest. Lasnek stumbled backward, looking as though he was withholding many screams, and he wrenched the trident out of his chest. He tried to stand but crumpled back down and dropped the trident. Haldel walked toward him, and the moment he was within reach, Lasnek launched to his feet, grabbed Haldel by the neck, and lifted him off the ground. It seemed as though the battle was over, that Haldel had made his fatal error, but something in his eyes told me he wasn't finished. The moon's light reflected from a miniature version of his sword. Just a tiny little dagger, small enough to hide in one's pocket but, I was sure, lethal if used correctly. As Lasnek squeezed harder, the light of Haldel began to diminish. Haldel didn't have time to hesitate; he swung the knife, but just before it reached its destination he simply disintegrated. Into a cloud of light-blue, glowing dust, which dissipated almost instantly. His tiny dagger was left behind, and it bounced across the ground, coming to a stop at my feet. I looked at Lasnek as he collected his trident, melting it back into his hand. The thought crossed my mind to pick up the dagger and fight him, but I knew it would be a losing battle. One day, I told myself, one day I would. I slid the dagger into my pants pocket and tucked the handle under my shirt, hoping it wouldn't stab me.

Lasnek now stood directly in front of me. His glowing red eyes burned into my plain old hazel ones. A smile crossed his ugly mug, and the next thing I knew, the back of his claw struck my face. The lights began to shut off, and the last thing I remember is floating up into the sky. This time I would not have dreams of candy and freedom from rules, but of this curious winged man named Haldel being slaughtered right before my eyes.

Chapter 3

The Wrong Idea

My eyes shot open as an icy breeze rushed up my spine. I could feel the cold of stone beneath my body, and the air was very damp. As I sat up I scanned the room, or should I say cave? I sat on a narrow path that dropped off on either side of me. About twenty feet from either drop-off was a stone wall, not like a natural cave, but carved and chiseled. Along the walls were torches, all burning very low. As my eyes followed the carved walls up the path, I saw a large throne at the end. Surrounding it, save for the path, was a sheer drop. I rose slowly to my feet, making sure I had my balance. The path was actually about five feet wide, but with no railing and no bottom to be seen, five feet seemed rather narrow. I walked toward the throne, but before I reached it a muffled cry rang out from somewhere below. Though it was just a faraway echo, it sent shivers down my spine.

I ran my hands along the throne and only then realized it was not just stone, but marble. Smooth as glass, with markings engraved into the armrests. They looked similar to what was written on Lasnek's trident. That was when it struck me, Lasnek and Haldel, I had been in the presence of an angel and demons. I spun around, suddenly dizzy. I flopped onto the throne, knowing right away it was probably an unwise choice. I didn't know much, but I knew that demons were not a good thing, and I was in their lair. My heart started to race as I looked frantically for an exit. There: at the opposite end of the path, a set of large, wooden, arched doors. I sprang to my feet and ran as fast as my legs would take me. I was halfway down the path when both doors swung open. On the other side stood a man. It was hard to see what he looked like, because the light silhouetted him. Another figure, towering above, could be only one creature: Lasnek.

Lasnek stepped forward, saw I was trying to escape, and bolted toward me. I scrambled backward, not certain of where I had to go, and lost my footing. I was now 100 percent certain that five feet was not nearly enough. As I tried to stop myself, the edge drew nearer and nearer. It was too late, I was too far gone, and I closed my eyes, took a deep breath, and readied myself to scream. The wind was knocked out of me when my back hit something solid. I opened my eyes and could now see that I was floating on nothingness, but a nothingness that sure didn't feel much like nothingness. I slid back to the path, only to be met by Lasnek's towering form. With a gleam in his eye, he reached his massive clawed hand down to pick me up.

"Enough, Lasnek!" the man commanded. His voice was strong, yet calming as well. "Leave the boy alone; he is our guest, yet you treat him as our prisoner."

"The boy was seeking to escape!" Lasnek growled.

"Because you treat him as a prisoner, which he is not." The man pushed Lasnek aside and looked down at me. "Josh." He paused. "May I call you Josh?"

"Whatever," was the best response I could come up with.

"Josh, you are our guest, though I must apologize for the means in which we 'invited' you here." The man smiled. "We have been searching for you for a very long time."

"Okay," I eloquently replied.

"Are you nervous?"

"Nervous? Why would I be nervous?" *I was only kidnapped by a demon, who killed an angel, who killed fifty demons, and then I was brought to a dark, dank cave with a creepy throne and dim candles and eerie echo screams and ... shall I go on?*

The man looked at me as if reading my very thoughts; he snapped his fingers, and the torches erupted, burning brighter than I had ever seen fire before. In the instant illumination I could now see that the walls were made of gold and silver and marble. The room was more beautiful than anything I'd ever seen. The throne was black, but not creepy black. And only now could I see that the drop-offs were not drop-offs at all, but glass floors. A million-mile drop below, but with glass to keep you safe.

"Now I'm nervous!" I was thoroughly amazed by the room, but the creepy man, that I could now see was very well dressed and looked much like a businessman, read my mind. I'll admit, though, he didn't look scary at all. He was clean cut and well dressed and seemed very proper, like an Englishman, but without the accent. There was something a little odd about him, though. He looked like a white guy, but his skin was dark at the same time. It wasn't as if he'd been tanning, though—just that his skin seemed shadowed.

"I apologize. It can be a little unsettling when I do that." He smiled, which somehow comforted me. "I did not read your mind, just your face and eyes. You would be amazed what people say with their faces and eyes. Josh, you don't need to be nervous; you are perfectly safe here."

I did not respond, merely looked at Lasnek.

"Lasnek!" The man's voice was overpowering. He did not yell but spoke with absolute confidence. "Leave! Your job here is finished. Please retrieve Haslo for me." Lasnek grunted and left, head held proud and high. With the crack of the big wooden door closing, silence fell again. "Lasnek is like a guard dog, useful but not to be played with. There are others like him here, but there are also those not unlike yourself. Haslo, for instance, whom you will meet soon." I stared at him, refusing to break eye contact. He was a man in league with demons; nothing could be less trustworthy. "May I tell you a story, Josh?"

"Okay."

"Millions of years ago, before humanity was even a thought, two races ruled the universe, each with an equal share. For millennia they ruled with justice and peace. The more densely populated of the two races were called Iyarians, and the other race was known as Cahirians. Neither had a king of their own race, so both sides looked to the one rumored to have created all things as their ruler. But one day that all changed, for an inferior race was born. A race you know as humanity, your own race. The Great King sent both races to watch over and help humans grow, to teach you and guide you. But the supervising races ran into a problem. The Iyarians did not believe humanity could handle the truth of the universe, so they locked humanity in a box, away from the truth. The Cahirians had other plans, but the Great King did not agree. So in secret they opened the eyes of the blind and sheltered, and showed the Iyarians that humans could indeed be told the truth. For this the Cahirian race was cursed for all eternity. Their once beautiful forms were stripped away, and what you see of Lasnek now is what they have become."

"Um ..." I replied, vaguely remembering the story from Genesis. Snakes and apples and curses. Dark stuff, I'm sure.

"Josh, that is the day the war began. The Iyarians, or as you better know them, angels, have been fighting to regain control of humanity, to again push them back into a world of ignorance and imprisonment. While the Cahirian race or, as most better know them, demons, an unfortunate name, have been trying to bring freedom and understanding to mankind for thousands of years."

This time I let my eyes do the talking. I gave the nicely dressed man the blankest I-don't-know-or-care-about-anything-you're-telling-me-right-now stare I could possibly muster. And it was a success.

"I'm sorry," he began. "I guess this is probably a lot to take in. I'll tell you what, stay here with us a few days. See a world you would never see. My words are meaningless unless my actions prove what I say to be true." He simply smiled for a moment. I thought of my mom and dad, worried sick about me. They would be panicked when they woke up. Plus, I'd be grounded for a thousand years. "What if I said your parents would never even know you were gone? You could stay here a while, then go back, and no one would ever be the wiser."

"Really?" I was curious now. "You can do that?"

"Well, not I, but I know of a few who could make it seem as though you'd never left." I thought a moment, not sure if it would be worth it, but my curiosity was bubbling over. Mostly I just wanted to know if he could or not. Even if I *was* risking eternal grounding. Finally I put out my hand, as if I were an eleven-year-old businessman.

"You've got yourself a deal, Mr. ..."

"You may call me The Curator."

"Well, that's a stupid name," I giggled. "I can't go calling someone that."

"That is what everyone calls me."

"Yeah, well." I thought for a moment and finally came up with a proper name. "For a few days you'll be Mr. Curry." I smiled. "And once I'm gone, you can have your stupid name back."

"Mr. Curry it is." He finally reached out and took my hand; it was a strange feeling. I suddenly felt a little more carefree about the whole thing. I wasn't really sure why, but what harm could a few days bring? I'd be home again before I knew it, my parents would be none the wiser, and what the heck—it would be cool!

A creak caught our attention. We turned to face the door. I had expected to see Lasnek walk through, so what I did see instead surprised me quite a bit. Such a misplaced thing, in such a strange world.

Chapter 4

A Friend

There in the doorway stood a small boy, and by small I mean about the same size as me. He smiled and walked over to us. As I looked up at Mr. Curry, he too smiled at me.

"Josh, meet Haslo. Haslo, meet Josh." Haslo, the curiously named boy, looked very similar to Mr. Curry, with the same strangely shadowed skin, but his eyes were so different. Mr. Curry's eyes were nearly black. Haslo's eyes were bright blue. Extremely bright blue. They were, unlike Mr. Curry's eyes, actually kind of creepy, but who was I to judge?

"'Sup, man!" Haslo said, like he was trying to be a little too gangsta for his plaid shorts and blue T-shirt. I laughed anyway.

"Not much. You?" I replied.

"I'll leave you two to have your adventures. If you ever need me, Josh, my office is just around the corner. Haslo can show you around and get you familiar with the compound." Mr. Curry smiled and headed toward the door.

"Thanks!" I called after him.

"You're quite welcome, Josh. Enjoy your stay," he replied without turning to face me.

"Enough of this crap, let's go do something fun!" Haslo said and turned to leave as well. I didn't move for a moment. I had yet to take it all in. The madness of it all, the story Mr. Curry had told me, the offer to stay here. I took a deep breath and smiled. What the heck.

"Coming?" Haslo tempted me.

"Sure am!" I said and followed him out.

I can honestly say I have no idea where the time went, between video games, TV, and whatever food we wanted, cooked by the nicest lady ever, Larasa. Haslo showed me around, but there was no way we'd ever see the whole compound. It was huge! And I think the entire thing was underground, because I never saw a single window. After the tour and games and all sorts of shenanigans, Haslo took me back to a room they said I could use while I was here. The door opened and my jaw dropped. Not really a kid-style room, but it was freaking awesome! A huge four-poster bed with red blankets, and a wood dresser with a mirror above it, and all lit by torches. Apparently they did not receive the safety-first training.

"And there are tons of clothes in the drawer that should fit you. Plus there's a closet over there"—Haslo pointed to the end of the room opposite the dresser—"that has fancier stuff. But like you'll need that!"

"This is sick!" I replied.

"Man, everything is sick about this place!" Haslo laughed, and I suddenly realized how much he reminded me of my best friend, Aniece. For a minute I started to miss home, Mom, Dad, and my friends Aniece, and David. But hey, it was only a few days, and then I'd be back with them. "Stop being crazy, Joshua, enjoy it, have your adventure. And stop thinking of home. You'll be back to all that soon enough," I said softly to myself.

"Huh?" Apparently Haslo had heard.

"Oh, um, nothing." My cheeks flushed.

"Well, I'm off to sleep. I'll see ya in the morning, Josh." Haslo closed the door behind him, and I was alone. I jumped onto the bed and felt a sharp pain in my leg. I had completely forgotten about the stupid dagger, and how on earth it hadn't stabbed me yet that day I didn't know. Quickly I pulled it out of my pocket and tossed it aside.

After a minute I realized I probably shouldn't leave it there. Everyone here seemed pretty cool, but I was sure they would not be okay with an eleven-year-old frolicking around with a razor-sharp dagger. Slipping off the bed, I headed over to the dresser with the dagger in hand. Opening drawers until I found the sock drawer, I dropped it inside and slid it closed.

The day's events had tired me out, and it was time I went to bed, but as I looked up into the mirror, I noticed I had a black eye. Stupid Lasnek, what an oaf. A second thing caught my eye, something carved on the top of the desk. I could not read it, but it was a phrase, maybe in the same language I'd seen on Lasnek's trident and on the throne I'd seen earlier that day. I wished I could read it. Realizing I would not learn to read a language by staring at the letters, I hopped into bed and pulled the blankets over myself. Feeling the tug of sleep, I allowed myself to slip calmly into the world of dreams.

It all started as quite normal, as we relived the highlights of the day, good food, adventure, even a little of the stranger beginnings of the day, but it all slowed as I sat in front of the TV. The image seemed to blur between stations; nothing actually made sense, but I was glued to it nonetheless. I could feel it pulling me in, and I did nothing to fight it, just gave myself fully to the fuzz of nothingness. Then with a crash Haldel smashed through the door behind me, sending the door flipping through the air. He dove over the couch where I sat and with one great slash of his mighty sword destroyed the TV. Sparks flew in all directions as he spun and looked directly in my eyes. He was about to speak, when from nowhere Lasnek's trident speared Haldel through the side of his ribcage. I watched as Lasnek walked over to Haldel to retrieve his weapon, but the moment the fire went out in Haldel's eyes, my body violently jerked out of bed!

I was awake! What a crazy dream.

"Ready for more excitement?" Haslo was standing right there, and I almost screamed. Haslo laughed, realizing he had freaked me out. "A perfect, good morning!"

"Give me a minute. I gotta brush my teeth and stuff," I said, dragging myself out of bed.

"No need!" Haslo said.

"Um, I dunno about you, but unlike most kids, I like clean teeth." I shook my head.

"No, I mean, while you're here, you don't *need* to brush your teeth." He smiled, showing off his pearly whites. "They just are always clean!"

I checked my teeth, not believing him, but to my surprise, no fuzz! Next I checked my breath: minty fresh!

"Okay, what the crap? That's just creepy!" I glared at Haslo.

"Don't ask me, man; it's just the way it goes!" he laughed.

As I walked out of the room, a strange glow caught my attention. But Haslo was dragging me forward, and I would not be able to discover the origin of the light. The next few days were generally the same: eat amazing food, do whatever I wanted all day, sleep in my sweet room, and dream of Lasnek murdering Haldel. That last part was a serious bummer, and it wasn't even like it was a repetitive dream: it was different every night. The only thing that was the same was Haldel showing up and Lasnek murdering him. But day three had come, and although I was loving it here, my vacation was coming to an end.

Chapter 5

The Eternity Door

I awoke in the morning and put back on the pajamas I had arrived in. The clothing here didn't belong to me, and I wasn't about to start stealing from Mr. Curry. I looked in the mirror one last time and saw that my black eye was a nice, shiny purple now. It was probably the worst it was going to get. And even though Mr. Curry might have convinced my parents that I was never gone, I doubted I would have the same ability to explain the nice shiner I got. Either way, my vacation in Wonderland was over, and home was calling my name. I left the room and headed toward Mr. Curry's office, which I soon realized I had no idea how to get to. The complex was ... complex.

I wandered through the halls, just getting more and more lost, until finally I came through a door into a courtyard. It was not outside, but it made you feel as though you were. There were grass and flowers and large rocks. It wasn't huge, maybe the size of a basketball court, but it was amazing. If you looked up, you could almost feel the warmth of the "sun" on your face. I wondered if there would be stars and a moon at nighttime.

I followed the path through to the other side of the room, finding another door like the rest, but a little more green than white. Peering through it, I could tell this was a whole different part of the complex. Maybe even a military part. It had the military-green feel to it all. Knowing that was not the direction of Mr. Curry's office, I turned back the other way, but about halfway back through the courtyard I noticed another path, much smaller than the main one.

"What the heck. One last adventure can't hurt." Famous last words.

I wandered down the path, soon coming upon a very different door, old and wooden. Its boards had split, and the crystal handle was yellowed from time and use. I made sure no one was watching, and with that, I turned the handle and pulled. The door let out a great squeal. Checking one last time to make sure I was still alone, I slid into the dimness beyond and closed the squeaky door behind me.

I was in a hallway unlike the other hallways; it was more like a cave. The walls were lined with old wooden doors, each having its own yellowed crystal handle. I tried to open the first but found it locked. Second, third, fourth—all locked. As I walked down the hall, I checked the odd door, but each was locked. Hundreds of wooden doors! What on earth could be behind them all? Soon, though, the little wooden doors didn't matter anymore, because there was only one door that mattered. In front of me, at the end of the hall, was a huge set of wooden doors. Unlike the rest, this set was in perfect condition. No cracking, no fading, no chipping, and no rusted hinges. For sure, this door would be locked like the rest, but as my hand spun the polished crystal handle, the doors broke loose and swung open as though they were as light as air.

Now, in this moment, I felt as if I were in a movie like *The Lord of the Rings* or something. Most awesome thing I'd ever seen! The room was easily the size of a football field. The ceiling had to be a hundred feet tall, with sixteen white marble pillars keeping it from crashing down, eight down either side. Each was about twenty feet from the outside walls, which looked like a mix between white marble and the stone that the cave had been dug from. In between the pillars against the outside walls were pictures, probably ten feet by ten feet, of sandy beaches, beautiful buildings, people enjoying life, and many other themes. I looked back to the ceiling to admire the chandeliers that hung about thirty feet above. Each held hundreds of candles, and thousands of crystals, sending the most brilliant light around this massive room. But something else caught my eye. At the far end of the room stood the largest set of doors I'd ever seen. The topmost point of the arched doors was just below the lowest point of the chandelier. I hurried my pace so I could see it closer, maybe even touch it or open it and see what could possibly lie on the other side. When I was just a stone's throw away, I stopped, able to see the whole door without moving my eyes. Mostly gold was what the door was made of, or at least that's what it looked like. The shiniest silver swirls streaked this way and that. And midway up the door was a word I could not read. It formed an arch from one door to the next. There was also a keyhole that I think I could have put my fist through, about five feet from the floor. But there were no handles anywhere on the door. Maybe they were like saloon doors, and they would swing open both ways.

On either side of the door was a picture. On the right was simply a picture of the door I was just looking at. But it was open, and walking toward the opening were a man and a woman, holding hands, smiling at each other. I looked to see if I could peer beyond the door, but it just looked black; the photographer must have left the light off in the far room.

On the left was a picture of an amazing tree. Tall and thick and full of flowers and a strange fruit, something I'd never seen before. And all around the tree were flowers more amazing than anything I'd seen in my mom's garden.

As I took a step toward the door, I got the feeling I shouldn't, as if it were somehow off limits or dangerous. But my curiosity was too much; I had to know. My hand reached out as I approached the door, as if the smallest touch would open it for me. Inch by inch I crept closer to it. Only three steps, two steps, one step ...

"Josh." I felt my heart leap through my chest. I spun around so fast I lost my balance and nearly fell. For a second my eyes went fuzzy, and all I could see was a figure walking toward me. My heart started to race, sweat began to form in the palms of my hands, my breathing quickened its pace, and ...

"Josh, it's okay, just breathe." That voice, I knew that voice, and it brought such calm to everything around me. Finally my vision cleared, and I could see Mr. Curry in front of me. "Sorry, Josh. I didn't mean to frighten you."

"It's okay. I guess I was just in La-La Land." I smiled. "P.S.: This room is awesome!"

"Thank you, Josh. It's one of my favorite places to be; it always reminds me of why we do what we do." Mr. Curry smiled.

"What's behind the big door?" I asked, too curious for politeness.

"As yes, the big door, more commonly referred to as the Eternity Door, but I guess you cannot read the language of the Cahirians. That is what that word says. In Cahirian it's pronounced *Teralla*, but in English it simply says Eternity."

"Sweet, but what's behind it?" I pressed for more.

"Ah, that is an adventure for another day, dear Josh. But I must ask you to venture through those doors only when you have been properly invited." Mr. Curry lost some points in that moment. He was still pretty cool, but, man, did I want to know.

"Well, I guess I'm leaving today anyway, so apparently I won't get to know." I tried to play the guilt-trip card.

"Ah yes, your vacation is at its end, isn't it?" Mr. Curry seemed disappointed. "But alas, I should have known, although the past few days seemed to fly by, didn't they?"

"That they did." I laughed a little. "I just wish it could have lasted a little longer."

"And if it could?" Mr. Curry tempted me.

"It can't. I have school and chores, and my mom and dad will want to know where I've gone. I'm sure you can't keep them blind forever. Plus, home is where I need to be."

"But is it where you want to be?" he asked, as if knowing the answer.

"Of course," I lied.

"Really?" he asked, and my mind started to whirl with memories of only a few nights ago.

I could remember lying on my floor in my room, with my ear to the vent. You could hear everything from anywhere in my house if you put your ear to one of the vents. My mom and dad were fighting. It wasn't the first time, but it was definitely the worst. And suddenly it reached a breaking point.

"Then you take care of *your* son!" my dad screamed.

"Just you wait! What is *that* supposed to mean?" My mom tried to stay calm, but I could hear her starting to tear up.

"You know exactly what *that* means!" Dad bit back.

"No, actually, I have no idea what you're implying." She had stopped yelling and simply forced the words through tears.

"Jessica, why must you always make things so difficult?" Dad was furious about something.

"Are you suggesting that Joshua is not your child? Do you really think I've been sleeping around?" Mom sounded offended.

"I don't know. Guilty conscience, Jessica?" Dad was icy.

"Cody, you can't really think that! This wasn't my fault; he came to me ..." I was in the middle of remembering, when a voice broke my train of thought.

"Is that really what you want, Josh?" His voice calmed me, shaking from remembering that night. "Is that really what you need, Josh?"

"It's the only home I have," I replied, not sure what else to say.

"Josh, do you remember what I told you about the Iyarians and Cahirians the other morning?" Mr. Curry asked.

"Angels and demons, yeah, more or less." I wasn't sure why he was bringing that up.

"Well, this is a perfect example of a time when the Cahirians, demons, tried to help your parents. Do you remember what the fight was about?" he asked.

"Some drunk guy kissed my mom, and my dad got really jealous, thinking she was cheating on him." I did not want to go into any more detail than that.

"And that is exactly what happened: some drunk guy that your mother had never met kissed her. It was not your dad's fault that he reacted that way, though. Iyarians and ..." He paused, seeing me figuring out which was which again. He let out a sigh. "Angels and demons can speak to humanity, influence them, guide them. But that night the Iyarians, angels, spoke to your father, pushing his mind to believe that Jessica had cheated on him. The Cahirians, demons, tried to convince him of what was true." He paused a moment, as if someone had broken his heart. "But, alas, with the curse placed upon the Cahirians, their voices match their looks, and therefore it is much more difficult to influence humanity."

"Why are you telling me this?" I asked, still not sure what to think of his history lessons.

"Give us some time to smooth things over with your parents, bring them to an understanding with each other. A few more days should do it, and then you can go home, and things will be the way they should be." Mr. Curry smiled, and for a moment I felt okay with his idea, but deep down I knew I had to go home. At the same time, I didn't really want to. Chances were that they knew I was missing, and if I went now they'd be angry. If I waited a few more days, they might be relieved. And they could work things out. It felt like my insides were fighting themselves, but I didn't want to get in trouble, and I didn't want to disappoint Mr. Curry either. Two birds, one stone. I made my decision. I stuck out my hand toward Mr. Curry.

"You've got yourself a deal." I smiled. "You can have your stupid name back in a few more days."

He laughed and shook my hand, and once again when our hands connected I felt like a giant weight had been taken off my shoulders. Like everything was going to be just fine, and so it was. Another few days passed, and I still wasn't ready to go home. I figured Mr. Curry would let me know when my parents were doing better, so I stayed for a few days more. And soon days turned into weeks, weeks into months, and my parents slipped into the back of my mind. I didn't need to think about them anymore. Larasa took the place of my mom, and she never complained or made me do chores. Mr. Curry, although he was busy most of the time, took the place of my dad. Haslo, Norton, and Gary, my three newfound friends, took the places of Aniece and David, friends from another life. The months slipped past without a dull moment to slow things down. There was never a time that I was bored or needed anything. Things were always different and new. Except one thing. Night after night after night, I would dream, and in those dreams I would watch Haldel be slaughtered a thousand different ways by Lasnek. Even though they were just dreams, I began to hate Lasnek. *Hate.* It was a new feeling, something different. I mean, I'd disliked people before, but this was not that at all. I would imagine myself older, taller, and stronger. Strong enough to kill Lasnek for the things he put me through every night.

And soon I would find just the thing I needed to get me there.

Chapter 6

The Teacher

Norton, Gary, Haslo, and I became really tight. Our adventures lasted late into each evening. The habit of sneaking through hidden passageways became a part of our daily routine. Larasa never even tried to figure it out but left us to our own devices. We would race all over and see who could find the fastest and coolest passages. Somehow, Haslo always beat us, but then again he was by far the most talented of all of us. Of course, the two hoodlums, Norton and Gary, were pretty good as well. I had never had so much fun in all my life. I had sunk into a world of forgetfulness: three fun kids my age, cartoons, food whenever I wanted, playing with dangerous things, and never getting in trouble. Mine was a carefree life of pleasure, games, and childish competitions. We must have played these foolish games for two months before Haslo ever introduced me to the real fun.

One day during an adventure, Haslo got that look in his eye. Norton, Gary, and I always knew when something crazy had just popped into his mind. Often it was something dangerous or a massive prank, usually against Lasnek, which I thoroughly enjoyed. But today I had the feeling it was his best idea yet. Even Norton and Gary looked a little nervous.

"What have you got for us, Haslo?" I asked, and Norton and Gary gave him their undivided attention.

"Fun, danger, trouble. You know, the usual." Haslo grinned.

"Usual, eh?" I smiled back, knowing he had something much bigger up his sleeve.

"Follow me!"

Haslo took off and Norton, Gary, and I took off after him. Peeling this way and that through the halls, we finally burst through a set of doors I knew well, into the massive courtyard. I would often come here alone to avoid what sleep brought me. Haslo continued to tear across the path toward the greenish doors on the other side. He stopped inches before the doors and slowly reached out to the handle.

"What on earth are you doing?" Gary could barely speak through his huffing and puffing.

"You know that's off limits!" Norton squeezed out between heaving. I smiled at Haslo, who didn't even look winded. I mean, Norton and Gary were most certainly not in any shape but round, but even I was a little winded.

"Scared?" I taunted them.

"Um, ahh ..." Norton sucked in his gut and tried to slow his breathing.

"... to death." Gary was still heaving and couldn't care less what anyone thought of him.

"Too scared?" I pressed.

"Never." Both of them smiled, finally regaining their breath. Haslo opened the door, and, like a pack of ninjas, we sneaked in. Haslo must have been here before, because he knew exactly where to go and when to hide, when patrols walked past. This was definitely the military section of the complex. Soon Haslo ushered us into a small room. I must have looked like a kid in a candy store when I looked at the walls. Not a square inch wasn't covered in something way too sharp for a child. Swords and daggers and clubs and axes and so much more. Haslo ran over to a drawer and pulled out four foam-padded swords. He tossed one to each of us.

"Let us duel!" he laughed. And Gary and Norton both ran at him, but I was mesmerized. Something about the feel of the sword in my hand was so perfect. The power, the control, the danger. Mom would kill me if she ... SLAM! Norton was thrown into me; I scrambled to my feet and blocked the next hit. It felt amazing, although I'm sure we looked like idiots. But we fought like warriors of old, defenders of good and slayers of evil! After hours of fun, we all limped back to our beds. Even though we were sore beyond belief the next day, we headed back again and again and again. It was addicting, and the more we went, the better we got. We stopped messing around and actually tried to get better.

Months passed and the video games got dusty, and the TV with them. Soon nothing else mattered. Who wanted to pretend when the real thing was so close? What I didn't know was that I'd only scratched the surface, and soon I would take the plunge.

One day Norton, Gary, Haslo, and I were practicing in that weapons room, and I was beating them all. Norton went down first, then Gary, laughing as they fell. Then it was on to my greatest opponent, Haslo. I had never beaten him before; I had gotten close, but he was so good. So it was he and I for the final battle. Today I would reign, and he would grovel at my feet. Locking eyes we engaged in putting fear into our opponent. Haslo would crumble at my sheer awesomeness. Yet he did not waver. Soon we lashed out, striking and blocking and trying to disarm the other. Finally I got a solid strike and knocked him to his knees. Now was the time. His sword was loose and his focus a little fuzzy. I spun full circle for my move of awesomeness, but when I came around, he was gone. Impossible! That could not be. I looked this way and that but soon realized Norton and Gary had bailed too. As if those punks had peaced out of my moment of victory.

In that moment, though, I heard a creak behind me. I spun fast as lightning; Haslo would feel the pain of my foam-padded blade strike him down! But as I turned I realized the figure before me was much larger than Haslo. It was too late; I could not stop the swing. The world around me slowed in that moment. There was nothing I could do but watch everything play out before me. I watched a twisted cane hook my sword, tossing it into the air, and at the same time the butt of the cane slammed me to the ground, blurring my vision and knocking the breath out of my lungs. I could see the same cane hook my sword out of the air, pulling it neatly into this tall figure's hand. From my spot on the ground, I watched the blur of a sword swing down to my neck. I tensed, only to hear the rattling crash as the cane hit the ground beside my head. It settled and the silence hung heavy in the entire room. Hard breaths interrupted the silence as I desperately attempted to soothe my seriously freaked-out lungs.

My vision cleared. I could now see an older man standing above me, a smile on his face. He must have been in his sixties; although his hair had kept its youthful black tone save for the two thin strips of silver along the sides. His grey eyes offered a kindness that seemed misplaced beside the violence he had just done me. I felt as if I knew him, that I had seen him before. It was like he would have been someone my dad knew. He extended a hand, stretching toward me from his brown old-school suit. He obviously had class and a sense of age, value ... something. His old, worn face kept smiling as he got closer. The skin around his eyes tightened, as if he were looking for something. When he got closer, I could see tiny black hairs; he must not have shaved this morning.

Finally he reached out his hand, and I put mine in his, noticing first how massive his hands were and how rough; they reminded me of my uncle Albert's hands, and the strength of his squeeze only fortified that thought. The strength of a farmer was in those hands. I stood to my feet with his help, and he eyed me up and down. I'm not going to lie; I was getting a little weirded out by this guy. I could see Haslo's silhouette in the door. He was chuckling, obviously a happy spectator to the whole show. I glared at him but was quickly interrupted.

"Interesting," the man said, sounding as if he had swallowed a truck full of gravel.

"What's interesting?" I cautiously massaged the back of my head.

"You have some skill in you, my lad. I am impressed."

"And you are?"

"Wouldn't you like to know?"

"My name is Josh."

"I am aware." He gazed into the distance, as if I hadn't said a word to him. Who was this guy? And why was he all of a sudden Mr. Big and Important?

"What is your name?" I asked again, becoming impatient.

"Ah, a good question finally." He turned slightly as if he would grace me with a glance.

"Are you going to answer me?"

"Hmm, back to the foolish questions, I see. Should have been able to figure that one out on his own." He was acting as if I were not in the same room as him.

"Fine. Don't answer. I don't care."

"Excellent."

"What are you here for?" I tried to change the subject, since he was being so difficult about his identity.

"Another good question. He's not as dumb as I thought." Again he ignored that I could hear him.

"Thank you?" I was getting a little uneasy.

"Well, dear boy, you have a lot of learning to do." He finally spoke directly to me, recognizing that I existed. "But I'm confident this will take less time than I anticipated."

"What will take less time?"

"Another good question; you're starting to get it. Ask the right questions, get the right answers." He smiled. "I will be responsible for your upcoming training. Haslo came to speak to me about your talent. You have learned in a few months what took, Haslo, Norton, and Gary two years to learn. Swordsmanship has proven to be a difficult skill to learn, and you have already mastered the basics. From this point on, I will be with you each day, refining your skill and honing your natural gifts. You will bask in a power beyond what you have ever experienced before. This all begins today. Unless of course ..." He started to drift off. "Unless of course you would rather just watch your cartoons?" He looked at me as if peering deep into my soul.

"Ah, no, I guess not. I'll do it."

"Excellent. Let us begin," he commanded as he handed me my padded sword. "My name is Harlstril, as you will address me."

The training began and within ten minutes I had regretted agreeing to this. My lungs were burning, my arms were shaking, and my legs felt like Jell-O. I was not aware of what Harlstril had planned for me. There was no backing out now, though. I could have bowed out earlier due to lack of interest, but now I'd have to quit out of lack of ability, and I sure as heck was not about to do something like that. I'd be the laughing stock. Plus, Norton,

Gary, and Haslo apparently all trained with Harlstril, so how could I not? And so the day continued. Sure, I was dead after ten minutes, but that didn't mean I couldn't go for another six hours. By the time the day was done, I stumbled back to my room and collapsed on the bed. Not one of my limbs worked, and I prayed to die while I slept, so that tomorrow I wouldn't have to go back. But soon enough, sleep crept over me, and the dreams of death came to me once again.

I awoke from my nightmare immediately after Haldel died at the hands of Lasnek. As had become the custom, a strange light flooded my room. It did so after every dream, but no matter how I searched, I could never find its source. This time it was accompanied by a scratching sound, a sound that came from my sock drawer. I was about to investigate, when my body protested and I slipped back into a slumber. Upon waking the next morning, I crawled out of bed, my body slightly rested. I knew this would not be a day filled with fun and excitement. Pain and agony were on tap for today, and after a deep breath I got myself ready for it.

After spending a little time in the courtyard and just enjoying the peace of it all, I headed through the large double doors into the halls of green and into the weapons room, where I would start my training every day. Looking at the weapons plastered on the walls, I wondered which I would choose when my training was done. Finally my eyes landed upon the most awesome weapon I had ever seen. It was a sword, and it was huge, probably taller than I was, and as thick as my leg. I walked over to it and picked it up, knowing full well it was going to go badly for me. The sword was immensely heavy, and once I had it cleared of the hooks, my arms began to shake, my knees lost strength, and I dropped the sword, jumping backward at the same time, narrowly missing the blade with my feet. With a great clang it slammed into the ground, sending sparks shooting in every direction.

"Ah yes"—Harlstril's calm voice interrupted my fast-beating heart—"the claymore, the ultimate destructive weapon. Enough weight behind it to knock a man's head off, even if it is dull as a butter knife. Joshua, I'm sorry to disappoint you, but no matter how hard you work, you will never wield a sword of such brute magnitude. That is a weapon for gargantuan men. You and I aren't built to fully enjoy its uses." Harlstril spoke kindly but with biting honesty.

"What kind of a sword would I use?" I felt slightly wounded by limitations.

"Those like you would use a sword of grace and precision," he explained as he returned the claymore with a grunt to its rightful place on the wall. "A sword of kings, not one of barbarians." He scanned the wall until he found the sword he wanted. Pulling it off the wall, he swung it in his hands as if it were nothing. Back and forth, this way and that, and then with one fluid movement he reversed the sword and slid the blade in between his fingers so that the handle stopped mere inches from me, with its point facing him. I looked down at the sword, able to see it more closely. The handle was about a foot and a half long, followed by a four-foot blade. It was of similar length to the claymore, but the blade was thin and had engravings the length of it. The handle was made up of two snakelike dragons, intertwined, and the wings created hand guards. I took the sword in my hand, and Harlstril released it. Although not nearly the weight of the claymore, it was still beyond my strength to move around. I could simply keep it from hitting the ground.

"This, dear Josh, is called the Long Sword. This is designed to kill your enemy cleanly and quickly, all the while upholding glory and honor. This, my young one, is the sword of kings."

"But I could never use it. It's way too heavy." I might be good, but not that good.

"Would you enjoy being able to one day carry such greatness and wield such a sword as if it were a paperweight?" Harlstril queried, instilling confidence in me.

"Yes." Who wouldn't? This was a dream. This had been a buried dream even before I knew it was possible.

"Then it's time we put down the childish training swords and get something just a little heavier."

Harlstril took the Long sword back and placed it on the wall, and then he looked through the drawers until he found a sword much smaller, yet still nearly twice the size of the one I had been using. For I moment I appraised it: simple, yet I knew the power that lay behind it. Looking to the wall, I again admired the sword full of glory and smiled. I would wield it one day. I thought Harlstril could tell what I was thinking, because he smiled too and drew his sword. The training was to begin; a routine would be built. And things like fun and games would become a faint memory.

"Five a.m. start in the gymnasium. Don't be late, lest you incur my wrath, Joshua." Harlstril always spoke as though he were ancient.

Each day, after two hours of intense workout, we would move straight into swordsmanship, which included learning with every type of sword, and then we would move to other weapons. I was to master the sword, but I needed also to be no fool with other weapons, for you never know which may save your life. After that it was class time: hours of lectures and war talk, strategy, planning, leadership, ownership, teaching me to not only *be* the ultimate weapon but to *lead* the ultimate weapons!

It was weeks before my body didn't throb in pain as I tried to sleep, and all the while my dreams of Haldel's death continued, and the strange glowing light and scratching from the drawer would wake me. When I looked there was never anything there but socks, and my dagger stowed beneath. Routine blended the days into weeks, and the weeks into months. Before long, three months had passed, and the day had come that I had been waiting for. Today there would be no class, no exercise, no lectures, and no training. Today Harlstril would tell me his story. The story of how he came to be.

I simply sat in the courtyard and listened as he spoke of the training that started when he was around my age, then of his first missions, with the Destiny Troops, the best of the best. They would sneak in and destroy the angels' strongholds. Nothing could stop them! He spoke of the many conquests, the battles he led, the wars he oversaw. And the final battle he fought. Thousands of troops on either side, and everything that could go wrong went wrong, until it was only Harlstril standing alone again the enemy. All of his best men had been killed off, one by one. In a rage Harlstril slaughtered every last remaining angel; he never fought again. He would resign his fighting and take up training. We must have been there all day as he divulged his tales to me. And I sat, eyes wide, soaking it all in, not wanting to miss a thing. But at last the day had reached its end, and Harlstril sent me on my way.

Lying in bed, I waited for sleep to come, but my mind was too full of all I had learned, my imagination was running wild, and sleep was not going to come easily. Hours passed before sleep finally consumed me. Once again I slipped into a dream, and here we go again, Haldel ... Lasnek ... Haldel's dead ... wake in a sweaty mess! This time was different, though. The glow was there, but the scratching had turned into the sound of breaking wood. I bounced out of bed and ran to the drawer. Pulling it open, I could see the point of my dagger digging into the edge of the drawer. I quickly grabbed the handle and pulled it out. I then noticed a considerable difference. There was no way that this dagger would have fit into my pocket. It was almost a sword now, the blade reaching fifteen inches. But daggers don't grow. This was ridiculous. And I felt heat emanate from the handle. Feeling a little odd, I dropped the dagger in a larger drawer and slammed it shut. Hopping back in bed, I fell asleep and waited for tomorrow's adventures to arrive.

Chapter 7

Seven Sets

You know that feeling when your head leaps off the pillow and you know you're doomed? That was my morning. I didn't even need to look at the clock to know I was done for. I had broken the number one rule. I was late.

I shot out of bed as if it were on fire. Frantically running around the room, I grabbed what I needed and scrambled for the door. As I reached it, I realized I was forgetting something. Now having already broken the number one rule, I sure wasn't about to break the number two rule: showing up unprepared. Each and every one of Harlstril's rules could be summed up like this: "You will respect me in everything you do." Being late was the ultimate way of saying, "I don't want to be here," and showing up unprepared was the best way to say, "You have nothing you can teach me." I looked around the room, wondering what I could possibly have forgotten, but nothing came to mind. I started tearing my room apart, trying to figure it out, but nothing was coming to me. Finally, I knew I had to risk it. I had to show up unprepared and late, before I didn't show up at all. I grabbed the door handle just in time to hear a click and then see the door swing open fast and hard. Had I reacted just a millisecond sooner, I would not have ended up with a black eye. But I did not. The door struck me in the eye, and I fell back onto the ground. Once my vision cleared, I could see Haslo standing over me, laughing at my pain and distress. That was when it hit me. Today was my day off. That's why I'd woken up "late," and that's what I was forgetting.

"Wow, workaholic, trying to sneak off on your only day off," Haslo laughed.

"Well, you sure kept that from happening!" I picked myself up off the ground.

"Ready?" Haslo smirked

"What do we have planned for today?" By the look in his eye I figured it would be good.

"Start simple: pancakes for breakfast, then waste no time in escalating, and prank Lasnek!" Haslo stuck out his hand toward me.

"Sounds like a plan!" I shook it.

"Breakfast it is!" We both headed down the hall toward the kitchen, where Larasa would be making pancakes for us. "So tell me, anything exciting in training, oh long-lost friend?"

"Sorry, it's just super busy, and by the time I get out, I pretty much eat, try not to vomit, and go right to sleep.".

"I didn't ask you where you've been, I wanted to know what you've learned." Haslo shoved me.

"Haha, just Harlstril telling me his life story and all." Mentioning that got me thinking about everything Harlstril had told me.

"Life story?" Haslo seemed overly concerned.

"Yeah, about his training and missions and wars and all that." I gave him a questioning look. "Why? Is that against the rules or something?"

"Oh." He seemed a little awkward. "No, no. Just random, that's all."

After that Haslo stayed silent for a bit, which was definitely uncommon for him. We ate our pancakes and then headed out for the mission of the day. I was to get rope and four fire extinguishers, and Haslo was going to break into the supply room for whipped cream. We would meet outside Lasnek's room. I got there first and started the trap. Step one was to set up the rope in front of Lasnek's door, then wire two extinguishers on my side and two on Haslo's side. Just as I finished, I could hear Lasnek rustling about in his room. Haslo had yet to arrive, making me a little nervous. Finally he got there, and we emptied four cans of whipped cream on the floor opposite the door. Haslo and I got into position, with him on one side of the door, rope in hand, and me on the other, rope in hand. And we waited.

It was a while before Lasnek's door opened, and as he stepped out we pulled the rope tight, snagging his foot. He headed forward, arms flailing, trying to grab something, but it was too late; his face slammed into the perfectly placed pile of whipped cream. In a rage he jumped up and spun toward Haslo. My friend dropped the rope and took a few steps back, and Lasnek foolishly stepped forward, right into my trap, hitting the trip wire. Two extinguishers opened up, blasting him in the face. Fumbling backward he spun around and saw me. I watched as his eyes glowed with red flames. Lasnek didn't like Haslo at all, but there was no hatred greater than his hatred for me. Again he foolishly stormed forward and hit the second trip wire, blasting him in the face with whatever they put in extinguishers. I had only a second to enjoy this, because I knew Lasnek would come cutting through the smoke and tear me limb from limb. So I spun around and took off down the hall, turning at every corner I could. Haslo and I had agreed to meet in the gymnasium supply room, our secret spot, where no one ever found us.

"I'll find you both and kill you!" I heard Lasnek scream from behind me, and I could hear his heavy feet smashing around, but once again he did not go the right way. I arrived at the supply room shortly after Haslo, and we hung out on the high jump mat and ate candy, laughing at Lasnek's whipped cream–covered face. Nothing brought us more joy then torturing Lasnek, and we never felt bad, because he was nothing but a jerk to us. After dinner Haslo and I parted ways. After a few hours of studying, I climbed into bed, hoping for a good night's rest before all hell broke loose again. My eyelids slid shut, and I was swept into the world of the unconscious.

It was bright. I was in a beautifully decorated room. Gold. Silver. Ivory. Two chairs of ivory and silver, one of which I sat upon, stood on either side of a table. The tabletop was shaped like a bowl and filled with the clearest water. The chair on the other side stood empty; it was as if I were waiting for someone to join me. I touched the water, and it spun to life like a whirlpool, the water lifting upward to form a waterspout. Tiny lightning bolts thundered from the sides of it. Thousands of them flashed around in a rage and fury, but finally a single flash flooded the entire room, and from inside its white-hot light I saw for a split second a lone figure violently fighting. I woke from the dream with light still flashing inside my head. I was brought to focus as I heard the noise of metal scraping metal coming from the larger dresser drawer.

I walked toward it cautiously; this was very unlike the scratching noise that usually entertained my evenings. Opening the drawer, I saw a bright light coming from the dagger sitting atop my clothing. Reaching in, I took the dagger and watched as strange symbols were carved into the blade by a bright white light. It was some kind of language, but I had no idea what it said. One word carved, space, a second word, space, third, fourth, fifth, sixth, seventh ... and with that the light slowly faded, leaving me alone in my dark room. I stood up to see the top of my dresser; there, engraved in the wood, was writing very similar to what was now in the dagger. Yet there was a subtle difference to it.

I placed the sword alongside the writing to examine it more closely, when suddenly the two began to react like two magnets pushing away from each other. I forced the dagger to stay put, and then the letters started to glow. The writing on the dagger went bright white, while the letters on the desk began to burn red-hot. Finally I pulled it away, and everything went dark again. I quickly wrapped the sword in the fine blue cloth sitting on the dresser and dropped it in the drawer. There it would stay, and no one would hear about it. I didn't know why I cared, but I knew it wouldn't be good to bring that to training. At the sound of footsteps coming down the hall, I slammed the drawer shut and hopped back into bed. Closing my eyes and focusing on the noise of my heartbeat, I slipped back into the darkness of sleep.

Again, days turned into weeks, and weeks to months, and months to years. That strange dagger soon grew into a sword. That freaked me out at first, but eventually I just gave in to the fact that the sword was not content with being little.

The strange markings on it never changed again, but they did grow with the sword. My life became consumed by training. Sleep soon became less and less, for when I slept I dreamt, and when I dreamt I would have to witness the slaughter of Haldel. Granted, my Saturdays were all reserved for things like pancakes, games, shenanigans, and, most of all, pranking Lasnek. Retribution for his nightly torture to my mind. I was only two months shy of my sixteenth birthday when Harlstril came to me and told me about the test.

Chapter 8

The Impossible Test

I stared into the mirror above my desk, barely recognizing the young man before me. Even though years had passed, I still pictured myself as that eleven-year-old boy in the forest. But now my face was fuller, and my dark hair was getting a little too long for Harlstril's liking. There was a time when he'd hold me down and shave it off, but now that proved difficult for the old man. He could still hold his own against me, but not enough to chop my shaggy hair. My eyes still held their indecisive hazel, switching from brown to green and everywhere in between. My scrawny arms had filled out, and although I was no body builder, there was no lack of strength in me.

Opening the drawer, I pulled out my strange, growing sword; it was almost an exact match to Haldel's sword, excluding that it was not as big, and mine had that strange inscription. Admiring the beauty of it and the perfect craftsmanship, I spun it this way and that. It was as if the sword had been designed just for me. Better than any I had ever used, the sword was virtually weightless, and its balance was spot-on.

A creak at the door snapped me to attention as I dropped the sword back in my drawer, slamming it shut.

"What were you looking at, Joshua?" Harlstril asked.

"Um ... n-nothing, just ahh, checking out my clothes." *Really, that was the best excuse you could come up with? Smooth move, man!*

"Hmm, I see." Harlstril knew full well I was lying, but he didn't push the subject.

"I am definitely in trouble if you're visiting me on my day off, especially seeing as how you had 'pressing business to attend to.'" I did my best Harlstril impression. Years ago that would have gotten me double duty on everything, but now Harlstril and I had a slightly more comfortable relationship.

"Which I have completed." Harlstril ignored my mockery. "But to my current affairs: I have excellent news for you."

"Not in trouble, and good news? Well, well, let's hear it!"

"It has been discussed with the Council ..." The moment he said "the Council," I was fully focused. This was a group of elite generals, tested through time to be the best of the best. They were the warriors who never fell, the leaders who kept their troops alive, and the generals who won wars. Every few months I would be permitted an audience with them, where I would sit and listen and never speak. For them to even mention my name was one of the greatest honors anyone could expect. Suddenly I realized that my full attention was not on Harlstril but on thinking about the Council. I refocused in time to hear " ... test!"

"Test? What test?" I was really hoping he hadn't just told me while I was daydreaming.

"*The* test, Joshua. The test that will prove you as a warrior, as a leader, but most of all as a man!" he said, a look of confidence in his eyes.

"I'm not even sixteen yet. I'm no man," I replied.

"Joshua, you are more a man now than most men will ever be. You *are* ready for this." Harlstril's voice held such confidence, but I was not entirely sure I agreed.

“So, what kind of test are we talking about here?”

“This will be a series of tests that will push you in every aspect of who you are. Your body, your mind, your spirit, your very soul will be tested, Joshua! The classroom has taught you all that it can; you have already surpassed me in your abilities. You must now take your training to the next level, and that is to teach oneself.” He looked at me as a proud father would. “Joshua, you will go through each test in succession, you may attempt each test as many times as you like, but you may not move to the next until you succeed. They are dangerous tests, so do not be foolish; you will be protected from death, but you could still be seriously injured.” Harlstril gave me “that look,” the “I’ll kill you if you get yourself killed” look. “These tests will push you to your limits and well past them, but if anyone can do this, it’s you!”

“Are ... are you sure I’m ready?” I asked, a lump growing in my throat.

“Are you sure you’re not?”

“I ... I ...” I knew Harlstril believed in me, but to be honest, I didn’t know what to expect, and the last thing I wanted to do was let him down.

“If your certainty of being ready is unsure, then surely you are ready. Joshua, I have given you all that I know, taught you all that I can. You have already surpassed me in every way, excluding your continual choice of speech.” I smirked at him, knowing how much it drove him crazy that I refused to speak all spiffy-like. “The time has come for you to take your destiny into your own hands; you must forge your own path from here.”

This was the opportunity I had hungered for. This was the moment I had envisioned. Nervousness grew in the pit of my stomach, but this was no time to look weak. I focused my attention, stood tall, and looked directly into Harlstril’s eyes.

“I accept.”

"Excellent! Then we will both rise to greet the darkness at four o'clock in the morning, for that is when your testing will begin." Harlstril shook my hand, then left the room, leaving me with my nerves and racing heart.

The rest of the day was spent pacing the room, trying to study, but my mind would not slow down; I did not even know what to prepare for. The first test could be anything. I pulled my notes from classes with Harlstril out of my cherrywood chest. I remembered the days Harlstril taught me to make things out of wood, because it would sharpen my finesse. This cherry chest was the rickety reward of my own making. It might not be very nice, but it was the only thing that actually belonged to me. No matter how hard I tried to read my notes, they all looked like a blur to me. Finally I just sat and stared at my cherry chest. Morning quickly faded to afternoon, in what seemed like no time, and before long, night arrived. When sleep is most important, it is always most difficult to find. My eyes finally closed, and I welcomed the annoyance that came with sleep.

As I opened my eyes, I saw a forest, thick and full. I took in a deep breath, and the scent of cedar and pine brought back memories of something, but what it was I could not tell you. I looked around for Haldel, who would be followed by Lasnek; then Haldel would die, I would wake up, and then I could sleep the rest of the night. Seems cold to think of it that way, but when you see the same scenario played out over and over, you get used to it.

Thinking about Lasnek made my head spin. There was not one redeemable quality about that guy!

My thoughts of loathing were broken by a bright light speeding toward me. I knew immediately that Haldel was on his way, carving around trees as he flew toward me at an incredible rate. I waited patiently for Lasnek to cut him down; you'd think Haldel would have learned after his more than a thousand deaths, but alas he continued into the inevitable trap. Just before reaching me, he snapped his wings back, catching the wind in them. His feet hit the ground, and he slid to a stop directly in front of me. His eyes were burning bright yellow, and his breathing was heavily labored.

"Joshua, I don't have much time. I must tell you ..." Lasnek's fist slammed into Haldel's face, sending him soaring through the air. He crashed into the ground and rolled back to his feet, ready for a fight; he grabbed for his sword but found nothing but an empty sheath. Lasnek raised his mighty fist, and in a burst of red flame his vicious trident appeared. Haldel was weaponless, but his message was more important than the fight at hand.

"You need to know ..." Lasnek rushed at Haldel, wanting desperately to keep him silent. But Haldel was far too agile; he rolled to the left, narrowly avoiding a fatal strike. "Don't ..." Lasnek struck again, but Haldel kicked the trident away. " ... Listen ..." In the moment Haldel took to say "listen," Lasnek had planted his foot in Haldel's chest, crushing him to the ground.

"Nooo!" I screamed as Lasnek buried his trident in Haldel's chest. I fell down by his side, looking into Haldel's dying eyes.

"To the lies." Haldel forced out those last words before blood filled his lungs and the fire in his eyes went dark.

I expected in this moment to wake up, but for the first time I stayed in the dream. Rage began to fill me as I looked up to see Lasnek standing victorious over his fresh kill. It was then that I felt warmth at my side. Looking down, I saw my growing sword. The seven sets of markings glowed white-hot. Lasnek would finally feel my wrath. Pranking would no longer satisfy me. This time Lasnek would die. I snapped the sword up and ran at him, but his reaction was way too fast. He swung his trident around and knocked me back to the ground. I quickly regained my footing and prepared for a less foolish approach.

"And what do you plan on doing with that, little boy?" Lasnek spat.

"I'll kill you, that's what. Sound good?" I readied myself in a proper attack stance.

"Perfect!" Lasnek smiled. His confidence was slightly unnerving, but I couldn't care less. "I've been looking for an excuse to finish you off, and now it's dropped in my lap. 'I was just defending myself'? Yes, I think that works perfectly."

With that he took a cheap shot, but having seen Lasnek fight many times, I knew to expect it. I bent backward till my hands touched the ground. As the prongs of the trident passed by my stomach, I kicked my legs into the air, wrapping them around the shaft of the trident. Used the momentum to rip it out of Lasnek's hands, I dropped it to the ground on the other side of me. Before Lasnek could figure out what I'd done, I was on my feet, sword ready. With me between him and his favorite weapon, I readied myself for a fight.

"So that's how you want it?" Lasnek glared at me and reached down, drawing his sword.

"The claymore, sword of the barbarian." I laughed. "Suits you, Lasnek: all brawn, no brains."

"Pity your brain can't swing a sword; then maybe you wouldn't have to use a girl's sword," Lasnek shot back.

"Just makes it all the better when my girl's sword kills you and your oaf sword." Deep down I was a little nervous; that sword was a monster. I'd even say it was bigger than the claymore I had tried to pick up all those years ago. The handle, or hilt, as I'd been taught to call it, was the body of a dragon. Its tail led to the tip of the handle and was razor sharp, meaning both ends of his sword could be fatal. The wings of the dragon were fully outspread, making for two magnificent hand guards, and out of the dragon's open mouth jutted the great claymore blade, with writing similar to what was on Lasnek's trident. I knew there would be no blocking of Lasnek's strikes; I would simply have to try to redirect them, which actually was a much more effective method anyway, as it often forced your enemy off balance.

Lasnek wasted no time in the attack, immediately going for the strike, and, considering his sheer size, he didn't really have to worry about being hit back. He could swing at will and not worry about me hitting him unless I walked fully into the striking area. Which is foolish and bad for your health.

But arrogant as he was, his first strike was a full-force swing, with every ounce of his strength in it. The blade looked like it was literally bending under the force. I ducked, narrowly missing it, and allowed his own sword to do the work for me. Having put too much force into the swing, and having nothing to slow it down, he was swung off balance by the momentum, and he hit the ground. I got quickly to my feet and spun around, but Lasnek was already on his feet again. His eyes blazed with fury.

He now chose to fight slowly and accurately; the only problem with that was that I was *fast* and accurate. He swung and I redirected; again he swung and again I redirected. Now here was my problem: Lasnek could keep this up a hundred times longer than I could, and as fast as I was, I would never get close enough to strike back. I had to outthink him somehow, or he'd exhaust me and I'd lose. Finally it hit me: I would play to his pride. I turned and ran, and foolishly he followed me. I got going as fast as I could and forced Lasnek to press himself to his fastest. Swerving in and out of trees, I allowed Lasnek to catch up slowly. My timing would have to be perfect, or else he would see what was coming. He got within swinging distance and raised his sword; now was my chance. I ran up the closest tree and snapped back toward Lasnek, sword straight out in front of me, my body fully horizontal. With Lasnek's sword in swinging position, it left his chest wide open, and my sword buried itself deep. With the change of momentum, I curled around, bending my back in a direction it was never meant to bend; I would regret that in the morning. I clamped my legs around Lasnek's head, and then, pulling the sword out of his chest, I leapt off of him just before he slammed into the tree I'd ran up. I hit the ground and rolled to a stop. Frantically, I got to my feet to position myself and find Lasnek. But as I spun around, I could see nothing but the splintered trunk of a tree. Impossible! Where could he have gone so fast? But then the world around me started to melt away. The trees turned into walls, a large rock into my bed, and the splintered tree trunk into my cherry chest, or, should I say, what was left of my cherry chest. It was shattered.

What had I done? How did I ... Suddenly I felt something in my hand, and looking down I saw my sword. It was covered in a black liquid, much like the blood of Lasnek. But it was a dream, wasn't it? Not sure what to think, I wiped the sword clean, placed it back in the drawer, and walked back to my bed. Climbing under the blanket, I closed my eyes, but my mind was not ready to sleep. Once again I lay there, mind racing, eyes closed, waiting for sleep.

I awoke early the next morning exhausted and sore, but I knew I could not be late. Dressed in my training clothes, I headed to the kitchen to grab some food. I filled my pouch with a handful of grapes and a bag of trail mix and headed off to meet Harlstril. Passing the courtyard, I breathed in the fresh air, feeling the morning dew. There was no time to waste, though. I had testing to do, and there was no time like the present. I opened the door to the barracks and headed to the training room. I saw Harlstril sitting on a stool in the corner, eyeing a sword, a solid black and magnificent piece of work. I had never seen it before, but when I looked at the far wall, I saw a drawer that had been left open. I assumed that was where it had been hidden. It was a very simple blade, nothing special, just elegant in its simplicity.

"This is the sword I used when I took the tests. It served me very well." Harlstril looked up from the blade and into my eyes. "I would be honored if you were to use it for your testing."

"The honor would be mine." I meant that statement with everything inside of me. Harlstril had become like a father to me over the years. Sure, Mr. Curry was awesome and all, but he wasn't around that much, and Harlstril was always there.

"You are ready, you are willing. Now go make me proud, Joshua," Harlstril said with his oh-so-rare smile.

"I will do my best." As I said this, I watched his smile diminish. "I *will* make you proud." With that his smile returned, and he helped me don my armor.

"You must know that this is the last time I will help you with this, for it is the honor of a man to don his armor in the morning and remove it in the evening." He said this and stopped for a moment, as if remembering something. I watched a tear well up in his eye before he shook it off and continued to work. Once my armor was all strapped on, he clipped the sheath to my side, and with an epic ring I sheathed the midnight-black sword.

"Follow me," Harlstril said and led me out of the room, down the hall, and back into the courtyard. From there we headed to the small door off to the side, the doorway leading to the hall of doors and finally to the Eternity Door. Entering the hallway, I was flooded with memories of when I had first come here, when I first found the massive golden doors, when I was first taught about the angels and demons and their true history. Although I still was a little uneasy with the whole idea, most of the Cahirians who lived here were really nice, excluding Lasnek. And Haldel was the only Iyarian I'd ever met, and he seemed awfully nice—dumb for dying so often, but nice nonetheless.

We stopped in front of one of the wooden doors in the hallway, and Harlstril spoke. "Joshua, I do not expect problems for you in this testing period, but if you have reached the limitation of your ability, you must but speak 'Enough,' and the test will end, and you will start again the next day. Remember, do not be foolish; pacing oneself is the key in the search for success." Seriously, I wished this guy would just say stuff like a normal human!

But what I said was, "Harlstril, you've taught me so much. For that, thank you. I will make you proud." Harlstril looked me in the eye, put his hand on my shoulder, and smiled.

"You have already made me proud," he replied.

"I'm ready." With that, Harlstril opened the door in front of us, revealing nothing but blackness.

"Your destiny awaits you." Harlstril motioned to the open door.

"What is the test?" I asked.

"You'll just have to figure it out." There was no turning back now. Nervousness filled me, but I refused to show it. Standing up straight, I put my hand on my sword and walked into the blackness.

Chapter 9

Dreamless?

Success, absolute success! Only one day in, and I'd already completed the first three tests. Lots of running and jumping and falling and fighting. Thoroughly exciting stuff! I would have continued, but Harlstril made me go see Larasa, and just like a mom, she gave me a vicious tongue-lashing about my newly bruised ribs. After that I headed off to bed. I tried to lie stiff as a board, so my ribs would not protest my sleeping habits. It was difficult, but after the day's adventure, nothing could have kept me awake for long. I closed my eyes and slipped into the world of the unconscious, and for the first time I slept in complete blackness. Silence was my only companion. This night seemed as though it would be full of nothing but peace.

Bang!

My body lurched straight up, and I quickly stifled a scream as my ribs disagreed with my sudden change of position. I slipped quickly out of bed and opened my drawer, retrieving my sword from beneath my clothes. Then I tuned my ear to find whatever made that horrid racket. A low whimper came from the hallway, almost like that of an injured dog. Light as a feather, I floated across the room, soundlessly cracking the door open. Just down the hall I could see that something had been knocked over and was now strewn across the floor. And just beyond it was what looked like an overgrown dog. Although the hall was dark, I could tell that this creature was no dog. The creature limped around the corner, and I slid out the door, opening it ever so slightly to keep it from squealing. Then, as silently as possible, I ran along the hall to where the doggish thing had disappeared. Stopping just before the turn, I checked behind me and then peered around the corner. I couldn't tell if my eyes were planning tricks on me, but it looked as though the thing had wings on its back, very tattered wings, but wings nonetheless. It pushed its way through the door at the end of the hall, and I took off after it. Sliding to a stop mere inches from the door, I cracked it open and looked through into the hall beyond. This thing was curled against the wall, trying to stand, but it seemed terribly wounded. I could tell now that not only did it have wings, but also its front legs looked to be large talons instead of paws. I wiped my eyes, wondering if I was seriously slipping, but, alas, when I looked again, the dog did have tattered wings, and talons for front paws.

It was then that I noticed something dripping off its hind end, which I could only imagine was blood. The creature looked in pain. But I was not sure if this was a moment for compassion. Injured animals are often among the most dangerous. I would not have a chance to consider the options; I heard footsteps coming down the hall.

"Nowhere to go. Why try an escape?" the Cahirian spoke. With that the beast rose up on all fours, and the lowest, meanest growl burst forth from deep within. "Puppy wants to play, does it?"

The creature lunged at the Cahirian, but it was far too weak. The Cahirian easily slammed it to the floor.

"Try to escape again, and I'll put you down for good." He grabbed the creature and dragged it off into the darkness. I considered following, but really had no reason to other than curiosity, and that was not enough to risk falling asleep during tomorrow's test, so I went back to my room.

It didn't take me long to fall asleep, even with everything that had happened. I was tired. And although I would have enjoyed more blackness, I was not granted such a reality. I could feel cold water rushing around my feet and a cool breeze floating in from the east.

As I opened my eyes, I could see that I was in a valley, trees up either side and grass along the bottom. The river I stood in was neither deep nor wide. On either side there stood a pack of demons, or I should say Cahirians, armored up and ready for a fight. In unison they drew their swords, sending a shivering ring through the air. I could not fend them off while trying to get out of the river, so I decided to try to outrun them. Taking off down the stream, I noticed my reflection in the water. I wore all-white clothing and had pure white armor. Over my left shoulder draped a long white cape.

There was no outrunning the Cahirians. They jeered and spat from either side of my creek, and to make matters worse, just ahead was a large boulder in my way. It was at least three times as tall as I was, and four times as wide as the creek. But a plan formed in my mind, a plan of genius and complete logic. I drew my sword and leapt toward the boulder. As I flew through the air, the blade ignited in white flames. The moment the tip struck the boulder, there was an explosion, and bits of stone were sent in every direction, clearing both sides of my little river and sending me flying backward. As I rose from the water, I could see steam all around me. The end of my sword was in the water, boiling everything it touched. I withdrew the sword and watched as the east wind carried away the steam that had formed around me.

Before me stood a warrior, about my age, my size, and dressed completely in black. His clothing was black, his armor was black, and, almost like me, he had a cape, black and over his right shoulder. His face was down, so I could not see his features very well, but deep down I could feel a hatred for him. He seemed to stand there and wait for my assessment. His hair was long and black, his hands were dirty, and his breathing seemed labored, but that didn't seem like it would be to my advantage. Finally he looked up and peered into my eyes, and I into his, his solid black, hollow eyes; his cheeks were sunken in as if he were half dead. Then he smirked, showing his teeth, his fangs.

With a snap he lunged at me, his sword lighting in black flame, and I raised my sword to block him, but I was slammed back, once again hitting the water. Once my blade hit the water, it sent a cloud of steam into the air, shielding me from further damage. I snapped to my feet and surveyed the area. Now my adversary was standing closer to the bank of the creek, placing me at a disadvantage, because he would continually have the better footing. But that wasn't about to stop me. I pressed him hard and fast, but with skill and accuracy. His fighting seemed like pure rage; he cared not whether he was injured, as long as he won the fight. I pressed him hard and began to push him back up the shore, but once he was on dry ground, I could not push the fight. The ground beneath me was spongy and slick, which infuriated me! I began to fight viciously, taking hits, just so I could deal out worse ones. I finally got an opening; I grabbed his cape and pulled him forward, planting a head butt square to his nose. He stumbled and fell flat on his back, giving me time to emerge from the creek and onto dry land. With a kick, he rolled up on his back and sprang to his feet, like a bloody ninja.

I had had enough of this fight. I turned off all defensive play and went fully for the attack, pounding him hard, until he played the defender. I attacked him again and again, as the rage poured out from my every fiber. As much as he tried to block me, he was weakening, and at last I knocked the sword from his hand and followed that up by planting my boot in his chest. Once he hit the ground, I dropped the point of my sword to his throat. My breathing was heavy, my lungs were burning, and then I saw it. Looking at my arm, I could see that I no longer wore white but was completely in black. I watched in bewilderment as the white flames on my sword were consumed by black. Then I looked down at the enemy I had defeated and no longer saw that warrior dressed in black, but the angel I knew as Haldel. I backed away, but as I did a force shoved my sword forward into Haldel's chest. Horrified, I pulled the sword back, hoping I could reverse what had been done, but it was too late, and I watched as the light began to fade from him. Rage filled me and I spun around to see Lasnek walking toward the valley hill. I was about to go after him, when I heard a voice.

"It's taking you." A pained breath. "Joshua, do not allow this." A round of painful coughing halted Haldel's words. "Do not listen to them ... they are lying ..." With that, I heard a final release of breath. I dared not look back at his lifeless body. I had grown used to Lasnek killing Haldel in my dreams, but for it to be done by my own hand filled me with such rage for him that I could feel the heat rise through my whole body, as if I were about to explode or burst into flame. I tore after Lasnek but made it only a few steps before ...

"Wake up, Joshua." Harlstril's voice brought me screaming out of my sleep. "Whoa, are you all right?"

I took a second to gather my surroundings and caught my breath. "Um ... yeah. Sorry."

"Good dream, I assume." Harlstril smiled but then drifted for a second, as though remembering something, much as he had when we first met.

"You okay?" I asked him back.

"Yes ...," Harlstril replied, collecting himself. "Get up. Get ready. Daylight is providing you with your next test."

Brushing off the emotions from my frantic dream, I got out of bed and got ready, dressing once again in my training gear. My ribs were still in agony, but I refused to show any weakness. I would complete these tests, no matter my condition.

"Are you ready for the second day of your testing, Joshua?" Harlstril asked

"Bring it on." I smiled.

"Let's move on, then. Your armor is awaiting you."

Chapter 10

A Friend in Trouble

We walked in silence, except for the clicking of our feet on the ground and the rings of my armor rubbing against itself. My heart still raced from the dream, and no matter how hard I tried, I could not calm myself. I felt as though my heart might pound out of my chest at any moment. I gripped the sword Harlstril had given me yesterday; it seemed to have a calming effect, but not enough to bring me to focus.

"Joshua?"

My attention was instantly on the thick wooden door that stood before me. Harlstril slowly opened it, and with no further instruction I walked through. Immediately my eyes were filled with green. I found myself in the middle of a thick evergreen forest. Ferns and soft moss covered the forest floor; I took a deep breath and just for a moment enjoyed the crisp air all around me. Everything about my surroundings seemed to bring back a memory, but it was an odd feeling, as if I'd been here before yet could not place when or why. Taking a step forward into the beam of sunlight squeezing through the trees, I simply enjoyed the heat on my face.

"Josh!"

I drew my sword instantly. Spinning on one foot, I stopped just in time, as the edge of my ebony blade made contact with Haslo's neck. His eyes were wide, and his breath was held tight.

"Are you insane?" Haslo scolded me.

"*Me*? What on earth are you doing here? And why would you sneak up behind an armed man?"

"Just came to wish you luck. Jeez, someone is a little testy today."

"Thanks ... you might wanna get out of here before the test starts, though." I pointed to the door I came in through but suddenly realized it was nothing but forest floor and trees now. "Oh, for crying out loud!"

"What?" Haslo turned to see what I was pointing at. Once his eyes saw what mine saw, his shoulders sank. "Oops."

"*Oops*?" I was infuriated. Sure, Haslo would be great to have alongside on a mission, but there were two distinct problems. A: He didn't have a weapon with him, basically making him a damsel in distress. B: It might very well be cheating to have him alongside me. So this whole thing could end up being a waste of time.

"Well, I guess I'll just hang out with you." Haslo smiled.

"Fine, but don't bloody well get in the way." I turned to walk on. "And way to show up weaponless!" I suppressed a laugh.

"Sorry. Didn't think I'd need a weapon to wish you luck."

"And look where that almost got you, D-E-D dead, by my sword!" We both laughed and walked on, neither of us knowing what to expect. Something was off, but the scene still looked perfect. I was actually kind of comforted by the company, even though he cut my peaceful lollygagging short. We walked along and I told him about the first three tests.

Haslo hung on every word. I had lost track of how long we had been walking and talking and was about to tell him about my dream, when all of a sudden I heard a thud. Haslo dropped to his knees and planted his face on the ground. My brain wasn't communicating as fast as my emotions. I wasn't making sense of what just happened. I had been so distracted that I had not been paying attention. I was about to wheel around to protect myself from Haslo's fate, when I heard a whirring sound from behind me. Feeling a sharp pain in the back of my head, I felt my knees buckle, and soon my face met the mossy ground. Blackness rolled over me, and the world was full of silence.

The first thought I can recall went something like this: *Sweet mother of all that is good and holy in life! That freakin' hurts!* I slowly crawled to my feet, expecting to have been moved or imprisoned or in a bonfire. But, alas, I had not been moved; I was in the exact same spot where I had fallen. Yet something was missing. I checked through my belongings; everything was still there. Then I noticed an indentation in the ferns and moss. *Haslo.* He was gone. I searched this way and that, yelling for him, but there was no sound. Then I saw it, only a few feet from where we had been standing. Pressed into the mossy ground was a print. Not a footprint of anything I'd ever seen, but a massive claw print. I could have easily fit my whole body inside it. My stomach turned, and I knew this would be no easy test. I drew my sword, took a deep breath, and began tracking this gargantuan beast. It wasn't difficult, at least; I just had to follow the path of utter destruction: ground torn apart, trees uprooted, but luckily, no giant scary monster poo.

I must have walked for most of the day—this creature sure didn't mess around—but I finally heard the sound of rushing water ahead. I hoped it lived near water, or I would need to make camp and wait till morning to continue the search. As I got closer I was halted by thick, vine-filled brush. From the look of the creature's tracks, it must have leapt over the brush. I, on the other hand, did not have jumping power like that. So through was the only way. With my sword at the ready, I began swinging, cutting through the brush, foot by painful foot. After nearly an hour, I made it through the twenty feet of brush and found a large chasm on the far side. I could see the rushing water below, about 150 feet down. Along the edge of the cliff were claw marks and scrapes, but why take Haslo to the river? Then my eye caught where the marks were headed. Just down the way a bit, there was a large cave mouth. And clearly, no way to get to it. The edges of the cliff were not fit for climbing unless you had thirty feet of reach. Short for my age, I wasn't quite there yet!

That left just one way down ... jump! I backed away from the cliff and removed my armor; it would have been nice to keep it, but I'd be sitting at the bottom of the river if I did. So I strapped my sword and sheath to my side, pretended that I wasn't going to die attempting this, and took off running. It's always easier to make big jumps when you do something dumb like run. I reached the edge of the chasm and jumped. I flattened out my body as much as possible, to catch maximum wind to help slow my descent. The air was moving too fast to breathe, which would have been nice to do before I hit what might be only three inches of water. At the last second I pulled into a dive and closed my eyes; the moment I hit water, I arched my back, to try to curl back to the surface before hitting bottom, but I realized very quickly that that was not going to happen. The river was more than three inches deep, but it still wasn't deep enough. I hit the bottom hard, slicing my arm wide open, and blood filled the water around me. Frantically I righted myself and kicked off the riverbed. I finally got myself above water, but the racing river was carrying me very fast toward the cave. Problem was, it was going to carry me very fast *past* it. Coughing frantically to clear my lungs while swimming with one arm was not an easy feat, but if I didn't make the cave, I had no idea if I would ever make it back. Finally I threw my other arm into it, pushing back the nearly unbearable pain, until I was safe. My adrenaline was filling my whole body, as it were life and death whether I made it or not. Reaching the very edge of the ledge that led to the cave, I grabbed hold of the rocks and pulled myself up.

I could already feel my mind slipping as I watched the blood pouring out of my arm. I tore the sleeve off my shirt and wrapped my arm with it, using my teeth and free hand to tie a tight knot. Sure, I might lose my arm if I couldn't find another way to stop the bleeding, but I'd lose my life if I did nothing. Once the tourniquet was tied, I stumbled into the cave, hoping for anything helpful, but my vision soon diminished to nothing, and my legs gave out from under me. I had enough strength to pull myself into a small nook against the cave wall, and then I slipped into nothingness.

Chapter 11

The Chunya

The long silence of unconsciousness finally ceased. I thought for sure with this dreamless blackness that I had passed into the next life. But, alas, I was brought back to the land of the living. I knew this because I could feel the pain all over my body. Before opening my eyes, I realized that I was not where I had fallen unconscious. I had been moved, and I could tell that I was on some form of rudimentary bed, probably made of some kind of wood, with nothing to soften it. I slowly opened my eyes and began to scan the room, hoping no one was lurking in the dark. Apparently I was alone in here, but I could tell I was in no hotel, and definitely not back in the compound. The roof over me was thatched straw, the walls of rock and mud. In the corner was a child's rickety wooden rocking chair, and everything else seemed to be of the same tribal kind of design.

I began to sit up and felt the blood rush to my head and pain sear through my arm. I could feel it before, but now I thought I might pass back out. I gingerly pressed through until I was able to sit up and allow my body to circulate the blood properly. I looked around for my sword, but it was nowhere to be seen. Not that it would really do me a whole lot of good. I slowly peeled back the strange papery bark around my arm. Once that was off, I could see that the huge slice was filled with a yellow powder, which had a spicy aroma. I checked over the rest of my body to make sure I wasn't marinating for someone's tasty dinner. Lucky for me, the rest of my body was spice-free. The potential of being dinner was minimal, but I still didn't know who had me here. I began the painful process of stretching my muscles. Not really the best thing for me, but if it was between muscle damage and death, I'd take muscle damage! The pain was excruciating, and just as I was feeling like moving might be an option, the door burst open.

A man all of three feet tall stood in front of me. Old, with long silver hair and a full, silver, scruffy beard, he did not look as though he lacked strength. He leaned to the left, where his hand held a cane, keeping weight off his right leg. His grey cloak looked far from ordinary, and something about this tiny man screamed leader, chief, general, maybe even king, although he did not stand proud as a king would. His eyes were dark as dark could be, and kind as well. I think the whole time I was analyzing him, he was doing the same to me. I was snapped out of my focus as he yelled out behind him.

"He lives! He lives!" There was a sudden roar of cheers erupting from beyond the door, and it was only moments before the room was flooded with tiny people. Then I realized what was going on: I was clearly still asleep and dreaming about *The Lord of the Rings*. I was most certainly in Hobbiton. But after a moment I realized that one thing I knew well was dreams, and this was not one of them. The little people looked much like hobbits, yet none of them were as nicely dressed as the old man. They were not in rags or dirty; you could just tell that the old man was of some importance. He noticed quickly that I was not comfortable being hemmed and hawed over by hobbits, and he quickly ushered everyone out, closing the door behind them, and leaving the two of us alone in silence. He looked at me, and a smile crept across his face.

"Man of tall stature, you bring with you the tides of hope and freedom!" He looked to the door as if motioning to the commotion. "I must apologize for that, but my people, all my people, have longed for this day for many generations, from far before the times of telling stories. Before when we even know." Taking a step closer, he continued. "You see, it is said a man of tall stature will come, come to set us free!" He pointed his stubby little finger at me as he smiled. "And you are the first man of such size to enter our cave. Do you see? Do you understand? You are our deliverer." The little man was more like a child at Christmas than an old man in that moment. ... Christmas, it had been a long time since I'd thought of Christmas, I could feel memories slipping into my mind, smells of cinnamon and pine. Mornings full of sheer excitement ...

"Ow!" A sudden pain shot through my arm as the little man touched it.

"I am so sorry." He shrank back immediately.

"It's all right; it just hurt." I was a little mad, but he was so tiny, who could stay mad at him?

"Do you understand?" he asked with some level of calm.

"Um, no. ... What exactly am I saving you from?" I asked, not at all sure what I was about to deal with.

His face quivered, as if the question were sensitive, but if I had to be fighting something, I wanted details. "I must show you. Come."

I stood up and got my bearings before moving forward and out the door. As I looked around, I realized we were inside a massive cavern. The ceiling was a good sixty feet up and had a handful of holes to the open sky above, letting light in. The cavern was immensely wide, with dozens of huts, and was large enough to house hundreds of these little people. Along the walls were many caves leading in all directions, but which cave led out, I had no idea. Escape didn't seem like a realistic option. The little man led me into a second hut, much like the first, but this one did not have a bed or anything like that in it. It did, however, have a fairly large library and a strange glass device in the center. The little old man quickly closed all the blinds and lit a small fire in a dish, then gently placed it inside the glass device. Immediately an image spread across the wall in front of me.

It looked like a painting, a very accurate painting; it was a cavern larger than the one I was in now, but with natural stone bridges over a flowing river of lava. But this picture was much more than bridges and lava. All along the right wall were hundreds of those little people, dressed in full battle gear. Archers lined the walls with bows pulled and arrows flying. The floor was dotted with spear-wielding little people, but that was not what made this picture frightening. Standing against the left wall was a creature unlike anything I had ever seen before. The best and closest comparison I could make was a thirty-foot tall version of Lasnek, but to be honest, next to this creature Lasnek was as cuddly as a kitten.

This creature was birthed straight from the most evil of nightmares. Its rear haunches were pure muscle, and instead of feet it had truck-sized talons, like a scary mother eagle. Each talon was shiny silver, or maybe more like chrome, and razor sharp. Its chest was almost human-looking, and again of solid muscle. Its skin was jet black and looked like snakeskin, full of scales. Its arms fit well with the rest of it, black, scaled, and with nearly human hands. Like Lasnek, it had claw-tipped fingers; unlike Lasnek, its fingertips were shiny, like silver or chrome. What I hadn't noticed at first was its tail, thick as the trunk of a tree, until it thinned out near the end, where a silvery chrome spade the size of a small car awaited anyone foolish enough to enter its path of destruction. Two massive black ram's horns curled out of its head, while its face glared with the flash of razor-sharp teeth and an animallike nose billowed smoke. And those eyes! Blood red, as though they could very well suck out your soul if you connected with them! My heart began to race as I realized what these folk wanted me to free them from. Not in a million years could I defeat such a creature. Before I could say anything, I noticed that the little man was tearing up. I looked closely at the picture and realized this was not just any painting, but a painting of a historical moment.

"What happened?" I asked, not really sure I wanted to know the answer.

"Years we spent training, preparing our strongest to rid us of this monster. We had waited for as long as we could remember for you to come, but we would wait no more. You see, every year, before the cold comes, we must sacrifice one of our daughters to the creature. If not, the alternative is"—he paused and I could see the pain in his eyes—"much worse. But we would free ourselves."

"Why not just run away?" I asked.

"You do not think we tried? The creature caught up with us, and in a matter of a few seconds half our people lay dead across the valley floor. In that moment we decided that we would fight for freedom or die trying, but no more would we live this way." I could see him holding back tears. "I once had three daughters and a son; now I have only one daughter. The time had come. Lots were thrown, and it was again I who lost, so not only did I lose my first daughter, but now my second daughter would lie upon the altar as well. We moved our forces into the caves and searched until we found the cavern of the beast. Then we waited; for three days we sat in silence waiting for the beast to leave.

"How did you know it would go?" I asked.

"Because my daughter was on the altar, and the beast would go for her." I watched as tears rolled down his cheeks. "Once the creature was gone, we got to work. The main bridge down the center of the cavern was the only bridge big enough to carry the weight of the beast, so over the next three days, we worked until the bridge was weak enough that it would collapse with a great deal of weight upon it, sending the beast to his death in the boiling river of lava. On the third day, though, we heard cries echo through the caverns. My son and I nearly lost our minds in that moment, but luckily the men kept us quiet, so as to not ruin our trap." There was a moment where he could not continue, but once he gathered himself he pushed on. "Three days we sat in wait for the beast to arrive. Archers scattered throughout the small tunnels in the walls, men with spears hidden in the shadows of the corners. Finally the creature came into the cavern. We waited and watched as it walked right into our trap. The bridge crumbled and down it went, slamming into the lava below and sinking to its doom. A great cheer erupted, for freedom was ours at last. In our moment of victory, we were all interrupted by a low groan emerging from the lava below, and as we looked over the edge, an arm appeared from out of the river, and slowly the beast pulled itself free and unharmed. Shock ran through us all for a moment, but we had come prepared for more! So I screamed out, "*Fire!*" and every archer released their arrows. Hundreds of arrows filled the air, and not one of them missed their target. Once the beast made it to the top, the spearmen viciously attacked it. They stabbed over and over again, until its blood flowed like a river of black. Over and over they stabbed, until their spears broke. Every arrow was shot. And the beast slunk back into a corner. We had hoped it would die, but then a laugh bellowed forth, a laugh that turned our hearts to ice and brought a fear like none other over us. Then we watched as all its wounds began to heal themselves, and in one flick of its tail."

The little man turned the glass device, and a new picture came up. Same cavern, but the floor was stained red with blood. The picture was blurry, and for that I was quite thankful; my imagination knew what I would have seen otherwise.

"Half my men were dead. Within a few more seconds it had clawed every archer from the walls; none were left, not even my own son." His eyes welled up with tears, and he tried many times to continue before he found success. "The creature knew I was there but did not harm me. It is no animal; it is intelligent and cruel. In that moment it knew my greatest pain would be to live on after losing so much of my family. That I would have to explain to the remainder of my people that we had failed. That we would have to bring another girl to the altar, year after year, and that none of them would have fathers, because of me." Finally he could not take any more and sat down of the floor to weep. I did not know his people, but I could feel my eyes well up with tears, imagining the pain these people must have gone through.

After a few minutes he stood, a fire in his eyes. "But you," a slight smile crept across his tear-stained face, "you were the one prophesied."

"Wait, what prophecy?" I asked.

The little man spun around and walked to the bookshelf behind him. He ran his hands along until he found a very old, tattered book. Gingerly he removed it from the shelf and opened it easily to the page he was looking for. Clearly it was a commonly read page, and a memory had been made in the spine to open to it.

"Then a man of large stature," he read, "once he has changed that which haunts himself, will bring deliverance and freedom.

He will take from them evil, pain, and fear, and replace it with goodness and peace. He brings you deliverance, so welcome him and help him."

I glanced over at the book to see it held a great deal more writing, and if I was going to be pegged as said hero, I wanted to know as much as possible. "May I see that?"

He looked at me cautiously, as if he were about to hand over his most precious gem, but then softened and gently handed it to me. As I skimmed over it, I saw what I was looking for. The prophecy made no sense; something was clearly missing. So I read, "Then a man of large stature," after which a word had been burned out of the book. Clearly there was something that someone didn't want these people or me to know.

"What was written here?" I pointed to the missing word.

"No one knows, but the prophecy is clear, and how important could one word really be?" He smiled, and I was about to press on, when I saw something that caught my curiosity. The simple fact that this remote tribe, with no contact with the outside world, could speak English was amazing, but as I looked at the bookshelves, I realized something more. Every book seemed to be in a different language, many of them not even in my own alphabet. I recognized a few, like Spanish and French, but most I could not. Some looked Asian, and others were just crazy-looking. One near the bottom was in ancient Egyptian hieroglyphs!

"Can you read all of those?" I asked, amazed.

"Yes, why?"

"How many languages do you know?" I was even more amazed.

"We do not know. But every seventh day, a book appears in the middle of the village, and when we pick it up, understanding is brought to the Chunya." He paused. "Is this not common among people of large stature?"

"That is not common in anyone, ever." Whatever they had, I wanted it, but I had a feeling deep down inside that I would never be granted such a gift. Suddenly I realized I did not even know who this guy was. Terribly rude of me, I know. "Wait, who are you?"

"Oh my! I am embarrassed with being so impolite." I could see the red flush into his face. "My name is Rahas." He bowed as he said this. "Chief of the Chunya peoples, and your humble servant."

"Um ... thanks. I'm Josh," I replied.

"Joshua."

"No, Josh," I corrected.

"Yes, Joshua! Sir Joshua!" He was ecstatic.

"No, it's just Joshua. I mean Josh ... oh heck, whatever." I wasn't in the mood to argue with him any longer. He was far too excited, anyway, and I didn't dare burst his little bubble of happiness. "Sir Joshua" stuck very quickly as we continued to talk long into the night. We had gathered around the fire near the center of the village, and Rahas told stories. The light from the sun had long since stopped flooding the cavern, and you could see the stars up above. Once in a while you could see the moon through one of the holes in the cavern ceiling. Finally the Chunya people started thinning as they headed off to bed, and finally Rahas took me back to my hut. The excitement had not worn down, but Rahas knew I would need my sleep and healing if I were to free them from this monster. The idea of slipping away in the middle of the night seemed tempting, but at the same time I felt for these people. Plus, Haslo was still out there. As I rubbed my rewrapped arm, I thought, *If not for the Chunya, at least for Haslo. Haslo, my friend, where are you?*

Chapter 12

Love

I slipped, as usual, immediately into a dream. I stood on a stone path high above a flowing river of lava. Near the far end of the path, I saw a throne cut from the rock. It somehow drew me toward it, as if beckoning me to sit upon it. I walked slowly forward until I stood before the seat. As I turned to sit, I noticed three figures floating before me. Each was the size of an average man, but they had no bodies, just transparent floating cloaks. They did not frighten me; maybe they set me a little on edge, but I was not really afraid.

As I sat on the throne, one figure floated toward me, and, with a snap, its head faced me. Although there was no distinct face or eyes, I could feel eyes boring into my own. The entity shot toward my chest and vanished inside me, instantly filling me with a rush of fury. My hands clenched, and I banged my fists on the stone armrests.

Immediately two men appeared before me, firmly holding a chained and gagged Lasnek. He was lashing about furiously, but the men easily held him. I watched as my hand rose in front of me. Like a caesar, I held my thumb to the side and then dropped it, sending Lasnek to his doom. His eyes opened wide in shock, and then the men lifted him off the ground and tossed him into the lava below. I watched for a moment as his body dissolved in the liquid fire.

My attention was drawn away by another of the dark cloaks floating toward me; again it turned its invisible face in my direction and then disappeared into my chest. The wind was knocked out of me, and anger filled my every fiber, but soon a deep satisfaction permeated me. As I thought about the death of Lasnek, I was filled with a dark sense of pleasure. Leaning back in my throne, I basked in my own glory and greatness.

Soon, however, the two men reappeared, this time holding Rahas. He was not the happy, joyful Rahas I remembered, but ferocious and flailing about. He broke free of the men and raced toward me, pulling a blade from behind him. I did not react. When the blade was mere inches from me, the men once again captured him. Rahas screamed at me, yet I heard only silence. Once again I watched as my hand lifted and the thumb went down. As the two men lifted Rahas off the ground, he only closed his eyes, ready to die with pride. The men tossed him into the fiery abyss.

I would have watched, but the final cloaked figure came toward me and again bored into my eyes with its invisible ones before vanishing into my chest. Waves of depression swept over me; I felt hollow and empty about what I had done. But then a greater feeling of success surged through me. I ran my fingers through my hair and focused on slowing my breathing, to no avail. My emotions overwhelmed me, deluging my mind and heart. Rage. Success. Fury. Victory. Hopelessness. Challenge. Fear. Triumph. Loss. Victory.

My hands clenched the armrests, and the men appeared once again. This time they were not holding anyone but merely escorting Haldel. It was clear they dared not touch him, yet he came willingly. My body reacted without orders from my mind as I stood and walked toward Haldel. The two men vanished immediately. Unlike them, I did not fear Haldel. As I walked toward him, he spoke in seemingly soft tones, yet all I heard was silence. His eyes welled with tears that would not fall. I stood directly in front of him, my insides feeling as if they would be torn apart by the rage filling me. I reached slowly to my left and grabbed hold of my sword. For a moment I wished what was happening to stop, but my anger was too great. I buried the sword in his chest. I watched his eyes close and open again, letting loose the tears that had waited there. Heartless, I twisted the sword and watched him fall to the ground. The light that usually shone about him vanished, and he was nothing but a dark frame.

With that the men reappeared, and I waved my hand to them to clean up the mess. But as they threw him over the edge, a sudden regret flooded over me. I could not believe what I had done; as I started to realize this, I felt a hand on my shoulder. Soft and warm it was, and I was comforted for a moment, but then my veins were filled with ice, and that soft hand turned cold and clawed as it dug into my shoulder. I felt fury and confusion and depression and power! Power like I had never felt before, as if nothing could stand in my way. The hand vanished and I heard a whistling, like the sound of an arrow cutting through the air. I watched as it whizzed by me and into the throne.

A small blue ribbon unfurled from it, and I saw the word *LOVE,* with a white tree behind it. As I approached it, I could feel its heat. But I had to get closer, I had to have it. My skin burned as I approached it, until finally I grabbed hold of the arrow. The pain was beyond anything I could remember, but for some reason it was comforting; I felt truly alive. I pulled and pulled on the arrow, as ever fiber of my body felt as if it might explode at any moment, yet I knew I was too late. The cavern around me began to melt away. And my dream was soon to turn into the world of the awake.

With a jolt I sat up in my bed. A cold sweat soaked my body. All of the emotions I had felt still surged inside me. I noticed a figure lingering in the shadows, reached for my sword, and realized again that it was not there. The figure took my momentary slip and bolted for the door. I took off after it, but after two or three times of the figure ducking behind a hut, he or she had disappeared. I looked for a few minutes but soon realized that whoever it was, was long gone. Something about that figure seemed familiar, but for the life of me I could not figure out what or who it was. Giving up, I walked back to my hut, thinking about the dream. Questions rattled around in my head as I tried to understand why I would send Rahas to his death, or why I would kill Haldel. Killing Lasnek was clear enough; I hated that guy! I'd gladly send him to his death any day of the week, but Rahas and Haldel—that just seemed illogical. Disturbed by the dream, I crawled into bed and hoped for peaceful sleep until morning.

I was pleasantly surprised when I woke and felt more rested than I'd felt in quite some time. It was as though that stiff bed of wood was better than my king-size bed back in the complex. I could hear a ruckus going on outside my door, but I cleaned up and dressed before going outside. As I opened the door, I saw baskets everywhere, with all sorts of oddities in them. Fruits and vegetables and blankets and trinkets. Suddenly I heard a few girls squeal, and as I looked they bowed, noses to the ground.

"Oh, no ... wait, I ... thank you?" I stammered like a bloody idiot. *This is new,* I thought to myself. I gathered my voice and tried again. "Thank you very much, but please don't bow to me," I said kindly, kneeling in front of them to show I was no king or hero or anything of the sort.

"We are showing our respect to you, Great Deliverer," one of them spoke as they rose.

"I have not yet delivered anyone; why bow now?"

It was the smallest of the girls who spoke, brushing her long dark hair out of her face. "We believe that you *will* deliver us, for that is what was spoken in the prophecy."

"Well, thank you very much." I felt a little uncomfortable. "I'll do my best."

"Joshua! Sir Joshua!" I heard a voice I recognized well by now.

"Rahas!" I called back as I watched the four little girls scurry off. He reached me and threw his arms around my waist in a very awkward hug.

"How is your arm, Sir Joshua?" His grin extended from ear to ear, and it was not until then that I noticed the lack of pain in my arm. I slowly took the wrappings off; my gaping wound had turned into a very manly scar, all the way from my wrist to my elbow. I moved my arm this way and that, and it seemed in perfect health.

"You are healed now. You can free us, Sir Joshua." Rahas waited for my excited "Absolutely!" in reply. I racked my brain for an excuse, but I was full of energy, completely healed, and ready as I could ever be for this fight.

"How did you heal my arm so fast?" I tried to change the subject.

"Me? Oh no, we Chunya have not the ability to do such amazing things!" He smiled a very mischievous smile. "I was visited by a man late last night, and he said you would awaken this morning ready to fight. When I told him you needed time to heal, he said you were already healed!" He clapped his hands. "And you are!"

"Who was this man?" I pressed.

"I cannot tell. I was sworn to secrecy, and I would never break my word." Rahas's smile grew, and I knew he was still waiting for my reply. As much as I wanted to run, I would never find my own way out, and Haslo needed me. I would have to fight this beast sooner or later, and I was only wasting energy by waiting.

"I will need a guide, for I will not waste time and energy searching for the beast."

As if Rahas finally was released to get the ball rolling, he called out, "Dersolo!" and a little boy came running over. He could not have even been two feet tall. "This is my great-nephew, Dersolo. He will be your guide to the beast's lair."

"A child?" I was disturbed. "You would send a child to a place like that?"

"Do not doubt what lies before you." He placed both of his stubby hands on Dersolo's short shoulders. "He is exactly the one fit for such an adventure. Besides, he is the only one other than I who knows how to get there."

"Why don't you guide me?" I asked, a little troubled.

"Ah, yes. That would suit, now wouldn't it? Except for the fact that the beast knows my scent all too well now, and we would both be dead long before we ever reached his lair." I could tell in his eyes that if it were possible, he would have been my guide. "Do you not trust my judgment? Do you really think I would willingly send another of my kin into the lair of that beast if it were not the only way?" He paused to let me think on his words. "No, my friend, I may live a life full of joy and innocence, but I do not make such decisions rashly." Rahas crossed my path, reaching for a pack, which he carefully attached to Dersolo's tiny back. "Sir Joshua, my great-nephew will take excellent care of you and lead you silently into the lair of the beast. I can only hope for a swift return of you both."

Dersolo looked me confidently in the eye; he was willing to be entrusted with such a task, restraining any fear of or anger for the creature. I looked back to Rahas, who seemed slightly uneasy.

"I will protect him and make sure he is returned to you safely," I promised, and fully meant it.

"I have made you each a pack with food and blankets." He pointed to the other packs, which were lying near the entrance of my hut. "It is a day-and-a-half-long journey. Good luck." Rahas gathered himself, gave his great-nephew a firm hug, and then ushered us out of the cavern village. We each waved a short good-bye, then headed deeper into the caves.

Chapter 13

The Scream

The longer the walk took, the more it seemed to fray my nerves to nothingness. There was a part of me that understood why I felt this way. I was about to fight a creature unlike anything I had ever seen before. But at the same time, size was not always the determiner of a battle. Sure, this thing was colossal and slaughtered an army and was built like a Sherman tank and had weapons coming out of every end of it, but hey, what could possibly go wrong?

As we walked, I started to notice everything, whether it was there or not. I found that the fire from our torches was playing tricks on my eyes, and I realized Dersolo was probably feeling some of the same things I was. Finally I broke the silence and asked the only thing I could think of.

"Tell me, Dersolo, how is it that you know how to get to the beast's lair?" That didn't really distract us from what was making us nervous, but it was my best attempt.

"I was never supposed to know, but when I was a kid I followed the warriors, hiding in the shadows for three days and eating the scraps left behind. I knew full well that I was asking for a serious beating when I made it home. But I had to see it." He paused and I could see him imagining the glory of what should have happened. "The downfall of the great beast. Our people rising against it, to finally take our freedom: such a glorious day could not be told in paintings and carvings but had to be seen. I was hoping that celebrations would be so amazing, that punishment would have been forgotten." He paused a moment. "But it would not work out like that. I was caught before the creature came to the cave. I was reprimanded sternly and sent home alone."

"They sent you home alone?" Definitely not great parenting in my books!

"They had no choice. Every soldier was needed for this. And none could be spared for babysitting. It was not a choice made easily, but one that needed to be made. Besides, it was only a day's journey home. It took us three days to find it the first time, because of the number of Chunya, and we had never been there before. Once I arrived home, the punishment I received was severe and well deserved, but it did not compare to the punishment of watching Rahas return alone. We knew immediately what had happened, and for seven days we mourned and fasted for the dead. Mostly we fasted because no one wished to eat. It was then that the tribe decided to wait for you, the prophesied one. We would await upon your deliverance, but I would not."

"What did you do?" I asked, curious as to what little Dersolo planned on doing.

"I began training, researching. You see, one day I will take Rahas's place as leader and chief. And I will bring about an end to this fear." He stood tall and proud.

"Then why am I here?" I asked.

"Because of the prophecy. I will gladly allow you to free us, but in the case that you do not, I will not lie down and die." Dersolo was a fiery little guy, and I was certain he would make a proud leader one day.

"Do you believe I can do it?" I asked.

"Defeat the beast?" he asked back.

"Yes."

"I believe you will bring us deliverance, which everyone assumes means you will deliver us from the creature, but the prophecy does not mention anything about you killing it. So I hope you can."

"And what of the missing word? Someone clearly burnt a part of the prophecy out, but why?" I asked.

"I do not know. It really could be anything, and I'm sure it's terribly important, but we'll never know. So we do what we can."

"How old are you?" I asked him, seeing that he seemed awfully wise for the age I thought he was.

"I am fifteen years old, nearly a man." He looked at me curiously. "And you, Sir Joshua?"

"I am sixteen years old, nearly a man as well." I smiled at him, and we both cracked up laughing. The rest of our walk was a great deal less serious. As we were both "nearly men," we figured we'd live it up and be kids a little longer. Soon the shadows became a game, and the noises became like music and the fear began to drain away. I knew I would have to face it soon, but now was not the time. Dersolo told me much about his people and their customs and celebrations. As heartbreaking as their lives were, they always sought to find the best in everything. But soon it all came to an end, as we saw the reddish glow at the end of the tunnel.

"We are here, Sir Joshua."

"Then you need to go," I replied.

"I can stay! I can help you fight." He stood strong.

"If anything happens to you, who will lead your people? Dersolo, you have a greater responsibility, and I have a promise to uphold. Now go, protect your people, and if I fail, succeed where I could not!" I went to shake his hand, but he swung his arms around my legs and clamped tightly.

"Do not fail, Sir Joshua!" With that he turned and headed into the darkness, and I turned and headed toward the reddish glow. The tunnel opened up into the cavern I recognized from the strange projection machine. In the middle of the room, the large stone bridge was broken and caved in. Far below was the river of lava, hence the reddish glow of everything. Above and below were large stalactites and stalagmites.

I found a bridge along one of the edges and crossed over it until I was on the large open platform on the far side.

"Hey, Ugly! How about we do this thing before dinner? I've got places to go and people to see!" I yelled this into the darkness beyond, really hoping the beast would just run away in fear. Obviously, a well-thought-out plan.

I realized Plan A was not going to work when I heard the worst sound in the world. It was the sound of footsteps coming toward me, not normal footsteps, but footsteps that were literally shaking the ground beneath me. Following the footsteps came a blood-curdling shriek, echoing off the walls of the cavern. I could tell it was from the beast, and it had a certain high-pitched sound coupled with a mighty depth. I had never heard a noise quite like it, and I immediately felt my heartbeat triple the speed. Next came the eyes, piercing red dots in the blackness. They grew larger and larger until its face appeared in the light. Not like the face of an animal, but almost human—tormented, deformed, and black as oil, and somewhat human. Near the temples were those horns, those massive curled horns. As its body came into the light, I realized that the picture gave this creature no justice. Its sheer size was beyond anything I had ever seen. My heart sank, and I could feel my knees weaken. How anyone ever expected me to defeat this creature was beyond me.

Finally the tail, swaying back and forth, came fully into the light. From the massive, razor-sharp talons, to its bared fangs, to the silver spade swaying back and forth, hypnotizing me with its sheer awesomeness, to the black spikes riddled along its spine, this creature seemed impossible to defeat. And yet here I stood, staring back at it, sweating bullets, ready to die for a people I barely knew. It stood up tall on its hind legs and stretched out its leathery, ebony dragon wings. The creature easily stood thirty feet tall, but its wingspan was nearly sixty. This creature was a beast of sheer magnificence.

I drew my sword, breathed deep, and readied myself for battle. As quick as a flash, the beast whipped its tail at me. I leapt out of its way, narrowly missing a clean cleaving. Back on my feet, I looked for the tail. There it sat, wedged between two rocks, the creature heaving to release it. I bolted fast and hard, knowing I would not get another chance like this. Ducking and dodging as the creature tried to slash me with its talons, I reached the tail and sliced hard and fast, digging the edge of the sword deep into the tail, nearly cutting off the spade. But it was not enough, and the added pressure of the beast's pulls wedged the sword in place. I pulled and pulled, and in my moment of distraction, I was slapped by one of those massive claws.

I skidded across the ground but then noticed that the creature's tail had finally come loose, and my sword was sent bouncing across the floor to me. I shot to my feet and snapped it up, but not in time to miss the next claw. I spun to avoid connecting with the talons but was still sent flying into the air. Connecting with a stalactite, I then fell directly above the creature. But I readied my sword and dug it into the side of its foreleg on the way down, burying the sword all the way, and slicing down until I was near the ground, where I pushed off and hit bottom. I tucked and rolled as best I could, but I knew it was not enough. Something in me cracked, probably a rib, but I couldn't be sure. Before I could react again, I was slammed by the broad side of the creature's spade, which send me soaring through the air again, and into the same stalactite. This time I fell all the way to the ground and crumpled when I hit. I knew for sure I had broken multiple ribs this time, but my arms and legs were still semi-intact. Slowly I got to my feet; it was as fast as I could move. I looked this way and that, but the creature was gone. I looked around the entire room, but there was nothing to be seen. Then I heard the sound of a large droplet splashing. I turned to see a puddle of black blood on the ground and knew what was about to happen. I looked up in time to see the creature dive down. I tried to roll out of the way, but I was too slow. Its talons closed around me like a cage, knocking my sword away and pressing me tightly to the ground. Its face lowered to me, baring its teeth as if mocking my feeble attempts. Then a deep laugh emerged from the beast, low and evil, filling me with the realization that I was finished.

Far above, one of the large spikes from the ceiling was swaying back and forth. It must have been the one that I had hit. It could break at any moment, but with a little help, it would break now, planting itself cleanly in the creature's back. But how? I was stuck here, unable to move, and even if I could move, I could never throw something that high. Then a small object soaring through the air caught my eye. I watched as it smacked the spike, which broke free and fell silently. The beast mocked me, unaware of the natural weapon about to spear it. With great force, the spike drove itself into the creature's back, sending it rearing up on its haunches and roaring in pain. The spike fell out with a mighty crash, and the beast backed up into the darkness.

I very slowly got to my feet, feeling every broken rib scream in protest. I turned to see Dersolo running toward me.

"Are you okay, Sir Joshua?" He scrambled to my side and helped me up.

"I've seen better days." I laughed a bit and realized quickly what a foolish thing that was. "I thought I told you to leave."

"You might have said something along those lines." Dersolo smiled. "A thank-you would also be fitting here."

"Thank you!" I looked at the leather strap in his hand. "How did you learn to do that?"

"Read about it in a book, about the power of a tiny stone that could conquer a great enemy. So I made one and have been practicing to take down the beast." He smiled, showing off his little leather sling.

"I need to find my friend Haslo. I think the creature took him." I started walking toward where the creature had gone.

"Who is Haslo?" Dersolo asked, and I explained the story of how we had both gotten knocked out and he was gone when I'd awoken. So we searched the caves, following the trail of black blood all the way, until finally we came upon a low-lit room. It had many thick wooden doors, with barred windows, clearly a small jail of some kind. Looking through the windows, I could see that most of the cells were empty, but one held someone curled up in the back corner.

"Haslo! Haslo, is that you?" I asked, opening the door.

"Josh?" Haslo replied weakly. "Josh, help."

He was covered in blood, and his clothing was torn. I gently picked him up, pressing through the immense pain that seared my ribs.

"Dersolo, can your people help him?" I asked.

"Yes, but what about the beast?" Dersolo pressed. I realized he wanted us to be certain that the creature was beaten, but Haslo's life was more important at the moment.

"We will have to come back for it. I'm sorry, Dersolo, but Haslo's life is more important right now." I could see his eyes grow dismayed, but I had no choice.

"But if it comes after the people in the village, we will all die!"

"I'm sorry, Dersolo. We'll just have to hope that doesn't happen."

I walked back toward the village, when suddenly my ears where filled with the strangest scream, like that of a child, but the sound was muffled and distorted. Suddenly, the walls around me started melting, and all sound ceased. In a flash, I was no longer in the cave, but back in the hall of doors.

CHAPTER 14

Retaliation

I stood there, knees shaking, as two men took Haslo from my shoulders and gently set him on a gurney. I could see now not only that the blood poured out of his back, but that his arm looked torn apart as well. It was a miracle that he was still alive. Before I could say anything, they had whisked him away, and Harlstril and I were left alone in the hall of doors. I turned to face him.

"Are you all right, Joshua?" He eyed me for injuries.

"Well, I've sure had better days, but I think I'll be all right." I quickly redirected, for I had more pressing questions to attend to. "How did you know about Haslo?"

"Joshua, we've been watching you this whole time, trying to pull you out of the test. Once Haslo went through the door, everything went haywire. We lost all control of the system." He shook his head in amazement. "You were never meant to fight that creature. It was merely a test of courage, to see if you would run or stand and fight. Once you made the decision, one way or the other, you were supposed to exit the test." Something about his eyes told me there was more to all of this, something I wasn't being told, or maybe Harlstril wasn't being told either. Something was certainly not right, though.

"Wait!" Sudden panic came over me. "What about Dersolo? I swore I would get him back safely! It was he who must have been screaming, but why? What happened?"

"Joshua, calm yourself!" Harlstril's forceful tone yanked me into focus. "The tests are merely scenarios, not actually real. Dersolo, Rahas, and all the rest do not exist. They are all fiction."

"But he saved my life," I replied.

"All part of the program, backups to keep you alive in case of problems. And it's a good thing too, or you'd be mincemeat right now." Harlstril put his hand on my shoulder, and immediately a flash of pain raced through my body, my knees buckled, and Harlstril picked me up moments before I hit the ground. "All right, are you? You sure don't seem overly right!" As Harlstril spoke, my eyes slowly closed; the pain, shock, and exhaustion were overwhelming, and my conscious mind slipped away, wanting the safety of the unconscious. Pity that neither was a safe place anymore!

My eyes opened into a dream, where I was looking down upon the Chunya village. But it was no longer a happy place; huts were fully engulfed in flames, bodies of the Chunya were strewn across the ground, blood was everywhere. I felt as though I should be sick, but for some strange reason, I felt deep satisfaction. Then, out of the corner of my eye, I saw someone running and ducking behind huts. I started to move, but it felt as though I were a good twenty feet off the ground. As if I were some kind of giant. Again the figure came out from behind a hut, but this time I recognized him, little Dersolo, with his sling whipping around. I watched as a stone came flying straight at my eye. The stone was traveling too fast for me to react. Then, amid great pain, my right eye lost its sight. I felt the deepest roar come from the depths of my insides. Rage coursed through my veins; I would destroy that little swine!

Again he darted out from behind a hut, and a second stone came, again with too much speed. Everything went black. I felt myself stumble on something and slam into the ground. Then I was overwhelmed by this pulling sensation, as if my entire body were being pulled in on itself. Slowly my body slid inward across the ground, as I got smaller and smaller. I was shrinking, I had been massive before, but I felt my body shrinking to my regular size.

My eyes opened to find myself back in my room, under my blankets, eyesight intact. But I was not alone: a warm, damp breathing flowed over my face. I turned my head slowly, until I caught the eyes of the beast. It turned to run, but I leapt out of bed, bolting out the door after it. As soon as I got into the hall, I recognized it. It was the same doglike creature I had seen before, the wounded one. Tattered wings, talons for front paws. Seriously, what was the deal with everything having talons for paws? No wonder there were no hardwood floors around here; they'd be destroyed. The thing was fast, but I pressed hard to keep pace. Finally I came tearing into the courtyard and ran off toward the Eternity Door. Excellent! There was no way out of this hall. Sure, this thing could push open doors, but it wasn't about to get through the Eternity Door, locked, sealed, massively huge. Oh yeah, this critter was mine!

I reached the entrance to the room with the Eternity Door and opened it slowly, slipping in. I only took a few steps before I heard something behind me. People were coming! I ducked behind a pillar and waited, peering around as two men came through, pushing a gurney. Lying on it was someone who had been seriously wounded. Blood was all over his face. I sneaked along, pillar to pillar. Where could they be going? I realized quickly that there was only one option. This room had only two doors: the entrance and the Eternity Door. I looked around the pillar, and the man put a key in the door and then slowly opened it. I strained my eyes, thinking this might be my chance. I might get a glimpse of what was behind that massive gold and silver door. The crack got wider and wider until ...

"Should you not be resting, young Josh?" Mr. Curry made me jump.

"Uhh, well, um, yes!" I'm pretty sure my voice cracked fifteen times in those four awkward syllables.

"So what are you up to, wandering about at this late hour?" Mr. Curry was not angry, merely intrigued.

"Well, there was this creature in my room, and I followed it, and it led me here, and there was a man, and a gurney, he was bleeding, what happened?" I rattled off everything on my brain in one breath.

"Easy, Josh; everything is okay. You need not worry." Mr. Curry's voice brought absolute calm to me. "The beast is just Jeshual, more or less like a dog. She is usually very safe, but like any dog, she can be defensive and dangerous. Do not be foolish around her." Right, perfectly safe, yet dangerous as all get-out. Sweet. "The injured Cahirian was merely doing his duty. He should be okay in time, but that is the cost of what we do, Josh. To uphold freedom is often to lay one's life in the line of slavers."

"I see," was the best response I could muster.

"Before you go, I have a question." Mr. Curry smiled.

"Ask away."

"How do you feel?" With that he began to walk away, and I suddenly realized my ribs were fully intact. Other than being tired, I was back to normal.

"But how?" I asked before he got through the entrance.

"You need not know the how, simply that it happened. Rest up, Josh. You have much to do tomorrow." He smiled again. "By the way, excellent work on the tests, most impressive."

"Thank you, sir." I smiled to myself as he walked out the door. Mr. Curry was rarely around, but I knew everyone there respected him an awful lot, and to receive a compliment from him was unheard of. I enjoyed it for a moment before heading out. I made it back to the courtyard and realized that I wasn't going to be sleeping anytime soon, so I just sat on one of the benches and enjoyed the peace and quiet of it all. As I sat I heard low breathing getting closer to me, and out of the corner of my eye I could see Jeshual walking toward me. Not menacingly or anything, just like a dog who was looking for love. I snapped my fingers, and she came alongside. Such an odd creature, and I could see why she wouldn't receive much love. She didn't have fur, just black scales, and the wings were merely black spines, without any flesh to actually hold air when in flight. Her back paws were actually normal-looking paws, and the rest of her was mostly dog-looking. Except the bright yellow eyes, almost like a cat's, but there was something unique about them. As I stroked her back, I found a large scar near her hind end. So this *was* the creature I had seen before. As I ran my hands along her back, she slowly curled up and fell to sleep. As much as she looked scaly and frightening, she was soft as silk and calm as ever. I kind of wanted to keep her.

I left after a while and headed to bed, knowing that if I did not rest, I would regret it in the morning. I woke early and got ready. I felt good again, but not like I had felt in the Chunya camp. There I felt amazing, but here, I just felt good.

"You're early," Harlstril said as I walked into the hall of doors.

"Couldn't sleep," I replied.

"You will not need to worry about that this evening. This test will make sure of that fact." He smiled.

"Encouraging. Have we got all the glitches out?" I asked.

"This is a fairly straightforward test; nothing could possibly go wrong in this one." Harlstril seemed very confident.

"What could possibly go wrong?" I replied sarcastically, knowing there were not many worse questions you could ask in life.

"Exactly!" Harlstril replied, not catching my sarcasm. "Well, if you're ready now," he said opening the squeaky door, "there's no time to waste."

"Apparently not." And with that I stepped through the door.

Chapter 15

Cause and Effect

It was clear to me why Harlstril said I'd be sleeping that night. This test consisted of a race up a mountain, in excessively dry, hot, desertlike conditions. But that wasn't the exciting part. You see, the key was not to get *me* to the top of the mountain, but a super-crude wheelbarrow full of rocks. A ridiculous test. I was in no mood to race two men twice my size. One of them was dark-skinned and wearing nothing but a butt-flap and his tattoos, and the other was fairly light-skinned, wearing a beige shirt and light pants. So I did what any genius would and built a catapult out of trees, rope, a banner, and some TLC. It was a moment of utter artistic awesomeness, and I wish I'd had a camera at the time.

So the plan was, launch the wheelbarrow over the mountain. That was so close to impossible that is was easily in the ridiculous category. The wheel barrow almost made it, but two problems arose. A: It shot about ten feet shy of the summit. B: The two other racers were right there. The wheelbarrow smashed them both, so, alas, I would have to run to the summit anyway and push the wheelbarrow ten more feet. I was about a quarter of the way up when I felt the ground start to shake. Which was odd and made me a little nervous, but I was not in a position to stop now. I broke through a small thicket of trees, and my heart sank. Problem C had arisen. Apparently the impact of my wheelbarrow was enough to break loose a large area of rock, which was now sliding at breakneck speed toward me. It took me only a split second to decide which way to go. If I went down, I would never outrun the rockslide, and it was far too wide to run around it. But just ahead was a small ledge, and it might just provide the cover I needed. I bolted toward it, hurling myself at the last second as the rockslide crashed above me. My head collided hard with the rock face, and everything went black.

I was dreaming again. But now I stood at the base of the mountain. I could tell that this was a different side than I had been on before. I stood in a straw hut village; it must have been somewhere in Africa, because everything seemed like the African art I had learned about from Harlstril. The village was full of dark-skinned people; most of them, women included, had tattoos all over their bodies. Small children ran about playing and laughing. But the attention of most in the village was on the summit. It was then that something caught everyone's eye. And I immediately recognized it: my wheelbarrow flying through the air. With a thud it impacted the far side of the mountain, and a mere moment later the ground began to shake. The villagers panicked, racing around to grab their children. They ran away from the mountain, yet I simply stood there, eyes fixed. That was when the whole side of the mountain shifted and began to move. The earth beneath me shook even worse than it had on the far side.

A crying child caught my ear, and there, in between two huts, stood a child, crying for his mom. My body moved of its own free will toward the child and snatched him up. I looked back to the oncoming tsunami of rock. It was too late to run, I would never make it. But a strange feeling bubbled up inside of me. A power like I had never felt before. My hand rose of its own accord, and I could feel my mouth shouting something. But the world around me had gone silent. Again I shouted, hand raised toward the rocks as if they would obey me. Again I shouted with all my might and passion, and then I watched as that little boy held in my arms raised his hand to the rocks. Mere seconds before they overtook us, an invisible wall was put in their way. Soon the rocks completely encompassed us, and I woke up.

My head was throbbing, and I could feel the blood trickling down through my hair. Nothing fatal, just kind of gross. I got to my feet and surveyed the area; everything at the bottom of the mountain was wiped out, and there was nothing but a heap of rock spread out a good thousand feet. My eyes traveled up the mountain to see that I was still a way from the summit. I took off running again, and as I neared the top I watched as the two men started to stand. Both were badly bruised and bleeding, but I was not about to lose for the sake of them. I bolted past and grabbed what was left of my wheelbarrow, dragging it over the top of the mountain. As I did, though, I looked down on the far side to see what was apparently not my imagination. There at the bottom of the mountain was half a village; the first half was now buried in rock, and most of the second half was destroyed. How had my dream been real? Was my subconscious truly that powerful, or was it just dumb luck. My heart sank, as I realized what had I done, what was I thinking, how could I have been so thoughtless of consequences... everything around me started to melt, and again I remember that this was only a test. The world around me turned into the hall of doors, and there stood Harlstril, staring deep into my eyes as if looking for answers to something.

"Harlstril?"

"Yes." He realized he was staring and regained composure. "Sorry, what would you like?"

"Just curious why you were giving me the creeper stare."

"I apologize. I was merely thinking." I could tell he was lying; Harlstril was good at many things, but lying was not one of them.

"May I ask you a question?" I asked.

"You just did."

"You know what I mean. If these tests are merely simulations, why was there a village on the far side of the mountain? Seems kind of pointless."

"Continuity, Joshua. So you may see that every action has an equal and opposite reaction. You must always choose wisely what you do, for you never know what effect it may have upon another."

Have you ever had a teacher who was a genius, but you stumped them once, and they just started making stuff up? And as much as what they made up made perfect sense, you knew they were holding out on you? That was this moment. Harlstril was amazingly good, and he was absolutely right, but somewhere inside I knew the test had nothing to do with that, so why tell me this? I left it alone, knowing full well that if Harlstril did not want to answer, then he never would.

"You were certainly right. This is the only test I'm doing today." I smiled. "I'm going to bed!"

"What can I say? It is just the way I roll." Harlstril attempted to steal one of my phrases and butchered it, but it made me laugh. "Rest, Joshua, and I will see you tomorrow."

With that, I headed off to my quarters, stopping only for a moment to pet Jeshual in the courtyard. After cleaning the blood out of my hair, I climbed into bed. Every muscle in my body felt as if it were on fire, and I could not wait to fall asleep. Apparently sleep couldn't wait either.

In no time I found myself back in the village after the landslide. I stood on top of the rocks, looking down at the unburied village until I heard a noise. The sound of a child's cry came from somewhere behind me. Frantically I searched the rocks, trying to find where it was coming from. Finally I narrowed it down and started moving rocks, as carefully as possible, but without wasting any time. After pulling one of the rocks away, I could see down into an opening. There stood a man holding the little boy from my last dream. He was dressed in a white button-down shirt and khaki pants. After removing a few more rocks, I reached out and pulled the man and child free, just as the rocks started to cave in. We scrambled out of the way before we were all pulled in. The rock settled and we stood and hugged one another.

But the joy was short lived as we turned around and saw the tribe standing behind us. In the front stood a tall, strong man with a long, thin shield and a spear. I assumed he was the chief. He spoke to us, but I had my usual in-dream deafness. I generally got the message, though, from his angry face and pointing of the spear. It was probably something like "You guys have made me generally upset, and I'd like you to relocate to somewhere other than here." Just a rough translation. A woman came up and took the boy, kissed the other guy on the cheek, and walked away. We turned toward the mountain and left the tribe. For a moment I turned to look back, only to see Haldel standing among the people. I could see the sadness on his face, but it lasted only a moment, as Lasnek joined in the scene and drove his trident through Haldel. He did not even fight back, just lay down and died. The dream swirled into blackness, until I heard a faint noise in the distance. It grew louder and louder, until finally it boomed in my ear.

"Wake up, Josh!" Haslo yelled, and my eyes flew open.

Chapter 16

Tricking the Darkness

"Holy sweet mother of Hannah!" I yelled as I bounced out of bed, my eyes wide and wild. I looked at Haslo, but only subconsciously did I know it was he. Three ... two ... one ... and I was back in the world of the living. "*Haslo*!" we both started laughing at my overly dramatic awakening. "Oh man! Are you okay? What happened? Do you have any scars? Have you been in the hospital this whole time?" Haslo took a deep breath and wiped his brow dramatically, as if I had worn him out with questions.

"Easy, Josh. More important things are at stake right now." I knew that look in his eyes: it was the look that meant he had mischief planned. "I've got something sweet to show you, Josh!"

"Bro, it's the middle of the night. Can't this wait till morning?" I asked, as sleep started to call me back.

"Just get up! I'll tell you on the way." With that he slipped out of the room, giving me only a second to throw on some pants and tug on a shirt before bolting out the door. Haslo was already running down the hall, and I had to take off at full speed to catch up.

"Tell me," I whispered once I'd caught up.

"Dude, you gotta see it! It's just not the same to tell you." Haslo smiled.

“At least give me a hint. *Come on,*” I prodded him as we turned a corner.

“All right.” Haslo looked around him to make sure no one was around. “They are making you something for when you finish your tests.”

“What is it?” I was getting excited now.

“I’m not tellin’ ya.” Haslo was enjoying this too much.

“Come on, I’m gonna see it in a second anyway,” I pushed.

“So I guess you’ll just have to be patient for that long, won’t you?” Haslo smirked. “All I can tell you is it’s the sweetest thing I’ve ever seen. They’ve pulled out all the stops to make this perfect for you.”

“What, what, what?”

He stopped abruptly, making me run into the back of him. “Ouch. Josh, focus here. Just through these doors is the coolest thing you’ll ever see.” Haslo paused for effect. “Are you ready?”

“Open the dang door!” I was going to open it myself in a second. But Haslo cracked it open and peered inside. And then stopped.

“What the heck?” He sounded frustrated.

“What?” I said, trying to peer in, but his big head was in the way.

“It was just here, not ten minutes ago.” He stepped back and I looked in to see an empty room.

“Mmm, yes, pretty awesome, Haslo,” I mocked him.

“Your armor, I just saw it!” Haslo looked fuming mad.

“Dude, armor?” I was excited to know what it was, at least.

“It was so sweet! They want it perfect, because you’re supposed to ...” The look on Haslo’s face was a dead giveaway that he had said something he shouldn’t have.

“Supposed to?” I hoped he might finish what he started.

"Um ... nothing ... I've said too much." Haslo turned to walk away.

"Aw, come on!" I called after him.

"No can do, Josh." He didn't even look at me. "Sleep soundly."

Haslo vanished into the dark hallway, and I was left alone, wondering what he could have possibly meant. I walked back to my room and tried to sleep, but I had never thought that all of this training was actually *for* something. At least not for something important. I wasn't sure if I liked the idea of being trained for something I didn't know, but soon sleep swept over me and the blackness seemed to wipe away all the thoughts of what Haslo had said. Morning had enough challenges to offer.

I woke in the morning feeling as if I'd been run over by a big rig. I crawled out of bed and considered calling it an early day, and by early I mean a nonexistent day. But I pushed the thought aside. I would not be seen as weak, not in any way. I dragged myself out of bed and put on my equipment. Once I was ready, I headed off for some food and then to meet Harlstril in the hall of doors. I knew the moment he saw me, he knew.

"Are you okay, Joshua?" He eyed me up and down. "Wisdom maybe saying today is not your day?"

I shook it off and stood taller for a moment.

"No, I'm fine," I lied. "Don't worry about me."

I was well aware that he knew I was lying, but it was as if his thoughts were saying back, *Okay, son, if you are going to pull the stubborn card, you are more than welcome to be tested under strain. After all, it's your test, not mine.*

"All right, then. You know what to do." Harlstril smiled as he opened the door and I walked through.

Instantly I was soaked, which is always a great start to anything. Lightning streaked across the sky and lit up a castle upon a hill lying directly in front of me. A tall, thick wall surrounded the base of the hill. It was not your pointy-roof girly castle; flat-topped towers all made of stone stood straight up, medieval-like. I walked toward the front gate and thought about finding a secret way in, but then thought, *Maybe I should knock.* Just another genius plan. I banged on the door three times, and a voice boomed out through the rain, "Who goes there?"

"My name is Josh!" I yelled back.

"Josh, we have been expecting you." The gate swung open just enough for me to walk through. On the other side was a man dressed in full rain gear. "Follow me."

He led me up to the castle doors and opened them for me.

"Up and to the left, Josh, and fourth door on your right." With that the doors closed behind me, and I was alone in a massive foyer. Marble floors flowed into marble pillars in each of the four corners. There was also a marble staircase at the far end that went up and then split ninety degrees left and right. The entire ceiling was made of glass, and the room was lit by torches and the lightning outside. There were many doors that led out of the foyer, but apparently I was looking for one upstairs and to the left. So I ventured forward, glad for marble floors; had they been carpeted, I'm sure the owners would not have been happy with my dripping-wet ways. As I reached the plateau where the stairs split left and right, I looked left.

Suddenly there was an explosion just down the hall. I ran fast toward it. Sure enough, fourth door on the right, blown to pieces, and on the left side there was an old man crumpled on the floor. His clothing was singed, and his beard and white hair were smoldering. I checked to see whether he was breathing, and he seemed okay, just unconscious at the moment. Suddenly the hair on the back of my neck stood tall, and my head swiveled to see inside the room. Thick black smoke was filling the room, and

I could barely see within. Glass lay strewn about the floor amid a few strange tubes here and there. I looked back at the man and made the connection. His white clothes were those of a scientist. Clearly an experiment had gone wrong, but something else was not right here. In the darkness I thought I saw something move, but my attention was pulled away.

"What are you doing here?" I turned around to see a girl standing there glaring at me, her bright green eyes trying to strike fear in me.

"I'm not really sure, to be perfectly honest with you." I found my tone a little snippy, but I didn't really care at this point. She took a step closer and was about to say something, when her eyes drifted toward the old man crumpled on the floor. How she hadn't noticed him before, I have no idea.

"What have you done to my uncle?" she screamed.

"What?" I took another step back, realizing this was not going to go well.

"*What* have you *done* to my *uncle*?" She clearly had attitude issues, and I was not about to deal with that.

"Listen, crazy!" I could tell that comment wasn't about to help anything, but it felt good to say. "I didn't *do* anything. I found him this way."

"Right. You just happened to find my uncle beaten and bruised on the floor." I heard a noise in the room that stole my attention. And I could see a shadow moving toward us. "See? You can't even look me in the eye ..."

"Quiet!" I hissed at her. Her chin sharply drew back at the insult of being given a command. "Wow, attitude."

"Don't tell me what to do. This is my house!" She fumed, but I was more focused on whatever was creeping toward us. I gathered my patience and looked her straight in the eye.

"Listen, you *need* to be quiet. There is ..."

"Who do you think you are?" She waved her index finger in the air as if it would add to her point. "You do not tell me to be quiet!"

"*Shut up*!" Man, this was the worst test ever. I was certain this had to be a patience test, and Harlstril was going to get it when I got back. He had never taught me anything about dealing with annoying, bratty girls full of attitude.

"What are you ..."

She was cut short by a creature much like Jeshual, but about three times her size, leaping into the hallway. Its head was nearly at the same height as my own. The clicking of its talons on the marble floor sent a shiver down my spine. And I could tell right away that this creature was not going to be a kind companion at all. Maybe a little more like a radioactive Rottweiler hopped up on speed. I didn't have time to discuss anymore.

I grabbed the girl's hand and bolted down the hall. She was yelling something, but I really didn't care anymore. She was far too slow, so I spun around and threw her over my shoulder, then continued to bolt down the hall. Lucky for me I got more traction on the marble than Beasty did, so even carrying this girl and all her attitude problems, I was able to put some distance between us. I jumped and slid down the banister. But I had too much momentum to turn and head down to the foyer, so I headed up the other side, taking three steps at a time. Behind me I heard a large crash and was certain the creature had wiped out at the bottom of the stairs. I took this moment to find the first door and push through it. I closed the door behind us and then finally set down Miss Attitude.

"What is wrong with you?" She took a moment to brush aside her long, dark brown, curly hair. And for a moment I thought I'd seen her before. It was the strangest feeling. "Is it normal practice to break into other people's homes, attack them, and then run around like a child?"

"Or ... how most people say it: 'Thanks for saving my life,'" I sniped in return.

"You"—she stuck her nose up all snooty-like—"are an idiot."

I stood there completely dumbfounded, mouth agape, eyes blinking, wondering what she was talking about.

"Retrasla is our pet; he is perfectly harmless. Or at least he *was* perfectly harmless. You'll find him ..." She paused for a moment. "Overly protective of me."

The door suddenly burst open and hit me in the back, sending me to the floor. I got to my feet in time to see Retrasla enter the room. I knew he could see me, but he did not come after me; he advanced on the green-eyed girl. Retrasla bared his fangs and growled, and Miss Attitude backed away in shock. I had to act quickly, although a little bit of me wouldn't have minded being rid of her incessant whining. I ran forward and thrust my shoulder into the beast's head. I tried to draw its full attention to me. Two birds, one stone. I'd draw the beast away from the girl and be rid of her at the same time. But when I looked back, Retrasla was lying comfortably on the floor, like an obedient dog.

"So who might you be, lad, and what are ya doin' in me home?" an aged voice inquired from behind me. I turned to see the old scientist leaning against the doorway. He looked a little younger now that he was awake, but he was still at least sixty.

"And therein lies the problem. I'm not really sure. I was merely told to come here; no one ever tells me why," I answered honestly.

"Your name, lad?" he asked, in his thick Irish accent.

"Josh."

"The same Josh who sent me a letter last week?" he asked, and I considered lying to him, but honesty was working for me so far.

"No, not that one," I answered.

"So you're not the Josh I'm looking for, and you don't know why you're here, and you've seen me work." I began to realize I should have lied. "That leaves us only one solution, Josh."

I stepped back and bumped into a large object. Retrasla was standing right behind me. Two options presented themselves, two simple choices: fight or flight. I chose the latter. But to assure myself I wasn't fighting two battles, I punched the old man in the face as I ran past him. Unfortunately, I turned the wrong direction down the hallway, heading not for the exit but deeper into the castle.

At the end of the hall was a square spiral staircase. I ran down it hard and fast and could hear Retrasla trying to navigate the slippery marble stairs, smashing and crashing the whole way down. After four flights of stairs, I bolted into a large, glass-topped room. As lightning flashed, I saw balconies high up and massive, regal felt banners that hung from them. Perfect for climbing. I climbed the twenty feet to the balcony. Just as I got in, I heard the clicking of Retrasla's talons on the marble floors. I looked over for a moment to see where he was, lightning flooded the room, and I watched as the beast sniffed around the room. A second lightning flash showed me that Crazy Girl had entered the room as well. She crossed the room and stood near the far end. Lastly, her uncle entered the room.

"Have you found your prey yet, Retrasla?" he asked, and the beast growled deep and low. Sounded like an "Oh yeah! Tasty, tasty prey." But that made no sense, the sound of the creature was moving away from me. "Good. Then kill him."

It was then that lightning flashed again, and both her uncle and I realized what was about to happen. The creature was once again going after the green-eyed girl. Clearly, this creature was a little bipolar. In a split second I decided to act. There was only one way down, and it was going to suck. Leaping over the edge, I wrapped my arms around the banner and slid.

"*Nooo!*" the uncle screamed, bolting across the room.

I hit the ground and could feel the skin on my arm burning; I was certain that was going to add to my growing scar collection. I turned in time to see the uncle running to his niece's rescue. I ran that way as well, though I knew I'd be too late to save her. I just might be able to save him. For some reason, her back was still turned to the beast. It was nearly pitch black, so I could barely see what was going on, but I watched as her uncle slammed into her, just in time to feel the wrath of his own pet. I reached his side and grabbed him to set him down gently on the ground. He tried to speak, but nothing came out. I drew my sword, ready to slay the beast, but it was nowhere to be seen. Then a low light slowly filled the room. Torches around the room seemed to light themselves. I looked around to find the green-eyed girl standing by the wall. She had just flipped a switch to light the room. I looked down at the man desperately trying to breathe, and I realized I still had my sword drawn. I looked back up to the girl, as tears started to well up in her eyes. Finally, a diamond trail of a single tear traveled down her cheek. Her eyes shifted from her uncle to me, and there was no more sadness, just pure rage.

"Kill him."

Before I knew it, I saw the shadow of the beast's talons flying toward me. I ducked and rolled to one side, then got back to my feet and ran. Racing out of the room, I turned for the stairs and ran four flights up. I was exhausted and my arms had started to bleed from my banner stunt. The creature also seemed much better at ascending the stairs than descending. I was barely keeping ahead of it this time. Getting to the hallway, I made a beeline for the foyer; with every step I could hear the creature getting closer. I would have to act fast, and there was only one way to do this. I reached the stairs and jumped. Drawing my sword again and spinning, I landed facing the creature. As soon as it leapt, I knelt down, then lunged forward, driving my sword into its soft underbelly. The momentum of the beast took us both to the ground, but I was able to get up, and Retrasla lay there, motionless. Even its breathing had ceased. I took a few minutes to catch my breath and enjoy my victory. Those were minutes I should have taken to leave, but foolishly I lingered.

My moment of victory was cut short by a searing pain in my shoulder. As I looked down, I saw the point of an arrow protruding from a pectoral muscle. I turned in time to receive a second arrow, but this one went in the front of the other shoulder. My legs gave way, and my eyes tried to close, but I forced them to stay open. There at the top of the stairs was the green-eyed girl. Tears poured down her face as she loaded another arrow into a crossbow. She was shaking violently, but she finally managed to load the arrow. She pointed it at me and walked down the steps. Her every step seemed to take the greatest of effort, as if all she wanted was to curl up and cry. As I looked into her eyes, a new feeling roiled within me. I did not know what it was, but it was as though I could feel her pain, her agony. But there were more pressing matters to deal with, like the last arrow that was now pointed at my heart. Her eyes held mine. They spoke. I listened. Their voice shredded any hope I had. Such anger, sorrow, rage, and sadness.

"For my uncle," was all she spoke as she pulled the trigger on the crossbow.

"Please," was the only word I could muster before my world went black.

I opened my eyes to find myself kneeling over the green-eyed girl's uncle. But as I grasped his hand, I realized I was not myself at all: my hands were female, the same hands that I was certain just delivered me to my death. I could feel the tears streaming down my face. As I looked at "my" uncle, he spoke. I could not hear him, but I shook my head and then watched as his eyes closed and did not open again. Emotions flooded through me, feelings I was not familiar with. My stomach twisted, my throat felt as though something were stuck in it, my eyes burned, and yet there was something so much deeper. I looked up and saw, through the blur of my tears, a weapons rack. I moved toward it. But something caught my gaze. Just to my right stood Haldel, arms open, as if to accept me in his comforting embrace. For a moment I considered it, but the rage was too strong, and I continued toward the crossbow hanging in front of me. In my peripheral vision, I watched Lasnek come from nowhere and slay Haldel where he stood. I picked up the crossbow and felt an icy coldness in my veins. Then everything went black again.

Chapter 17

The Light Inside

I woke up in a hospital room, where Harlstril explained to me that once again their test malfunctioned, leaving me in it far too long. He seemed genuinely frustrated with whoever was in charge of that department. Although I thought for sure I had failed the test, apparently I had passed it in a very creative way—something about taking command of the castle. Apparently, I wasn't supposed to rescue the girl. though. Oops.

The next two weeks were spent in recovery and getting myself back in shape for my next tests. First was a fighting test. I was put in a sparring room with Harlstril and Haslo and had to disarm them. Once I had both of them disarmed, Lasnek joined the fight. And I ended up only nearly killing him, which was thoroughly disappointing to me.

But once again I passed, keeping my streak of success going. Then Harlstril and I played the coolest game ever, for the next test. Each of us had command of an army of miniatures, and I'm not talking the miniatures that kids collect and paint. I'm talking about tiny little warriors that move and kill each other. I had to defend and destroy Harlstril's invading army, leaving no one alive. I almost lost but in the end pulled a Mulan and took out his retreating army with an avalanche. Thank you, Disney!

The next test was all about running. I was not sure if it was really a test or just Harlstril wanting to punish me. I ran through a maze, chased by an Indiana Jones–worthy boulder, then ran through a tunnel, avoiding poison darts shooting from the wall, fell into a volcano, narrowly avoiding getting burned to death, and then fell through an underground, Disneyworld-on-steroids waterslide full of muck. Next I outran an avalanche and then fell into a hundred-foot-deep ravine, where I almost got swept over the edge of a waterfall. But I pulled myself up onto a strange rock that came above the water and stuck out over the waterfall. Nice place for a picnic if you didn't have to risk death to get to it.

Once I was up on the rock, I took a moment to catch my breath, but I was already aware I wouldn't have much time. I could hear a noise behind me, and as I turned around I could see a creature crawling out of the water onto my rock. It was more or less human but covered in weeds. Maybe like the Creature from the Black Lagoon. I backed up a bit and reached for my sword, which I soon discovered was no longer with me. I must have lost it in the river. The creature was now getting up onto its feet in true zombie fashion. I looked over the edge and decided it was either hand-to-hand combat with a lagoon monster or jump the waterfall. Considering this didn't seem like a fighting test, and eventually I'd have to get out of here anyway, I chose jump. I ran down the rock, getting as close to the creature as possible, and then took off back up the rock. I wanted as much distance as possible from the falling water, so as not to be sucked into the never-ending undertow. I flew through the air only a moment before I hit something solid and fell backward. I was a little panicked as I looked around, but I soon realized I was back in the hall of doors.

I rose to my feet, breathing heavily and smiling at Harlstril, waiting for some kind of smile in return. But the look in his eyes was not like anything I'd ever seen. He looked proud of me, but at the same time horrified. I started to ask him what was going on, but he raised his hand to silence me. His eyes seemed to glaze over, and it looked like he was remembering something. I tried to ask him what was going on, but this time he just turned and walked away.

"What about the next test?" I asked, seeking any kind of response from him.

"Tomorrow," he said, as though he might cry at any moment, which was not something Harlstril would do. Something was very wrong.

"I'll see ya then," I said, with the strangest feeling that I wouldn't.

"Yeah." It was if it took all his energy to reply.

"Okay. ... Thanks." I tried to say more, but he turned straight around, and the look on his face was pure regret.

"*Don't!*" he boomed. Wide-eyed, he looked away again. "Please don't thank me."

With that he walked through the door and closed it with a cold, hollow thud. I just stood in silence, wondering what I could have done wrong. Harlstril had such control all the time, was so put together. The only emotions I had ever seen in him were kindness and righteous anger, and these new emotions seemed to defy him. I looked at the floor and saw my sword there, the one Harlstril had given me. Could he have been mad about that, that I was careless with his precious sword? It seemed beneath him, but so did his attitude. I sheathed the sword and headed to the courtyard. I wandered back and forth, trying to slow my mind. Jeshual joined me and nudged up against me as I walked. Finally I sat on the bench and relaxed.

It wasn't long before I was asleep, finding myself once again in the world of dreams.

I found myself back on the rock that was overhanging the waterfall. I looked down to see the mist collecting below. A noise from behind me caught my attention, as I turned and saw the Black Lagoon creature crawling up from the water; this time, though, I looked more closely. Its seaweed-like body seemed covered in oil and full of debris, as if it had lain dormant under the water for a hundred years, collecting all of life's garbage. I drew my sword and noticed that my hands were old, very old. I felt myself yell something, but as always silence was all I heard.

The creature continued forward, and I stepped into it, stabbing it in the stomach. In that moment something happened that I certainly did not expect. A light started to emanate from the creature, becoming so bright it blinded to me. Finally it dimmed, and before me stood Haldel. Again I spoke, but silence was all I heard. I looked upon his wound, which poured scarlet down his white robes. His eyes spoke so much, but I just didn't understand. Finally the light diminished completely, and Haldel fell into the river. My eyes followed him as he descended over the falls beyond my sight. But a new presence appeared; there at the point of the rock, Lasnek stood, proud, arrogant, tall, as if he had just won a great battle. I felt bitterness well up inside me, and again my mouth spoke words that I was not permitted to hear. Lasnek smiled a toothy grin full of fangs. He said something that was stolen by silence and then dug his claws into my shoulder, lifting me off the ground. The crushing was pure agony, but in that moment I looked into his eyes and felt something I could have never expected. Pity. Blackness invaded my dream as an icy cold overcame my body.

I awoke with a start as I found myself launching off the bench. I hit the ground and fell, then quickly snapped back to my feet, scanning the area to make sure I was alone. The only one who had seen was Jeshual, and she wasn't about to tell anyone. The emotions of the dream conflicted with my own. Who in their right mind would have pity on Lasnek, a creature of pure evil? I mean, I had gotten to know lots of Cahirians since I arrived here, and they all seemed a little creepy, but most were really nice. Lasnek, on the other hand, was just. .... My mind was pulled away from these thoughts by another. My sword, not the one from Harlstril, but the sword that hid in my dresser—for some reason, I felt a sudden overpowering connection to it. I ran out of the courtyard and down the halls to my room. Bursting through the door, I pulled open my drawer and drew the sword from it. It was glowing just a little and had become quite magnificent. In fact, it was getting a little big for the drawer. But there was something more important about it.

I immediately recalled the moment I took the little dagger, then the first battle of Lasnek and Haldel, the mob of Cahirians, or demons, as I knew them at the time. There was more, though. I pushed my mind to remember. The walk through the woods, the grass beneath my feet, pulling on my rubber boots, a flashlight. I pushed harder: I remembered my room, being so confused and curious by the flashes of light. Something was hidden from me, though, a memory I couldn't seem to reach. I pushed harder, forcing my mind to go where it did not want to go. Something I was forgetting, something I should have known, something I should have always known, something ... no, *someone*, someone I should know ...

"Josh!" Haslo's voice broke my concentration, and I dropped the sword, kicking it under the dresser.

"*What*!" I yelled, not meaning to.

"Woooww." Haslo took a step back.

"Sorry. What up?" I calmed myself.

"You ready?"

"For what?"

Haslo just stared at me like I was some kind of idiot. And then it hit me like a ton of bricks.

"Oh my gosh, of course!" My second-to-last test was today. I was nearly finished. "What time is it?"

"You've got five minutes to get ready, and you look horrible!" Haslo said laughing as he left the room.

"Well that's what you get for sleeping the night away on a bench." I said to the door.

I think I spent all five of those minutes staring into the abyss. I desperately wanted to search back further in my memories, but I didn't have the time. Luckily, I had never gotten undressed from yesterday's test. Frustrated, I headed off to the hall of doors to meet with Harlstril, hoping he had calmed down from yesterday, especially because I was going to be late.

Chapter 18

The Journey

I arrived to find the hallway empty. One of two things had happened: either Harlstril had not come back, or he too was late. All the years I'd known him, he had never been late, not even a little. "Fourteen minutes early is one minute late, Joshua," he would always say, and it drove me crazy. I began pacing up and down the hall until something caught my eye. On one of the doors there was a small note. I pulled it off and opened it up.

Dear Josh,

It is with regret that I must inform you that I cannot be here to welcome you to the first of your last two tests. This test is called The Journey, which is exactly what it is. Before you lies a simple test. Your only mission is to find the lair of the Hiltezion. Use whatever means you see fit in your journey. I would recommend you seek the wisdom and knowledge of the locals, but take caution: not all that you meet will welcome you with kindness. Josh, these are all the details I am able to provide you at this time.

With Luck,
Harlstril

With Luck? Since when do you believe in luck, Harlstril? Man, I didn't know what had happened to this guy, but he sure was off his rocker lately. Hopefully, he was off getting some therapy, and maybe he'd be back by the time I was finished with the test. Slipping the note into my pocket, I turned the doorknob and walked through the door, feeling a little strange doing that, as Harlstril had always opened the doors for me there. Instantly I was drenched in sweat. Great. Who doesn't love a walking test in the middle of a jungle? I scanned the area and realized very quickly that I was legitimately in the middle of nowhere, with nothing to point me in any specific direction. Not a mountain, not smoke from a village. And the only noises that could be heard were those of the monkeys swinging from tree to tree, plus the exotic birds, which caused enough ruckus to drive a man insane.

I put my hand in the air to feel which way the wind was blowing, but, alas, there was no wind to direct me. Awesome, this was going to be a great test. I looked to the sun and picked south, because "it feels like going downhill" (thanks, *Lord of the Rings*), and if I was already in the South, going south would make it cooler. Sure, it would take weeks to feel the difference, but I could dream.

With a direction in mind, I headed off, pushing through thick brush and vines and avoiding the venomous creatures all around. Finally, after an hour of walking and sweating and wishing I'd brought more water, I found a path. It was covered in banana leaves and headed southeast and northwest. So, I continued with my original assumption and journeyed southeast. At least the traveling was easier now, although I was not so sure it was getting any cooler. Another hour passed and I smelled smoke in the distance: success! It was late afternoon when I found the village. I cautiously entered the open area and tucked myself behind a mud hut. The village was full of dark-skinned women and children, but there were no men to be seen. Probably off on a hunt, hopefully not for me. The women seemed very preoccupied, though, mending huts, cooking food, chiding the children for screwing around, tending gardens. It seemed like a busy little community here. Suddenly, one of the woman called out something in a strange language. All the women surrounded the fire pit in the middle of the encampment. Then they busted out some sweet moves, dancing and spinning and chanting and having all sorts of fun. I assumed this was some kind of daily ritual.

They chanted louder and louder, and then all jumped to face the east. They did a little dance, and then they all faced south and did yet another dance. They followed up with a little jig to the west, and finally, they all faced ... oh! Suddenly forty women were all staring at me. Apparently I'd gotten so into the show that I wasn't hiding myself very well anymore. They all froze and just stared at me.

"Um, hi." I waved awkwardly and panic erupted. Women went in every direction, grabbing children and running for the woods. That probably wasn't a good thing, but I sure wasn't scared of these tribal folk. I ventured deeper into the camp and looked around, hoping to find a map marked "Hiltezion," but I was distracted by the fire pit in the middle. It was as if something were calling me to it. I walked slowly, getting closer and closer. At the edge I started to look down into it, when a voice caught me off guard.

"I wouldn't do that if I were you."

"Pardon?" I spun around and saw a man, probably in his late twenties, early thirties. He was scruffy and dirty as all get-out. He was not dark-skinned like the rest of the tribe; he was clearly white, with just a bit of a tan, and his clothing was nothing like the tribe's; he wore torn khakis and what might once have been a white T-shirt.

"I wouldn't look into the pit." He gestured to it while walking up to me. "It's sacred to them, and to look into it is punishable by death."

"Seems a little extreme, doesn't it?" I asked.

"That it does, but they say it is the doorway to the afterlife, and to look into it would steal your soul. A body with no soul is an evil thing, so they say it should be put to death." He smiled as if he didn't take it too seriously. "Trust me when I say they will make sure death comes to you."

"Have you ever looked in?" I asked, now overly curious to look into it.

"Do I look dead to you?" He laughed a little.

"Touché." I smiled back.

"So, my friend, what has brought you to this forbidden place?" the man asked, pulling out his glasses to get a better look at me.

"My name is Josh, and I was sent here to find something called the ... um." I racked my brain, but suddenly drew a blank on what I was looking for. I pulled the note from my pocket and read it again, suddenly noticing that Harlstril had called me Josh, and he never called me Josh. It was always Joshua this, Joshua that. Drove me crazy, but this note was all sorts of weird.

"Were you planning on finishing your sentence, or should I just guess?" Four Eyes's sarcasm brought me back.

"Sorry." I quickly found the name. "The Hiltezion." As soon as I said the word, the blood drained from his face.

"Wh-why ..." He looked at me as if I'd lost my mind. "Why would you want to look for that?"

"No idea," I replied, eyeing him closely. "I was sent to find it. I don't ask questions; I simply do as I'm told."

"Foolish." He glared at me. "Trust me in this, the Hiltezion is not something you want to find."

"And why not?"

"Just trust me."

"Well, I don't know you, so I won't trust you," came my sarcastic reply. "So how about you just tell me how to find it and leave the rest to me?"

He looked around to make sure no one was watching, and then he headed out into the woods. I thought he assumed I would follow him, which I did.

Finally he stopped and turned to face me but said nothing.

"Um, I don't know about you, but this is getting awkward," I bantered.

"Would you shut up for a second?" Clearly, his funny mood had left him. "I want to make sure we're out of earshot of anyone in the tribe while we speak about their god." I could tell he knew better than to believe it was a god, but still he seemed to have great respect for whatever it was. "Do you know *anything* about the Hiltezion?"

"No, or I wouldn't be asking." His face was hard to read, as though he were thinking about decking me and crying all at the same time. Finally he took a deep breath and began.

"Josh, the Hiltezion is a being that is deeply feared, and it is for good reason. He is not some idol, ancient relic, or idea. What these villagers worship is more real than I ever wished to experience."

My eyes widened. A creature. I was up for a good fight and had seen my fair share of demented things. Now, if I could only get Mr. Glasses to hurry up and give me a destination, the beast and I could have a nice date.

"Josh, I came here a year ago with six others. We came to understand the tribe and bring them the truth. We spent months living alongside them, learning their language and their traditions, until one day a young boy came to us and told us a story of the great beast in the forest, the god they worshipped, the Hiltezion. He told us to try to scare us off, but we knew better. We were wise and educated, and we were well aware that any creature could be caught, and it was probably just a simple idol that they bowed to." I could tell that what he was saying he no longer believed.

"We soon learned that the tribe offered their firstborn children to the creature to appease it, which made all seven of us quite angry. We decided to capture the beast and show the tribe that it was not a god, but merely an animal, mortal as all of us were. So we set traps. But every time we went to see if we had caught the creature, the traps were destroyed. So it was time to step up our game." His eyes lingered for a moment, looking into his own past. I could see tears welling up, but his emotions seemed quite cold.

"We split up into three groups. Jaden and I hid to the north with Sarah. Beth and Luis were half a kilometer south, and Carey and Mike agreed to hide in the brush nearest the trap, a little to the west and directly between my group and Beth's." As he said her name, I could tell there was something deeper with her than with any of the others. "We waited for three days, taking shifts to sleep. And then it happened. A sound broke the long silence, a piercing noise that will never leave my mind. Carey's and Mike's screams rang out across the night sky. The horror of it sank into me. We leapt out of the tree and ran to their help, but they were silenced all too fast. I realized then we had to get to the others, but before we could move, their screams reached us. We were too late; within a few seconds they were silent once more. I grabbed Jaden's and Sarah's hands and ran the opposite direction. There was a small alcove in one of the cliffs nearby. It would be the safest place. We climbed the cliff and curled into the alcove. It was small, with barely enough room for the three of us, but we made it work. As I looked at Jaden's face, I knew it wasn't good. He had gone completely white, and his skin was cold; then I looked to Sarah and realized she wasn't much better. They were both in shock. But we had to wait, wait for sunrise; maybe the sun would protect us. Soon, though, the creature came to us. We kept silent in our little niche and prayed it wouldn't find us. I could barely see it stalking back and forth, shaking the forest floor with its size. I remember seeing its body peppered with tranquilizer darts; there were enough in the creature to take down several elephants."

"What happened?" I asked—gently, as not to offend him.

"Jaden and Sarah both fell asleep, but not in a good sleep. They slipped in and out of a comatose state, shock overtaking their bodies. When the sun rose the next morning, the creature had left. I shook Jaden and Sarah awake, and we went back to the village. Once we were there, Jaden and Sarah collapsed. The tribespeople loved them greatly and tried everything to bring them back, but without proper medicine they slipped further and further into their comas. Eventually, their bodies just shut down."

"What about you?" I asked. "Why didn't you slip into a coma?"

"God's cruel joke, I guess. I don't know." I could sense the conflict in his voice, as though he still trusted God but hated him at the same time. That was not too far from the way I felt. "Either way, I survived, and once the tribe had buried the dead, they forced me into slavery, as repayment for offending their god. I was granted the time to search for my other friends, but I wish I had never gone." He paused as if trying to force the images out of his mind. "Let's just say there wasn't enough left to bury."

I shared his moment of silence, but I was not here to counsel; I had a mission.

"So what did it look like?" The more I knew, the better prepared I would be.

"It's hard to remember. I didn't go comatose, but the shock was still intense. Most of it is just a blur. All I remember is that it was massive. Even if I could describe it, words would do it no justice; you would have to see it to truly understand." Finally, we were getting somewhere.

"Can you show it to me?" I asked, with a little too much excitement.

He looked at me as if I had lost my mind. "What are you talking about? Did you hear *anything* I just said?"

"Of course, didn't miss a thing, but I still need to find it; that is why I am here. As I see it, you are the only one who might show me where this beast dwells. So you're the perfect candidate to help me find it. Besides, of all people, you should want this thing dead."

"You can't be serious. This thing will tear you limb from limb." He looked at me with a mixture of pity and confusion.

"Not if I get it first." I looked down at my sword.

"You're not getting it: this thing had enough tranquilizer in it to put a herd of elephants to sleep, and it wasn't fazed. You think you can take it down with a *knife?*" His eyes burned with passion.

"Well, I don't plan on putting it to sleep, do I? I plan on *killing* it."

He was about to reply, when his face suddenly changed, an idea forming.

"The tribe will kill me if I have anything to do with it, yet if I am released to you, we may have a mutually beneficial arrangement. Tonight, when the men of war return, there will be a celebration. At the end of each raid, there is always an open challenge between the chief and any man who wishes to assert his power and strength in a fight to the death. If you take on the chief and win, you can release me, and I will be happy to lead you to the Hiltezion's lair. If you lose, you were no match for the beast anyway, and I saved you the trouble." He smiled.

"Deal." With that we headed back to the village, which was now full of men and women and children. No one seemed afraid of me, now that I was with Mr. Glasses. I was introduced to many of them, and Four Eyes interpreted for me. As night fell, they heaped wood into the pit, and the smoldering coals soon lit the wood into a great blaze. Music and dancing ensued, and the night was full of celebrations. The day's kill was cooked and passed around for all to eat. It was delicious, but my mind was on the mission. All night I had seen no one that looked anything like a chief. But once the food was eaten, and the dancing was done, they brought out the drums and started to pound on them. And out of a far tent came a very large man, at least six and a half feet tall. With skin the color of night, and eyes to match, he walked with great dignity, yet he also seemed full of kindness. A good leader, proud and strong. He called out what I assumed was a challenge to anyone who felt they could be a better chief. One of the tribe members brought him a long spear with a spear head the size of his massive hands, and a shield tall and skinny, pointed at the top and bottom.

"That's your cue," Four Eyes chuckled. "Have fun."

I stepped forward and walked into the ring. I figured they would have a "three, two, one, go!" But apparently that was understood once I stepped into the ring. The chief threw his spear, and I narrowly dodged it, rolling to the side. I scrambled to my feet and was slammed by his shield. Back to the ground I went. By the time I was on my feet again, the chief had his spear in hand once more. He thrust it at me, but I simply batted it to the side with my hand. I thought of going for my sword, but I wouldn't need it. He thrust a few more times, but I continued batting his spear away. Soon I realized I was merely insulting him. He thrust his spear one last time, and I grabbed hold of it, pulled hard, and drop- kicked the chief in the stomach. His grip on the spear loosened, and I pulled it free. Spinning around, I smashed the back of his knees with the shaft, and he crumpled. Then I put the point of the spear to the back of his neck; he was beaten. He said something to me in his language, and Four Eyes interpreted for me.

"He told you to finish it."

"Tell him I don't want to take his tribe. I don't even seek his life. All I want is for him to be indebted to me, that I may find the Hiltezion, and that I will remain free of superstitious beliefs regarding my finding of the beast and any ties to this tribe," I replied. After the translation, the chief spoke back, and near the end his emphasis was quite strong.

"Your desire has been granted, yet he also called you a great but foolish warrior, for seeking the Hiltezion."

"Tell him thanks," I said and backed away, raising the spear in a sign of surrender. He stood and I handed the spear back to him. He bowed in recognition to my skill and then called to the crowd, most likely another challenge. I stepped out of the ring and sat down. A younger warrior stood and entered the ring. He was not as tall, but pretty close, and more than a fit challenge for the chief. Clearly, this easy defeat had encouraged the young warrior, but the fight lasted only a moment before the young warrior was dead on the ground. Once the body was carried away, the celebrations continued.

"It has been a great many months since someone challenged him, and I'm sure it will be a great many more before he is challenged again," Four Eyes said.

"We leave first thing in the morning. For now, I assume, I should rest." I smiled. "I will see you at sunrise, then." He smiled and joined the celebration. I headed to a small hut the village had kindly offered me, and sleep quickly came over me.

I was in another hut, a much more elaborate hut indeed. There were animal pelts lining the walls and floor, and in the center of the roof there was a small hole to let the smoke out of the hut. Beneath it was a small, altar-like pedestal, in which was a small fire. I walked toward it and bowed down, then came back up, then bowed down, up, down, up, down, until the flames changed color. Blues and purples and yellows and reds, and a single white flame danced in the center. The flames combined and swirled, then suddenly went out. Standing in the doorway to the hut was Haldel, his hand outstretched to me. But I knew it would not last. A moment later his light diminished, and he fell. Lasnek stood just behind him, sword in hand, a fanged smile splitting his face. He walked into the hut slowly, and I backed away. Falling backward I looked down at my legs and realized they were not mine. They were dark as night, and I realized in that moment that I was seeing life through the eyes of the chief. Lasnek raised his sword to strike, and I came fully awake.

Cold sweat soaked my body, and my breathing was heavy, as if I had just run a marathon. I was about to check on the chief, when I realized it was just a dream. I laid my head back down and slipped once again into the darkness beyond.

"Wake up, Josh!" My eyes snapped open, and I sat bolt upright. "If you want to see this thing, we must leave now."

"What ... why?" I asked Four Eyes as he was walking out of the tent.

"No time to explain. Just get up and let's go!" He was not in a good mood this morning, that was for sure. I got up and grabbed my things before slipping out of the tent. The sun had not even risen yet, although its glow was coming up on the horizon.

"We have to go now!" Four Eyes demanded, and then sped off into the bush. I bolted after him, knowing he was my only hope of finding the Hiltezion. We ran for nearly two hours before he finally slowed his pace.

"What is going on?" I demanded, breathing heavily, although not as heavily as he was.

"The chief is dead; he was murdered during the night. He told me to come to him early in the morning, before we left. He had had a final blessing for me. When the warriors find him, they will assume it was you and kill us both. No questions asked."

"But why? Why should they suspect us? I could have easily killed him in the ring, and you are free now, with no motive." I was dumbfounded.

"To kill the chief in the ring is an honor for both of you. To murder him while he sleeps is to insult both him and his tribe. You already insulted him once by beating him without breaking a sweat and making demands of him. They think of me as your slave now, so I would die for that simple reason alone," he said and continued walking, but I had had enough of this tribal superstition crap.

"That ... is the stupidest thing I've ever heard!" I was fuming mad now. "Let them come. They want to kill me, let them try!" My arrogance was raging now.

"I don't care what you do, but I'm going this way; follow or don't." He continued walking, and once again I realized I was beaten. The tribe was secondary; I had to complete the mission. Hours had passed by the time we reached the base of the mountain. There the path split left and right.

"Why is there a trail if no one wants to come here?" I asked.

"No one wants to come here?" He paused. "Well, that is only partially true; they would rather not, but every year they come to offer a firstborn child to the creature. It's part of ancient tradition and has lasted for centuries. That was the aspect that brought my group and me here, remember? It is a thing very few can grasp, so we wanted to understand it. Oh, and understand it I did," he said beneath his breath. That made me want to kill the creature even more.

"Why don't they just fight the creature? Their warriors must be skilled enough to defeat it."

"You and I see it as an animal, one that surely deserves respect, but they see it as a god, and gods cannot be killed, so why would they try? I asked God to destroy it many times, but nothing ever happened," he said with a tone of bitterness.

"Figures." With that he gave me an inquisitive look and was about to say something but then seemed to lose interest.

"Stay to the left, and you will be led straight to the beast's lair. I have no such desire to be near it again, so this is where I will take my leave."

"Wait ... where will you go?"

"This side of the trail cuts through the lower hills, leading to a mining town not twelve kilometers away. Prop planes come in once a week. Josh, it's time for me to go back to America." Despite the tension, he broke his bitter exterior and extended a hand. "It was a pleasure to meet you. I owe you my freedom." For a second he stopped and just stared at me. "You know, you can join me if you like. I don't know who sent you on this mission, but it will get you killed very fast. You don't have to do it ... you do know that, right?"

His sincerity struck me, but I knew I had to press on.

"Thanks ... but no thanks. Trust me; this *is* something I must do." Sensing my determination, he let it go and just nodded his head once in agreement.

"Once you get to the summit, you'll know where to look." Once again he stopped and stared. "If you are ever in America, and if you ever need anything, remember me. My name is Harold Grismold. I don't know where I will be, but wherever I am, you are more than welcome." He stared one last time from behind those glasses. I started to say something but didn't know what would be right. Before I knew it, he walked away down the path to the right. I watched for a moment, before beginning my own path.

Just as he said, I knew exactly where to go, for upon that flattened peak I found a slanted cave carved into the face of the rock. *So this is the beast's lair,* I thought to myself. I took a sweep of my surroundings, preparing myself to enter the darkness.

Apparently the Hiltezion was more than aware of my arrival. I caught first sight of the hallowed brute as his gnarled head emerged from the darkness of the cavern. His black and scaly body followed, as I drew my sword. My head tilted to the side as the beast's form began to hit the sunlight. The Hiltezion was almost identical to Retrasla, only bigger. His tail was longer and flicked back and forth in protest of his current disruption. His eagle-like talon paws were clawing the ground, as I clutched my weapon. Yellow eyes gleamed at my intrusion; his head tossed back and forth as he snorted his own form of curses.

The beast took two steps toward me, challenging yet still taking me in. Clearly, human confidence was not common to this creature. That is when he unfurled his broken and sickly wings, and I realized that this would be a new form of a brute, much larger, and a greater match than Retrasla had been. Each fibrous wing curled and bent in broken spines, as if this creature had been part of more brawls than even he desired. Sparse remnants of black, crow-like feathers hung in ill form. He bellowed a roar, revealing a mouth full of vicious animallike fangs. My body suddenly felt as though it were being pulled apart. I knew what was about to happen, and I winked at the creature.

"Another day, friend," I said as the world around me melted away and I found myself back in the hall of doors.

"Excellent work, Josh," came the overly professional voice of Mr. Curry. I spun around to meet him and to see which of his many suits he was wearing today. It was a silvery suit, with even a bit of a metallic shimmer to it. He took my outstretched hand and shook it, smiling proudly at me. "I am sorry Harlstril could not be here to congratulate you himself. He is currently indisposed. Tomorrow you will start your final test, but for now you should get some rest. I am sure you have already figured out what your final test is."

"Kill the beast," I stated.

"That is correct. Again, congratulations, and I am certain Harlstril would say the same." With that Mr. Curry turned and left.

I headed back to my room, and after cleaning up I climbed into bed. After tomorrow, I would be finished with my testing. But for now, I would simply sleep.

This night I was to live through the eyes of Harold. He shook my hand and then headed off around the right side of the mountain. *Flash.* I found myself at a tiny dirt runway, airport. *Flash.* I was boarding the plane, looking back at the mountain in the distance. *Flash.* I looked down and could just see the peak of the mountain where the beast's lair was. I shuddered and looked away. A feeling of freedom came over me, but it was tainted with such loss. *Flash.* Buildings towered over me, cars flew past, and horns were honking everywhere: New York City. *Flash.* I found myself in an alleyway, hunkered in a corner, under a pile of newspapers. Then warmth came over me. I looked up and saw Haldel standing just in front of me, hand outstretched, but as always his light vanished and he fell, to reveal Lasnek's evil smile just behind him. Cold filled the alleyway, the street lights dimmed, and everything went black.

My eyes flew open, and my room was flooded with light. I climbed out of my bed and pulled my sword out from under the dresser. The glow and warmth from it filled my body. Again memories of that first night flooded my mind. Flying through the air, the fight, the forest, my backyard, rubber boots and a flashlight, my bedroom, the flashes—but what of the rest? Again I pushed my mind to remember, but it was like there was a wall, thicker than any ever built, holding me from knowing what I couldn't remember. I desperately pushed back, but no matter how hard I tried, I could not recall. I held the sword close, as if it were my only link between the frustrations that are and the frustrations that were. But nothing happened, nothing would come, no revelation, no understanding, no comfort. I threw down the sword and screamed at the silence. Kicking the sword under my dresser, I climbed back into bed, my only solace, in the hopes that night would hold only blackness for me, and nothing more.

Chapter 19

Mixed Emotions

Silence woke me. It wasn't a dream or a stealthy intruder or even my own angst. For the first time since I could remember, I woke of my own natural accord. But resting was not what I was here for. I climbed out of bed and pulled on my clothing, donned my armor, and, for the last time, strapped on the belt that held my sheath and sword. Pulling out the black sword, I realized it would soon be too small for me; even now I should have moved up one size, but, alas, it was Harlstril's gift to me. I would not dare trade it for another when I was this close to the end of my testing. Plus, I had grown to quite like it. It was comfortable in my hands. Before heading to the hall of doors I pulled out my only possession from a life forgotten. From beneath my dresser I retrieved the once small dagger that belonged to Haldel. Although it was the perfect size for me, it just didn't feel right in my hands. I swung it this way and that and realized how light it was. Heavy enough to have great momentum, yet still light enough to swing in a lengthy battle without growing weary.

With the time close at hand, I returned my mystery sword to its home and headed on to my final test, dreaming of what might become of me after. I would finally be able to see this armor Haslo kept talking about, and the whispers about my future might finally cease. Often I had heard the elder Cahirians speaking of me, but they would hush their voices the moment they caught sight of me. Destiny. Warrior. Leader. Turner of Tides. And many other titles seemed to be bestowed upon me. As excited as I might be, I was not there yet, and Harlstril had always said, "Take caution when dreaming of such futures, for you may lose sight of the present and the battles at hand."

The hall of doors was empty. A great disappointment washed over me. I had not dreamed that Harlstril would miss this day, the day of my victory. He had been like a father to me in this place. Always pushing me to be better than I was. For him to miss this day seemed like an insult, but this was no place for self-pity. For a while I paced back and forth, hoping, waiting for someone to instruct me. After some time passed, I gave up on waiting and started trying doors, but up one side and down the other, they were all locked. I was about to give up hope and walk back to my room, when the door at the end of the hall slammed open. Lasnek's massive frame filled the hall. Instinct shot my hand straight for the hilt of my sword.

"Oh please!" His eyes lit up. "I would love that more than anything."

"Well, in that case ..." I drew my sword half out of the sheath.

"Put your little stick away, fool," Lasnek spat.

"Scared?" I mocked him.

"Of you?" Lasnek laughed. "Do you actually think your victories over me were your own?"

"I sense a hint of bitterness," I bit back but couldn't help but wonder if he was telling the truth.

"Foolish child." He smiled. "Anyway, I am not here to fight you, nor would the rewards of killing you be worth the punishment I would receive. I am here to send you to your test, and hopefully to your death as well."

"Where's Harlstril?"

Something in his eyes lit up. He knew something, and it didn't seem good. He took a moment to think, looking up and to the left. "Busy," was all he came up with.

"Big word. Take you a minute to form it in that little brain?"

He simply glared at me, as an adult would at a child, chastising mentally. He turned in silence and opened one of the doors, then walked away. I smiled to myself, but his look when I mentioned Harlstril still bothered me. Where was he, especially now?

I drew my sword and walked through the doorway, finding myself, as I expected, back on the top of the mountain where the lair of the Hiltezion was. I looked around me quickly to make sure the beast was not directly behind me, which I'm sure would have satisfied Lasnek very much, but I was alone on the plateau, or at least I was for a moment. I heard a low growl come from the darkened cave in front of me. I took a deep breath and readied myself.

Soon the creature emerged, his enlarged wolf's head stalking from side to side, angered at my presence. Then he stopped, standing rigid, full of pride, eyes burning into mine. He stalked closer, prowling, studying his prey, and willing me to make a move. Stopping, he sank his six-inch talons into the earth, ready to charge. With him standing so close and so still, I now realized how great of a challenge he was. The back of his body must have been several inches taller than I am, but with his head staring down at me, it must have been just shy of a foot above my scalp. This time, I would have to be careful. This time, I didn't want to play taunting games. The strength behind muscles like that would be enough to strike me dead if I made even one mistake. His tail kept flicking back and forth, willing the fight to begin;

he tipped his nose and tasted the air, as if to smell my very apparent nerves.

I had had enough of the cat-and-mouse charade, so I took my courage and went for it. Running full force at the creature, I readied my sword to swing. *Let us see just what you are up to; let's see if the legend can die.* Charging at full speed, I headed straight into the brute but then quickly side-stepped to the right, just dodging the deadly front talon that he swung in my direction. I steadied my feet and lunged at the creature, almost successful at making contact with my weapon, but the beast was too fast. Ducking to the ground, I poised myself to stand and strike; unbeknownst to me, his thick and scaly tail had sailed over my head and whipped back around, hitting me full across the chest. I was sent flying back about four feet, almost losing my sword in the landing. He was fast, and he wasn't just a mishmash of ugliness; the Hiltezion had a measure of intelligence and powerful force combined with a moody temper. I got to my feet just in time to see the immense creature lunging toward me. I dove forward, underneath his surging charge, and scathed his soft underbelly. He recoiled and howled in pain. I rolled from underneath him, hoping my task was complete, but I hadn't done enough damage to stop him. Just enough to make him rather testy.

Immediately he was back on his feet, charging to me. Before I could defend myself, he rammed me full in the chest with his scaly head and knocked me clean to the ground, my sword flying from my hand. When I opened my eyes, his black form filled my vision; his broken wings were snapping back and forth in an enraged display. I didn't even have time to think; my first instinct was to rearm myself. I tossed a fistful of dirt in his face. The brute recoiled, snorting and hissing at me, as I scurried to my sword. I grabbed it just in time to roll out of the way of the

Hiltezion's talon, now hooked into the ground precariously close to where my chest had just been.

No matter what I did, I couldn't get back to my feet. I slid and rolled on the ground, his body looming above mine, his hooked talons clawing around me. I took several blows but was fortunate to avoid the single piercing strike that could have ended me right then. I had to think, and I had to think fast, or else it was about to be all over. Timing it just right, I swung my sword around and managed to cut into both of his forelegs as they landed, delivering clean surface wounds, and causing the Hiltezion to rear up on his haunches, howling viciously at what I had done. As he landed, I extended my arm, aiming for his heart. I planted my sword right into his chest. He recoiled and I pulled my sword out. I was sure that with such a blow I had bested the beast. I managed to get to my feet, but as soon as I was up, he charged again. Unprepared, I raised my sword just in time to block his blow, but the Hiltezion quickly drove his head into my chest, knocking me once again on my back. It was almost as if I could see the creature smile as he lunged at lightning speed, bearing down onto my chest with talons outstretched. I closed my eyes, but no pain came. Everything was quiet, and the sounds of the jungle faded away. Even with closed eyelids, I could tell it was darker, colder, and suddenly safer. When I opened them again, I found myself lying on the floor of the hall of doors, my sword lying beside me.

"An excellent show," came the calm, cool, collected voice of Mr. Curry.

"What?" I asked as I stood and shook the dust and, hopefully, some of the nerves off of me.

"Although we are unable to consider that a pass, you still displayed excellent quick thinking and discipline with a sword." Mr. Curry smiled and helped me brush off a little dust I had missed. "You are dismissed for the day, and tomorrow you may attempt the test again. Take some time and think on mistakes you may have made, and how best to correct them."

With that he turned and left. I'm not going to lie: I was a little offended by the "mistakes you may have made" comment. That bloody creature was probably ten times my weight and twice as fast and had weapons coming out of every side of its body. But, alas, I must beat the thing. So I spent most of the day in the courtyard, going over the creature's movement, style, attitude, strength, and anything else I could think of. Also I looked at the surrounding area: what advantage could I utilize, and how was I to conquer such a creature? Once night came I headed back to my room and slipped into bed. With my mind calm, and my heart at peace with the defeat, I slipped into the dreams beyond.

The world was rushing past me. Yet everything was speeding in reverse. A rush of the feeling of familiarity swept over me. I had been here before. I had seen this before. I was here again. My skin tingled with the feeling of night air, as my tiny body was being carried by Lasnek's claws. My mind rushed backward to Haldel's and Lasnek's words filling the knoll behind my house with coarse taunting and shouts of boasting. The dream rushed again, as I felt my body running backward through the tall grasses, then up my steps, then to my bedroom, as it filled with white-hot flashes that I couldn't understand yet was so excited by.

Then it stopped in a flash. It was as if the dream had frozen. Somehow, for some reason, this time the dream went further, into where I had been unable to go for so long. It was as if someone pressed the play button, and that night began all over again, only earlier that evening, before the sun had set. Without the speed of rushing backward motion, I walked down the carpeted stairs, only to meet Haldel, standing with his hand blocking me from going into what I was certain was my childhood family room. I wanted to go; something important was just beyond the opening. There, just beyond, was something I had forgotten, something that should not be possible to forget, but indeed it was not there anymore. It had been wiped from my memory.

I tried to yell for him to move out of the way, but as usual my voice was of no use in this world. Knowing how so many of these dreams had occurred before, I started wondering where Lasnek was. I was agitated and beginning to grow angry at the Iyarian who was blocking my vision and stopping me from having a moment to understand what was really happening. Why did my understanding always have to be covered in mystery? Why couldn't I just *know*? For some reason, I began to wish for Lasnek more than Haldel. I knew that if he came, I would be able to see what was in the next room.

It would not be long before I got my wish. In that moment, Lasnek appeared at the top of the steps; the creaking of the stairs protested his large—or should I just say fat—body descending them. Haldel seemed unaffected and refused to move. His mouth was moving, and I could tell that he was trying to give me stern instructions, yet I could not hear him. Lasnek reached the bottom of the steps and snarled an insult. He grimaced as if disgusted that he would have to share the same breathing room as the Iyarian behind me. With narrowed eyes he raised his hand. The air thickened and obeyed his bidding; a burst of hideous flame shot upward, revealing his menacing dark trident.

Haldel turned to me, eyes full of stern pleading for me to do as he said, yet his firm voice was still muted. Tears streamed down his face; his emotions were almost begging me to heed him. But I was torn. My everything was being split in two, and the frustrations of my muted senses were sending me into a panic. I wanted to hate Lasnek, but I also wanted to know what was in that room, and at that moment Haldel was my only obstacle. I just didn't understand. Why? Why was he blocking me? Lasnek was near now, coming within inches of my face, taunting me with a plastered smile. With one fluid move, he cuffed the side of my body and threw me out of the way. In a rush, voices, sounds, scuffling flooded my being. Haldel's voice became the clearest.

"Wake up, Joshua." His voice was filled with urgent emotion, yet immensely calm. "We need you to wake up."

My hearing may have been restored, but my ability to respond remained frozen. I didn't know what to do. Lasnek bent back, poised for a killing blow, yet just before impact my eyes opened, and I was back in my quarters, lying in sweat-drenched sheets. It was as if the competing worlds were too much for my mind, and almost immediately I fell back asleep.

The next morning arrived, and I readied myself for the Hiltezion again. No one was there to send me on my way, not Mr. Curry, not Haslo, and not Harlstril. But I knew the door, and it stood unlocked, so I ventured forth. Again, victory was not mine, and there was no one to console me after my test either. My chance of victory seemed impossible, as day after day passed, each filled with loss and loneliness. It was as if the entire complex had emptied itself. No one ever came to speak to me. Haslo, Norton, and Gary just vanished. I would catch glimpses of Mr. Curry, but he was always busy or just too far away. Even Lasnek and Haldel visited me only in my dreams, which was the same every night: the same world in reverse, and Haldel blocking the door and me being angry. Days turned into weeks, and weeks into months, and soon a full year had passed. Some of the days I would not even get out of bed; others I would go against the Hiltezion three or four times in a row, just to release my anger at the world. But as the end of the year approached, something changed. Something shook me out of this gloom, and it all started with a simple dream.

Chapter 20

Give and Take Away

It started the same. They always did, as the dream ran in reverse, flying, fighting, yelling, running, the bright flashes in my bedroom. Nothing marked this dream as different. I felt cold and calculating; so much repetition can only turn someone's heart to ice. What more could this dream expect from me? I did not care what it revealed anymore, did not care what lay beyond, for I knew that mystery would never be revealed. But, alas, I stood before Haldel, who was blocking my path. I glanced around to see Lasnek, who had indeed become my freedom. As much as I loathed everything about the creature, he brought an end to the dream, and a beginning to another day full of failure. For once, Lasnek was not there, though. I looked this way and that, but never did Lasnek appear; finally I turned back to Haldel. He looked different, and in that moment I realized I could hear the sounds of the house, creaks in the floor, voices in the distance, a light breeze whirling around the outside of the house.

"Do not believe them, Joshua." Haldel's voice was full of concern. "For they seek to deceive you."

"Who?" I asked. "Who wants to deceive me?"

"You will soon understand. Do not forget my words, even when all seems lost and in despair. Do not let what I have told you slip away. Now go; see what you have so desperately desired to remember."

"Wait! What are you talking ..." Before I could finish, Haldel simply vanished. Slowly I walked forward, not trusting that I would actually see anything. I waited for that moment when I would once again wake up into my anger and disappointment. But I stayed in the dream, and forward I walked. Upon entering a family room with an attached kitchen that seemed so familiar to me, I saw my eleven-year-old self sitting on a couch, staring at a blank TV. Just behind him, with her back to me, I could see a woman with long, dirty-blonde hair and a flower-print dress. She was doing the dishes but seemed unfocused on the task at hand.

"Joshua, it is well past your bedtime," she spoke.

"But Mom ..." As he said that word, it stung my heart. How could I have forgotten? It seemed an impossible thing to forget, but I had. "Just a few more minutes."

"Joshua Williams!" Her tone was very stern, and I watched as my miniature self's eyes widened. "If your father comes home and sees you out of bed, he will not be happy to see you! You will see him in the morning; now off to bed with you."

Little Joshua's shoulders slumped as I watched him dawdle in the direction of the stairs.

"And do not forget your nightly prayers!" Mom called after him, but just then a pair of headlights filled the front hallway, and little Joshua came running back into the room.

"*Dad*!" he yelled, but his trip was cut short as Mom stepped into his path.

"I will not tell you again!" she scolded him.

"Fine!" Joshua snipped at her, and for a moment I thought she was going to scold him further, but I could sense there was some deeper meaning to her sending him to bed. Something was wrong. Little Joshua stomped away to his room, and just as Dad came through the front door in his brown business suit and carrying his worn leather briefcase. Everything seemed so right in the world as I saw the two of them together.

Suddenly, I was ripped away from the kitchen, and I stood in my old room. Little Joshua was just about to kneel for his nightly prayers, when heated voices came from downstairs. They were muffled and hard to understand, but I had a distant memory of what they had fought about. Suddenly, out of the corner of my eye, I saw a group of angels walking past my childhood room: four Iyarian warriors, two of whom stopped at the door to my bedroom as if to guard it, while the other two pressed on, toward my mom and dad. Slowly the arguments settled, and silence took over the night. A sense of peace filled the whole room, and I turned to see little Joshua climbing into bed and pulling the covers over him.

It was then that a feeling came over me like none I had felt before, or maybe I had felt it before and just pushed it away. Either way, there was no stopping it this time. Nor did I wish it to stop. I was, for the first time in so many years, homesick. I closed my eyes and just allowed the feeling to wash over me, and when I opened my eyes again, I found myself back in my quarters in the complex. As I looked around at all that I had, all my belongings, I felt it was all so fake, so superficial. Nothing of importance existed in this room, and so it was decided. When morning came I would find Harlstril, and if I could not find him, then I would find Mr. Curry. In the morning, I was going home!

Sleep swept over me once more, and peace flooded every part of my very being. In all the time since I could remember, I could not recall sleep like this. I almost didn't want it to end, but

I knew that at the end of this sleep, reality would be something worthwhile and wonderful. So morning finally arrived, and I leapt out of bed and got dressed. Not in my training clothes, but in something nice, something I wanted to wear on the return to see my family. Then I rushed down the hall to the kitchen, where I hoped to find Larasa. As empty as the complex had been in the last year, it suddenly seemed to teem with life. Hope filled me that I would indeed find Harlstril.

"Can you tell me where to find Harlstril?" I nearly shouted at Larasa by accident, causing her to spill the contents of her mixing bowl. "Sorry."

"It's okay, dear Josh." She smiled. "You just shocked me is all." She paused to think on my question. "I'm not sure, my dear. He has not been around much lately, and I believe he is gone at the moment." Her words stung, for what she said meant that he had indeed been back and had not once taken a minute to see me or find out how I was doing. But I focused on what was good and moved on to my second option.

"What about Mr. Curry?" I asked, and she chuckled as she always did, for I was the only one to call him that. Everyone else called him The Curator, which to this day I believe to be a ridiculous name.

"He should be in his office, dear." She smiled. "Breakfast?"

"No time!" I said and turned to leave. "But thank you!"

I bolted down the hall and around a few corners before finding Mr. Curry's office. Knocking three times on the door, I waited a second before going for a second attempt but was interrupted just in time.

"Come in," Mr. Curry's voice called to me.

I burst through the door and sat without being invited to. I was too excited for pleasantries.

"To what do I owe this pleasure?" he asked.

"I want to go home!" I said with all the joy that had been waiting to burst forth.

I wasn't sure what Mr. Curry thought. He waited a moment before responding, but that was like him, and as always he hid his emotions very well.

"Okay," he finally answered. "But may I ask why?"

"I had a dream," I said and then stopped to think about what I was saying. "Or maybe a memory. Either way, I saw my parents and realized in that moment that as awesome as this place is, it's not where I belong." I took a breath and continued. "I belong at home, with my mom, with my dad, and with people more like me."

I didn't want to offend him, but I really had no other way of putting it.

"All right, Josh, the choice is yours." I could feel a "but" coming. "But I must ask you if you are sure. For you may go home at any time you like, but once you go, you can never return here. So you must choose now: do you go home and abandon this life, or do you stay and seek home at a later date?"

"I am sure there will be much I will miss here." I smiled. "And I will never forget all I have learned and experienced, but I know with all my heart that home is where I am meant to be."

"Then it will be as you have asked," Mr. Curry replied with a smile. "Give us a day to prepare a portal to send you home, and in the meantime you can say your good-byes and pack your things. Take whatever you like from your room, for it all belongs to you. And know that you will be greatly missed, Josh. But who knows? In time we may see you again on your side of the world."

"Thank you!" I stood and shook his hand vigorously. "Thank you for everything!"

I darted off to my room. I packed what I wanted to take home and put my armor and Harlstril's sword back in the weapons room. As I set the sword back in its drawer, a memory washed over me of the first time Harlstril handed me the sword. He really did remind me of my dad, in a rough warrior kind of version. I realized then that I was about to give up any chance of ever seeing Harlstril again. As hard as it was, I knew it was what I must do. Sliding the sword into the drawer, I closed and locked it. I searched for Haslo and found him to be missing as well. No matter whom I asked, no one seemed to know where he was. So finally I wrote him a note and left it on his bed for when he returned.

The day was done, and I was packed and ready to go. There was nothing else to do but sleep in this bed one last time. As dreams swept over me, I found myself back in my childhood room. Flashes flooded it, and I watched my eleven-year-old self bounce out of bed. If only I could tell him to stay in bed, but I knew it was just a dream, just a memory. Another flash lit the room, and I saw the dreams of adventure in my younger self's imagination. Little me ran to the closet and grabbed my airsoft gun and flashlight. Then down the stairs he went. I followed him to the kitchen, where he threw on those little rubber boots. Then I watched as little Joshua slid out the door and into the night. I didn't follow. I waited, only a moment or two, before my mom came into the room. The look on her face indicated that something was wrong, but she could not tell what it might be. Mom walked out of the room, and that's when everything went crazy. The world around me started to flash and spin, the seasons outside flew past as if each one were only a few seconds long, and the calendar in front of me flew through the months and years, until it all came to a sudden halt. I looked at the calendar and realized the date was today, as if I were dreaming in the present time, seeing what was happening right now.

I looked around and saw my mom sitting on a worn couch. Her hair was frizzy, and her face seemed weathered, not as young and full of life as it had been. She stared longingly at a photo album, and I dared to see what she was looking at. As I looked over her shoulder, I saw pictures of me. My heart sank as I realized I had not even considered my parents in all this time. How must they have felt? How abandoned they must be feeling. I had left them without even a simple good-bye. From behind me, I heard the front door open, and I watched as my dad came in. His face too had become weathered. He noticed my mom and quickly rushed across the room to her. He wrapped his arms around her, and she began to cry. Dad took the photo album and set it to the side, closing it as well. Then he helped my mom to her feet, and they walked to the kitchen.

"I'll be home soon," I said, knowing they couldn't hear me. "I'm sorry."

But everything went wrong at that moment. The front door burst off its hinges. My dad panicked and pushed my mom into a closet, closing the door to hide her. He rushed to his briefcase and pulled out a small handgun. He shouted something, but it seemed as if all my senses had been muted in that moment. I turned to look at the intruder, and a sense of calm came over me. There in the door was an angel, with long blond hair, white eagle wings, glowing white and gold armor, and a white, hilted, silver-bladed sword.

The crack of gunfire brought my attention back to my dad for a moment. Smoke rolled from the end of the barrel. My eyes shot back to the angel. Something wasn't right. He smiled as if he enjoyed what was going on. I heard another crack of gunfire. The angel started to laugh and drew his sword. Four more shots were fired, to no avail.

I watched, unable to move, as the angel closed in on my dad. The angel stabbed him through the chest. My dad went to his knees, and the angel stabbed him again and again, until the floor was stained with his blood and he lay motionless on the ground. Then the angel turned to the closet and threw open the door, but he was not expecting an iron to fly at his head. The angel stumbled backward, and for a moment I thought I saw Lasnek in his place, but that was ridiculous. I just wished it were him. As much as I had been taught about the angels', or Iyarians', corruption, I never really believed it. The angel grabbed my mom and tossed her across the room. She landed in the puddle of her husband's blood. Lashing out, she grabbed the gun and pointed it at the angel.

Click. Click. Click.

It was empty. The angel gave no time for any other retaliation; he stabbed my mom, over and over and over, and no matter how much I wanted to stop him, I could not move. I was frozen in that spot. Acid tears stabbed at my eyes but refused to flow. My throat clenched and I could no longer breathe. I watched as the Iyarian warrior walked out of the house, leaving a trail of bloody footprints the whole way. Finally I closed my eyes and screamed, but instantly I knew I was awake. I opened my eyes, and standing over me was Mr. Curry.

"Are you okay, Josh?" he asked with a look of genuine concern.

My breathing was deep, as if I'd just run a few miles, and my eyes darted back and forth, making sure I was truly in my quarters. Finally I calmed down.

"It was just a dream," I said, knowing I would soon see my parents alive and well.

"Josh, I tried to wake you for nearly five minutes." I wished he had succeeded five minutes ago; he could have saved me a great deal of sorrow.

"It's okay, I'm okay." I sat up and breathed in deep. "Don't worry about it. I'll just be glad to see my parents again." I knew as I said this that something was wrong. Mr. Curry was excellent at hiding his emotions, but for a moment he slipped up, and I caught it.

"Josh, that is what I have come to talk to you about." Something was wrong, very wrong. No, no. It was going to be okay. The journey was merely going to be postponed.

"Will I have to wait another day?" I asked.

"No ..." he started slowly, and my heart began to lose hope. "Josh, yesterday I sent some men to inform your parents of your return ..." He took a deep breath, which only prolonged my suffering.

"And?" I forced him to press on.

"And when they got to your home, they found your parents ..." Again he stopped as if the news would be too hard to tell.

"Found my parents what?" I said with an edge.

"Josh, I don't know how to tell you this. They found your parents dead, murdered. Josh, I am so sorry." I know he must have continued talking, but I heard nothing more, nor did I care to hear any word ever again. All my joy was stolen away; things like hope and love and peace vanished and were replaced. Rage. Sorrow. Pain. Guilt. Fury. Indignation. Helplessness. Anger. Fire coursed into my emotions, and this time I let that blaze take me where it had always wanted to go. I held nothing back; I let it fill me, consume me, become everything I knew. I know Mr. Curry kept talking, but I didn't care what he had to say. I leapt out of bed, put on my training clothes, then took the edge of the dresser and, with inhuman strength, flipped it up and over. I grabbed Haldel's former dagger, the now fully grown long sword, and stormed out of the room. I flew down the halls, ignoring all in my path, then through the courtyard and into the hall of doors. I stopped and stared at the old wooden door that stood in front of me. My breathing was violent, sweat poured from my face, and my heart pounded in my chest.

"Josh!" Mr. Curry yelled. "Do not be foolish! You are in no right state of mind to do this!" He took deep breaths, obviously worn out from chasing me. "You don't even have any armor on, and if something goes wrong, we are not prepared to pull you out. You could be killed."

"Good!" I said without looking at him. "I guess it means this is a win-win situation." I raised my sword and pulled back the door. "Either way, I see it as gain. This will be the last time I cross this door. One way or another, I'll never take this test again!"

Chapter 21

Power from Within

Sword in hand, I swept through the open door, Mr. Curry's voice just a trailing memory. With only one focus, I stormed across the mountaintop plateau. The Hiltezion seemed ready for a challenge but was caught off guard by the furious speed of my attack. He reeled, trying to defend himself, but I swung hard at his face, slicing him from nose to ear and watching as black blood flew in a wide arc from my sword. The beast reared up on his hind legs in pain, and I took the opportunity to dart in from the side and stab at his soft underbelly. The feeling of my blade sinking into his flesh fueled the fire already raging within me.

There was no time for thought, merely action. I attacked again and again, pushing him back hard and fast. But then he switched from defensive to offensive mode, refusing to move and risking injury so that he might injure in return. He slashed forward with his great paw, and his talons grazed my cheek. It was too close for comfort, but I refused to back down, refused to change my tactics. I didn't care if I died; win or die, it was all the same to me. Another swipe of his claws ripped three deep gashes across my chest.

I stumbled backward and considered fleeing, but in a flash of memory I watched as the angel stabbed my father to death. The image fanned the flames of fury. Renewed strength and an unnatural power such as I had never felt before surged through my body and pushed me forward, swinging faster and harder. I pushed the creature back once more, farther and farther, until he was almost back in his cave. Choosing to accept injury rather than entrapment, he lunged toward me. I ducked down and sliced upward, digging my sword into his side beneath his wing, and he stumbled over me. The beast hit the ground and rolled in a tangled mass of claws and tail and crumpled wings.

I pursued the creature, not wishing him to have a moment's rest, not allowing any chance of escape. As he scrambled to his feet, I slashed at his tail, cleaving it clean off. The creature howled in pain. I tore around to get in front of him for a terminal blow, only to find his talons arcing toward my face. I recoiled, not quite ready to die at this moment, with my vengeance incomplete. But I was not fast enough; one of the talons sliced into my face from eye to mouth. Pain almost overpowered me as blood spurted out and splattered my armor.

In another flash of memory, I watched my mother murdered once more. Fear left me, regard for life slipped away, and any sense of mercy that may have been left vanished. Rage. Hatred. Vengeance. Those were the things I knew now. Power swelled in me once more, like a bomb exploding within me. I watched as the world around me slowed to a crawl, as if no matter how fast the creature was, I would be ten times faster. I watched as he raised his left paw to attack, and in a flash I sliced off the three talons. He reared back in momentary pain, then surged forward in attack, but I was too fast, dodging left and right, backward and forward as if fighting a child. The beast could no longer touch me. I struck again and again, until finally I cleaved off his right paw completely, removing the last of his weapons except for his teeth.

The beast sank back, knowing it was beaten, knowing escape was no longer a possibility, but unwilling to go down cowering. His eyes bored into mine, and mine into his. A barbarous growl rumbled forth from deep in his gut, but I growled right back. He bared his teeth, and I realized he could finish me with a single snap of his jaws. To be perfectly honest, I wished he would. Then we could both be released from our pain and anger. He had fought valiantly, without fear, and he deserved to win just as much as I did. I waited no more. I drove my sword deep into his chest, piercing his heart.

In an instant, everything changed. The creature's eyes were no longer just yellow; they seemed to burst into yellow flames deep within. I watched as his black scales flaked off, revealing white, glowing skin. Then the tatters of his wings turned to gold and developed a plume of white feathers. Finally the creature shrank to the size of a man, and there in front of me stood Haldel, with my sword through his chest. My eyes widened as I looked upon the angel I had seen in my dreams for so long, the angel I had watched die by Lasnek's hands thousands of times. And now it was by my hand. My knees grew weak as I realized what I had done.

But in yet another flash of memory, I watched as the angel who had murdered my parents walked out of my house, leaving a trail of bloody footprints.

I looked directly into Haldel's eyes, and I could see the reflection of my own rage-filled, hate-flooded eyes. I drove the sword a little deeper. He tried to speak, but I cut him off by driving the sword deeper still.

"Do not speak to me," I seethed. "I will hunt down every last one of your kind and kill you, one by one if I must. *How dare you try to speak to me*!" I screamed in his face.

"Lies. They are telling you lies." Haldel forced the words out through the blood already starting to fill his mouth.

"Lies?" I spat. "I watched my father brutally stabbed to death by one of your own. I watched that angel stab my mother through her heart, *and for what*?" My voice cracked. "I would have been home with them now. All of you would have been safe from me." I calmed myself and spoke with cold hatred. "But no. Not now. *I* will be the one to make this right." I began to shake as I started to lose control. "*I* will kill every last one of your kind. Starting with you."

I twisted my sword in his chest, breaking his ribs and shredding heart and lungs. I watched as the fire in his eyes dimmed. He tried to speak, but there was no hope of that. Nor would I allow it. I planted my foot on his chest and kicked him off my sword. As he slid off the blade, the entire sword ignited in black flame. Power, indescribable power, filled me. I felt as though I could tear the mountain from its very roots and toss it into the sea without breaking a sweat. But my sword began to shake violently. Something else from deep within me, some other force, surged to the surface. The powers did not mesh; like two magnets they pushed away from each other. My whole body began to shake so that I nearly dropped the sword. Suddenly everything calmed, and a white flame wove through the black for only a second; then both vanished.

An immense weakness came over me. My knees buckled and my vision blurred. My hands grew weak, and I heard the clatter of my sword hitting the ground. Then everything went black.

Chapter 22

Spark of Hope

I was dreaming. I experienced a floating sensation as I looked down upon the mountaintop plateau. I watched for a moment as the Hiltezion and I battled. It was one epic battle. I watched until I had beaten the Hiltezion, and then my head turned of its own will. There in front of me was Mr. Curry. He looked at me and smiled, proud of what he saw, but there was something else as well, something deeper. My head turned back to the fight, and I watched myself scream at Haldel, pushing my sword deeper and deeper into his chest. I watched myself finish the fight with a quick twist of the sword. As I watched myself pull free the sword, it ignited in black flame. Once again my head turned to Mr. Curry, and his smile grew into a devious curve. He turned his back on the battle and started to walk away, but my head turned to look down once more, just in time to see the jut of white flame shoot out from the black. Fear filled my heart, and I turned toward Mr. Curry and called to him. Mr. Curry turned and looked at me. I could tell that whatever I was saying was urgent, but as was the case in most of my dreams, the sound was muted.

I saw something I had never seen before. Mr. Curry seemed to erupt in rage. His strange, lightless skin seemed to absorb the light around him. Even the sun seemed unable to keep its brightness. The warmth in the air dissipated, and Mr. Curry walked slowly toward me. Fear filled me, but I had to make him see what I saw. I kept speaking but was silenced in a sudden moment as Mr. Curry's fist collided with my face, and blackness was all I knew.

The blackness was kind, though, kinder than my dreams, kinder than my reality. I wished to stay here in this blackness, in this nothingness. Forget my fears, forget my pain, forget my very existence, and simply float into the nothingness beyond. The great void would show me its kindness, the place where feelings are let go and sorrows have no grasp; there I would be safe, and there I thought I'd like to stay. But, alas, deep down I knew I would not be granted such a gift; I felt the void slipping away, and my eyes opened to a burning light.

I found myself in a medical room, feeling the air on my skin. Bright lights made it hard to see around me, but I could tell it was a simple white room, with my bed, a side chair and lots of wires and tubes attached to me and a machine that beeped and buzzed. I knew I was no longer dreaming, and I was fully back in my own skin. Slowly I sat up but stopped as my chest screamed with pain. I cringed and that too hurt. Bending as little as possible, I managed to get myself to a sitting position. Gently I swung my feet over the side of the bed and gingerly placed one foot on the floor. I was weak, very weak, but I was determined. Cautiously I rose to stand on both feet, breathing deep and making sure I did not pass out. Next I proceeded to remove my chains of wires and tubes. I left my heart monitor till last, and as I removed it, it blared with alarm. It was calling down all the nurses and doctors, I was certain. I was almost to the door when it burst open, nearly hitting me in the face.

"Josh!" Haslo seemed shocked to see me so close to the door.

"Hi," I wheezed.

"What are you doing out of bed?" he asked, dumbfounded.

"Thought I'd take a stroll." I smiled weakly.

"Think again; have you seen yourself?" He pointed toward a mirror. I knew now why he was so shocked. I was completely black and blue—well, at least the parts of me that were not covered in medical wraps. My chest was fully wrapped, and a good chunk of my face too. But everywhere I could see skin, it was bruised purples and yellows and blacks. It was actually disgusting.

"Wow, that's hot," I coughed.

"Very, and I'm sure it will make a great story, but you need to get back in bed before you ..."

Before he could finish, my knees buckled. Haslo caught me and lifted me back to my feet. He should have just carried me back to the bed, but he allowed me enough pride to simply accept his help. I wanted to be up and moving, but apparently even I have my limits. Haslo hooked up the IV again and then the heart monitors.

"I didn't know you could do that," I said.

"Well, once I realized I couldn't beat you with the sword, I took to learning other things." He winked at me. I laughed but quickly stifled it, as the pain was too great.

"Did you see that fight?" I asked Haslo.

"No, but I've heard many stories from The Curator and Lasnek, who were both there watching it." Haslo seemed to be imagining the battle as they described it. "Apparently it was the battle of the millennium. Even Lasnek was impressed, if you can imagine that." I couldn't help but remember the dream I'd had. Had I been looking through Lasnek's eyes then? Had it been real? "You know what this means, right?"

"What?" I asked, sure I could figure it out but far too tired to try.

"Once you are on your feet again, you'll be inducted straight away. You'll finally get to see your armor, and then you'll be set up to lead missions," Haslo said with a hint of jealousy in his eyes.

"Missions?"

"You'll see soon enough." He smiled mischievously. "And whoever stands in your way will surely regret it."

"That they will indeed," I said, remembering the promise I made Haldel on the mountaintop. I smiled but felt myself losing the strength to even keep my eyes open. Haslo must have noticed, because he backed away a bit and smiled too.

"Rest up, Josh. You'll need your strength soon enough."

With that he left, and I slowly slipped back into the abyss. Darkness enveloped me once more, but this time I could hear voices in the beyond. Two voices started to separate themselves as unique. Heated words were sent back and forth, but only a murmur seemed to reach my ears, tormenting the only form of sleep I had.

Chapter 23

The Argument

The murmur grew in my mind, becoming clearer and clearer until finally the voices rang out with absolute clarity. As soon as they became clear, I knew who was speaking, or should I say arguing. Lasnek's and Mr. Curry's heated voices battled each other.

"I know what I saw!" Lasnek snapped. "And he is not what you think he is!" With that I caught a flash of Lasnek's snarling mouth.

"Lasnek!" Mr. Curry retorted. "Don't toy with me; I am quite certain that I am a little more observant than you are." A flash of the man's eyes crossed my mind, stern and warning. "A little more in the *know* than you are, and a little more *in charge* than you are! I will tell you this only once more: this is none of your concern."

"You don't understand. You didn't see it." A glimpse of Lasnek's hand pointing into the abyss appeared before me and then vanished. "It is still there. It is still hidden inside of him. He will turn back. It must be removed!" Lasnek pleaded.

Silence filled the air for a moment, as if maybe Mr. Curry were gathering himself, or possibly it was the calm before the storm. For a moment I almost felt bad for Lasnek. But then Mr. Curry came back, with much more of a fatherly tone.

"Lasnek," he offered, "I understand how this must be difficult for you to work under him. I know that subservience isn't really your thing, but you *know* why this must happen."

Lasnek was clearly unwilling to be pacified yet held a deep sense of sincerity. His tone was laced with a deep sense of genuine concern.

"Look at Harlstril." His softened face flashed before me. My dreaming ears seemed to perk up at the mention of my old master. "Look what happened to him: he was with us, but we missed the tiniest fraction, and it almost ruined everything."

"Lasnek, I know people." He sighed in frustration. "You know as well as anyone how long I have watched people. I know things about them; I can see through them. And I have never seen anything like I saw in Josh!" I suddenly felt overly exposed, as I realized this conversation was about me. "Trust me. I know where his heart lies."

"Just like you knew Harlstril," Lasnek seethed under his breath.

"Excuse me?" Mr. Curry seemed enraged by the comment.

"Nothing." Lasnek surrendered what seemed to be a losing battle. I heard the thudding of his heavy feet walking into the distance and then silence, peaceful silence.

It lingered for quite some time. I could not tell whether it had been an eternity or just a few minutes, as if time had no hold on this place. I just seemed to exist within the nothingness once more. But as it always did, an end had to come. My eyes opened and light pierced them. Once they had adjusted, I slowly sat up; this time the pain was minimal, more of an annoyance. Once I was sitting up, I waited for the blood to move to its appropriate places. I did not want to risk too much and suffer for it. Soon, though, I was feeling ready, and I gingerly stood. The cold of the tile soaked into the soles of my feet. Strength seemed to flow through me. Although I was still a little unbalanced, I felt ready to move about freely. I removed all of my connecting chains and turned off the heart monitor before unhooking the wires. I cautiously stretched this way and that, careful not to reopen any injury. Once I felt confident, I removed the medical wrapping from my chest, revealing three long scars from my right shoulder to my left hip. They were still red and puffy, but they were closed up and healed. Another set to match my circle scars from the arrows that pierced my chest. The door opened and once again Haslo stood there, shaking his head at me.

"Josh, you tool." He smiled.

"Hey, Haslo, how are you?" I asked, my voice hoarse from lack of use.

"Not too bad ..." He looked me up and down to see how I was. "And yourself?"

"Alive, with a few sweet scars to remind me that I almost wasn't," I chuckled.

"Have you seen the one on your face?" he asked nervously.

"Ah ... no." Something about the way he asked made me nervous.

"You might want to check it out." He smirked and pointed to the mirror. Looking in it, I noticed that most of the bruising was gone, excluding a little around my right eye. I unraveled the wrap around my face until I could see the scar that started from beside my right eye and curved down to just above my lip.

When I saw it a new feeling came to me. It wasn't pain, yet it bit into my gut. It wasn't sorrow, yet it sank into my very soul. It was the same sensation I had harbored toward Lasnek for years, an undercurrent of hatred, rising up inside me. This was not directed toward Lasnek. A different face formed in my mind now, and I realized that the burning inside of me was an unfiltered emotion aimed at Haldel. As I realized the source of the feeling, a fire snaked through me.

I wanted them dead, all of Haldel's kind. Each one of them I would kill without mercy or regard. I swore to myself I would find and kill every last one of them.

"Josh!" Haslo interrupted my thoughts. "You okay?"

"What?" I asked, back to reality. "Oh yes, I'm fine."

"Well let's go; its time."

He kept talking, and a piece of me followed him as we began to walk down the hallways, yet my mind was filled with the satisfied imaginations of the race of angels, the Iyarian, upon the end of my sword. *Yes, Haslo,* I thought. *It is time indeed.*

Chapter 24

Induction

After I changed into something less revealing than my hospital robe, which left very little to anyone's imagination, Haslo guided me onward, to where I did not know. Wearing a suit was an unfamiliar feeling to me. Although it was very comfortable and perfectly tailored to my body, I was not a fan. I was used to things like armor and training clothes, not suits or ties or fancy things like that. We wove around this corner and that, until we were farther than I had ever had need of exploring. We finally came to a halt before two large wooden doors, which came to an arching point between them. Haslo eyed me up and down to make sure I was all in order.

"Seriously, you *had* time for a bloody haircut, you know." Haslo shook his head.

"I like my hair." I smiled. It had grown shaggy: not shoulder length or anything, just long enough to flop over my ears and move when I moved.

"Are you ready?" Haslo asked, smirking as if we were about to quest for mischief.

"Ready and willing?" I replied, not sure what I was supposed to be ready for.

"Alrighty, then. Onward!" He swung open the double doors, and we walked into an expansive room. To my right stood a large, solid wooden cabinet, alone in a corner, and to my left stood a massive great room–style wooden table, surround by twelve chairs. In each chair sat a member of the Council, the wisest and oldest of the generals. All twelve of them stood as they saw me enter the room. That in itself was a far greater honor than I ever deserved. Along the walls stood men and Cahirians alike, all dressed in their finest attire. They stood in respect and at attention. At the head of the table stood Mr. Curry, who motioned me toward him. I walked forward, soaking in the moment as the most respected beings in this place stood in respect of me. Who was I to deserve their respect? Who was I to be honored by them? Who was I to even be in this room with them? But I took the moment for what it was and basked in the glory of it all.

"Josh," Mr. Curry spoke, and I bowed my head in respect to him. "You have made me proud, more than I ever expected. Your determination is unlike any I have ever seen." He paused as if to measure his words carefully. "You, young sir, have completed every test and challenge we could put before you. Not only that, but you have finished each test with absolute excellence. Tests that have foiled some of our greatest warriors you put to shame as if they were mere child's play." He looked out over the crowd, eyeing each of them as if to make certain they did not miss what he was about to say. "But fight and talent are not enough. They will not bring about the destiny you are built for. And that is why you are so special. For all your talent, for all your intelligence, for all your fight, you have something far more dangerous. Something to be feared above all else." He looked back into my eyes. "You have vision, Josh. You know what needs doing, and nothing will stand in your way. No power, high or low, or anywhere in between, will stop you now."

He stopped and took a deep breath, then surveyed the crowd. "Now you have a choice to make, Josh. Will you venture forth from here, go home as you asked before? For that is still your choice to make. You can do much good in the world, Josh; you have many talents that will be useful. You can guide and teach people, change the world from the inside." A smile crept over his face, and I knew that whatever option two was, it would be the choice I would take. "*Or stay and fight*!" The crowd erupted in cheering. "Take on the enemy face to face! Destroy them where they stand! Leave none alive! Destroy this parasite from the root!" Again the crowd erupted, and I could feel fire in my chest. "Will you join us, Josh? Will you lead in this war? Will you take your vision, your talent, your gifts, and turn them against the oppressor of all time?" There was a lull, but I knew he wasn't finished; he was merely pausing for effect. The calm before the storm. The receding before the tsunami.

"For now is the time," he started calmly. "Now is the time to take your vengeance." His voice rose. "Now is the time for the reaper to rise." His intensity seemed to suck the very light and warmth from the room. "Now is the time to avenge the murder of your parents." My heart skipped a beat at the mention of my parents, but moments later all feelings of sorrow were swept away, replaced with revenge and hatred. "Now is the time for The Great King, the King of the Iyarians, the King of angels, the King of kings, and God of gods to feel your *wrath*! To feel your vengeance, to feel your retribution." His eyes pierced my own. While the crowd erupted, Mr. Curry and I shared a silent conversation. His eyes were full of pride, but they seemed to be searching me for my answer. What would I say, what would I do, how would I respond? My eyes narrowed and a smile crept across the left side of my face. Mr. Curry's eyes lit up, and he smiled in return.

"Tell me, Josh, where do you stand?" Mr. Curry asked loud enough for all to hear.

"*Speak*!" The twelve members of the Council shouted in unison and slammed their fists against the table. I took a moment to look around the room, making eye contact with everyone present, making certain that no one was left out. Then I spoke out, letting my voice fill the room.

"Mere days ago I was ready to go home. To leave this place for a normal life, a life with parents and school and sports and friends. A life full of pleasure and joy." I stopped and let the words sink in for a moment. "But the angels ... the ... Iyarians made a fatal error. I would have dropped off their radar, been nothing more than another of their pawns to do with as they liked, but they sent an assassin to slaughter my family. In a few swift strikes with their weapons, they have created their greatest enemy." My voice was not loud or agitated, but controlled and focused. "And now, nothing will stand in my way. Nothing will hold me back. There is no power that will bring my vengeance to rest. I will see every last Iyarian slain, and then, when his armies are gone, I'm going after their king. There is nowhere he can run, nowhere he can hide that I will not find him. To this I swear. Death itself will not be enough to stop me!" Silence filled the room for a moment. "So you ask me where do I stand?"

"*Speak*!" The Council cried in unison once more and struck the table with their fists.

"Where do I stand?"

"*Speak*!" they chanted back, slamming the table.

"*Where do I stand?*" I looked to everyone in the room.

"*Speak*!" the entire room roared back, the Council pounding the table and the men and the Cahirians stomping their feet.

"I am with you," I spoke coldly. "Till death and beyond."

The room erupted with cheering and applause, but soon Mr. Curry raised his hand to silence the celebration.

"Then it is time. Follow me."

He walked me around the table, and everyone's eyes were glued to us. Mr. Curry snapped his fingers, and a light lit up the corner of the room with the wooden cabinet. Slowly and methodically he unlocked the clasp and opened the double doors, at which a second light came on inside the cabinet and revealed the most magnificent piece of armor I had ever laid my eyes on.

I knelt down, running my fingers over the lengths of tall boots. I tested the material, intrigued by its hardened exterior, as if not even a Hiltezion talon could claw through it. Yet, as I slid my hand into the interior, I found it soft, ultra thin, and highly flexible. I was stunned at its design, completely in awe at its strength and power, yet mystified by its elasticity and ability to conform to whatever I would need it to become. The best parts about the pair were the knee guards that extended into a tall sharpened point. One swift blow with the knee, and it was game over for whoever dared defy me.

Beside the impressive footwear lay a pair of black gloves. I stood up and examined them, finding them to have the same feel as the boots. I slipped one over my hand and flexed my fingers, noting the perfect fit. Small yet powerful metal spikes protruded from each of my knuckles. The well-fashioned material slipped up my forearm, stopping just shy of the inside of my elbow. As with the boots, a wicked spike extended outward from the joint, fashioning my elbow into another fierce measure of destruction. I looked back to Mr. Curry, who seemed thoroughly content to watch my amazement as I went over each piece. He gestured slightly, beckoning me to the rest of the suit. My eyes locked upon the body work. Its liquid black gleam reflected my astonished impression. The craftsmanship astounded me as I picked up the breastplate, quickly realizing that it was complete with a tight-fitting back plate, both sides forming one solid piece, with locking hinges to the left waist and just under the arm. Well-formed pectoral muscles and abs were sculpted into the metallic armament. I stood there puzzled, trying to figure out how it could fit me, how one could know my exact measurements. Mr. Curry caught my eye and seemed to shrug off the silent exchange, as if to say that his craftsmen were just that good. I was most impressed with the protruded flanges that offered a sense of intimidation and additional protection. On the right, the wide guard arced around my neck, shooting upward to my ear, daring any opponent to try a lethal head blow at the risk of his sure failure. The left shoulder offered a similar flange, yet instead of a vertical arch, it was horizontal. With such a piece, I would definitely be able to maintain an edge in close combat. I worked my fingers over the back of the armor, only to discover sharpened spikes along the vertebrae. A smile drew across my face. They were pointless, but cool nonetheless. *Just don't pat me on the back after a battle.* I chuckled at the thought.

"You like it?" Mr. Curry asked.

"Indeed I do." I paused "May I try it on?"

"I thought you'd never ask." Mr. Curry snapped his fingers again, and a servant came in with a small box. Mr. Curry opened it and pulled out a black shirt and black pants. "You won't want to wear your armor against bare skin, nor will a suit do you much good."

"Thank you," I said and took the clothes and armor. The servant grabbed the boots and gloves and joined me in the side room. I was able to do most everything myself, but the armor was difficult to don by myself. Once the armor was on, I leaned over to put on my boots, realizing I had been foolish enough to put them on last. But when I leaned over, the armor astonishingly bent with my body as if it were made of rubber. Slipping the boots on, I stepped back into the main room, where everyone was in silent awe of the armor.

"What is this made of, Mr. Curry?" I asked. "It bends and forms like rubber. Is it even sturdy?"

"You need not worry, Josh. The armor is unique. It will bend and conform to your body, will grow and change as you do, and yet there are not many weapons that stand a chance of piercing it." Again he snapped his fingers, and another servant came out, carrying a large black piece of cloth. Mr. Curry swung around behind me and attached the cape upon the two clips on my right shoulder; it nearly touched the floor. A renewed feeling of power flowed through me. Mr. Curry stepped back and surveyed my appearance.

"You lack but one thing." He spoke and was about to snap his fingers, when the servant walked in with a long, thin wooden box, carved with all sorts of designs. Blue satin flowed from each of the four corners.

"Open it," Mr. Curry said, and I did. Light poured forth from the box as I gazed upon my perfectly polished sword, its long silver blade and ivory-white hilt, its perfectly placed diamonds. And, of course, there was that strange writing upon the blade. Haldel's little dagger was grown into a fully fledged long sword. I reached out to take it.

"Wait!" Mr. Curry commanded.

"Sorry?" I was confused as to why I could not take the sword he was giving me. I felt a nervous heat rise to my cheeks. This was an Iyarian blade, the metal poisonous to Cahirians. Was I about to be reprimanded in front of the Council? I breathed deeply, ready to accept the consequences of my actions.

"We had planned on making a sword just for you, one that would mesh well with your arrangement, but as we watched you battle the Hiltezion with this Iyarian blade, we realized that no other sword would do. A connection lies between you and this weapon." He picked up the blade and set the box in the servant's hands. The servant quickly moved away as Mr. Curry swung the sword this way and that. Stopping, he extended the hilt toward me. "As long as you carry this blade, you will draw strength from it. The strength of the Iyarians will be yours to wield against them. He looked into my eyes, and they pleaded with me to listen well. "Josh, don't ever lose it."

With those words I wrapped my fingers around the hilt and took it from Mr. Curry. Immediately a black flame enveloped the sword, and immense power stirred within me. All of my senses heightened at that moment. I held the sword high, and the room erupted in cheering. Even Mr. Curry was clapping—in his calm, cool, collected fashion, of course. In that moment I became one of them. Although my experience was not as extensive as that of the generals, I would be respected as one, and soon my actions would earn me the respect I was given now.

I brought the weapon down and realized I was not complete. I looked up at Mr. Curry, who had already called the last servant in. He bore a solid black scabbard, and once it was belted on me, I sheathed my sword. Yet in that moment I realized that Haslo was not in the room. I scanned the crowd to be sure, but, alas, he was not there.

"Haslo?" I asked Mr. Curry.

"Ah, my apologies. He has been on a very important mission for me, and even bringing you here was much more than he should have done. He, like you, though, is unswayable once his mind is set on something. He will return soon enough, but for now, Josh, follow me."

It seemed strange that everyone of major importance was here but Haslo could not be. Still, I was glad he was here for as much as he could be. Mr. Curry led me through a few halls and then out onto a large veranda that overlooked a massive valley. As I looked down, I saw a multitude of Cahirian warriors, dressed and ready for battle. There were groups of what looked like five hundred each, but as I tried to count the groups, I realized the number was beyond measure. It went on and on, for what looked like forever. Finally, Mr. Curry put his hand on my shoulder and then raised his other hand out over the multitude below. The cheering erupted and shook the very ground beneath me. The power of so many voices could literally crumble foundations.

"This, Josh, is your future." He looked at me and smiled. "These are the men who wait for you to lead them into battle." As he said this, my first instinct was to pull back; although this was a great honor, it was a greater responsibility. But then I realized that this was exactly the way it must be. They would merely be an extension of my hand, an extension of my wrath. They would be the ones who make my vision possible. Together, we would destroy the Iyarian race and their king.

"Your first mission is a small but very important one." Mr. Curry led me away from the cheering army and back into the complex. "You must lead a small reconnaissance team. There are specific people who hold high importance to our victory that need saving."

"When do I start?" I asked, eager to begin my mission.

"You leave at first light tomorrow, but right now it is time to meet your team." We turned another corner, walked down a long, doorless corridor. "Do you remember Harlstril telling you of the Destiny Troops of old?"

Did I remember them? Of course I did; those were the fighters from whom legends were born. My mind began recalling Harlstril's epic stories of his missions.

"These are the new Destiny Troops. You will find each one to be of great value to you; each warrior has specific strengths and talents that will be of great value to you. Your time has come, Josh, to pave this road to the final battle. The time to bring freedom to man is here. Josh, meet your troops."

Chapter 25

The Destiny Troops

Mr. Curry walked through the door, and I followed him. Standing before us were seven Cahirian warriors, but unlike the multitude I had seen before, these troops were geared for their specific talents. One Cahirian generally looks just like the other, except for maybe a small height difference. These warriors were no different, save one. The second-to-last in line had solid black eyes; the rest had fiery red eyes. Also, he wore no armor but had a strange aura that shimmered around him. Mr. Curry walked me to the beginning of the line and introduced me to the troops.

"Josh, meet Derus, most certainly the finest swordsman, next to you and Harlstril, I've ever met." I nodded to Derus, and we moved to the next. "This is Restas; she is more than capable with any weapon, but her weapon of choice is the tongue. If ever you find yourself captured, Restas can speak but a few words, and anyone will fall under her spell." Female Cahirians were rare, and they always carried a strange beauty about themselves. "This is Tartesol, who is indeed not standing here at all, is he?" Mr. Curry seemed to ask the air, and suddenly the apparent mirage of Tartesol vanished, and we heard a noise from behind us. "Ah, yes. The illusionist: not an enemy you would want, but a great comrade." Tartesol moved back into line, and I made sure to keep him in my peripheral sight at all times. "Zanos. You may notice that his eyes burn brighter than most; do not stare into them unless you wish to lose your mind completely." I nodded to Zanos, cautious to avoid prolonged eye contact. "This is Forseth, a unique addition to your troops. A skilled warrior, but do not lose him in the thick of battle, or you will lose him altogether. Forseth is a master of planning and coordinating, and although you must protect him in battle, you will reap the rewards of fighting smarter, rather than harder." If Cahirians had nerds, Forseth would have been one. He was smaller than the rest and a little awkward, but I could see in his eyes that his mind was working a million miles a second.

Finally we came to the black-eyed Cahirian. Just standing close to him, I could feel his thick aura sapping my very essence. "At last we get to the powerhouse of your team. Before you is Serstis. As I'm sure you have already noticed, he is unique among any Cahirians you have ever met. Serstis can control the elements, bending the natural and the supernatural to his will. A mighty foe, and a powerful ally." I nodded to Serstis, and it seemed as though he looked right through me.

"Leraska." Leraska reached out his hand and took mine in his, which is an uncommon thing to do in Cahirian culture, and even more uncommon to do with a commander. But I took his hand and shook it nonetheless. "He comes with my highest recommendation. He will be your second-in-command until you choose one of your own, but I am sure you will find him more than capable. He is skilled in weaponry of any kind and an excellent leader, and even Serstis here would not dare defy him." I watched as a wry smile crept across Serstis's face, as if to say, "I might just."

"It is my pleasure to meet all of you. I spoke with authority and without fear of any of them. "I look forward to leading you on such a valiant mission." I looked to Mr. Curry. "Speaking of which ..."

"For now get your rest; tomorrow at first light we will meet, and I will give you all the details then." He shook my hand and left the room, followed by the Destiny Troops.

I was alone with my thoughts once more: thoughts of where Haslo could be, of what was so important that he had to miss the armor presentation. I thought of Harlstril and the fact that he seemed gone from my life. I would have liked for him to do this introduction. As much as I liked Mr. Curry, Harlstril and I had an ongoing relationship; and that seemed to have come to a grinding halt. Would the same happen with Haslo? Would missions and whatever he was doing drive us apart? Would I ever see him again?

I made my way back to my quarters and unpacked my belongings, after putting my dresser back in its correct place. Memories of what I almost had came back to me, and I couldn't help but think about that. This time, though, I had nothing to get angry at, nothing to kill—not yet, at least. Tomorrow I would receive my vengeance, but not yet.

"I will make you proud, Mom and Dad." I paused, breathing deeply. "I'm sorry I wasn't there, I'm sorry I left, I'm sorry."

As night fell I climbed into bed and slowly slipped into a dreamless sleep. No Lasnek, no Haldel, just nothingness, blackness. When morning came I rose, only to realize I had gone to bed with my armor still on. What kind of idiot goes to bed with armor on? I laughed at myself and realized I didn't have time to lollygag; I sped off down the hall and met Mr. Curry and the Destiny Troops in the room where I had been inducted. Without need for introductions, Mr. Curry got straight to business, for which I was most pleased.

"This first mission sends you to one of the most thriving cities in North America. Your goal is to find Robert Wistel. He is a prominent businessman there, and his corporation holds together a large portion of the North American economy. Millions of families depend on his business, and even more depend on his products. The Iyarians know this and have targeted his business and him. Tonight is an especially important night, as he has a major decision to make."

"What are we to do?" I asked.

"Make sure he is able to make his decision unhindered. Once the Iyarians are dispatched, head back to base, and we'll prepare your next mission."

"With pleasure," I replied.

"Follow me. I'll take you where you need to go." Mr. Curry smiled, and I fell in step with him, as the Destiny Troops fell in step with me, Leraska in the lead. Soon I realized we were heading toward the hall of doors. Mr. Curry took us to a door I had not been through before. When I gave him a funny look, he realized my question.

"The doors can lead to scenarios and also act as portals that can send you anywhere in the world in the blink of an eye. Once there Leraska knows the portals that can take you back to base." He smiled. "Make me proud, Josh," he said as he opened the door. I nodded and motioned the troops to follow me. *New York City, here we come.*

Chapter 26

Losing a Member

Night had fallen on the city. I scanned the area and realized night would not provide us a great deal of cover. This was the city that never slept. We kept to the alleys and darker shadows, keeping clear of street lights when we could, although I doubted New Yorkers would give the strange group a second glance. Nothing fazed these people, but I figured it was better safe than sorry.

"Leraska, what are we looking for?" I asked, knowing he had been well informed as to locations.

"It won't be far from here. Opposite end of the street, maybe two or three blocks away. A skyscraper called Wistel Towers."

"Excellent. Sounds easy enough," I replied.

"It is an enemy stronghold, has been for quite some time," Leraska warned, but I smiled. Enemy strongholds held a great number of the enemy; my vengeance would have its fill this night.

"Move out," I ordered them. We made our way down the street as silently as possible, until finally we saw it there: a soaring skyscraper, guarded by only two Iyarian warriors. As I looked through the building's windows, I could tell that many angels roamed those halls.

"Tartesol, take the left flank; wait for my order. Zanos, same thing on the right. The rest of you stay here." Tartesol did his strange vanishing act and suddenly was lurking in the shadows on the far side of the street. Zanos had to be slightly more stealthy but apparently had a few tricks of his own. He climbed up the side of the alleyway and then leapt across the road, silent as ever. Just before landing he stretched his wings like a parachute and softly landed on the large overhang above the main lobby doors. That was my cue. It was time for a little arrogance. I stepped out of the shadows and walked across the road.

The two Iyarians just ignored me, which made me a little annoyed.

"Hey!" I yelled to them, which made them look at each other, a little confused. "Yeah, you two."

"Can you see us?" the one on the left asked.

"Clearly." I smiled. "And so can they."

I motioned for Zanos and Tartesol to attack. Tartesol appeared directly in front of the one on the left, and the angel moved forward to strike, but he struck at a mirage and found a knife planted firmly in his back. As the angel on the right went to his friend, Zanos leapt onto him and bored into him with his burning eyes. The angel quickly went limp. Wasting no time, I motioned for the rest to move in. We entered the lobby, which lay empty.

"Forseth, find out where Robert is." He swiftly ran to the front desk and planted himself in front of the computer, where he began typing furiously.

"Leraska, why did the Iyarians assume I could not see them?" I asked.

"Because most humans cannot, unless they are permitted," Leraska replied.

"Can the humans see *us*?" I asked.

"You are human and thus appear to them clear as day, but the rest of us are also invisible to them, unless we allow otherwise." *Interesting*, I thought to myself. *That could be a useful tactic.*

"Fourteenth floor," Forseth said, and we headed for the stairwell.

Together we swiftly moved up the flights, but as we passed the seventh floor, we heard heavy footfalls from above us. Quickly motioning everyone to stop, I looked up and saw two sentries descending upon us. We could easily overtake them, but I was not in the mood to risk losing anyone. I pointed to the door, and we rushed through it. I would have closed the door quietly, but it seemed pointless now: twelve Iyarian warriors stood in front of us.

"Take them out; no one survives," I ordered and turned back to head off the sentries coming down the stairs. As I turned, the two stepped through the closed door as if it weren't even there. *Cool trick, but let's see if they can do it backward.* I kicked the first angel hard in the chest, sending him slamming into the door, which burst open. The Iyarian tumbled down the stairs behind him. The second tried to defend himself, but I was too fast, and with two quick blows he was dispatched. Chasing after the second, I ran through the door and down the stairs. Only a moment later he lay dead on the floor. I turned to head back when I heard dozens of feet descending the stairs. Apparently our location was revealed. I ran back into the room to see my team standing over the strewn bodies they had slain.

"Fight's not over." As I said this, a dozen more Iyarians walked through the wall in front of us. For a moment they just stared us down, and we did the same to them. Eight of us versus twelve of them: easy victory. But that was when Serstis did something very strange. He flung out his hand and sent a strange black aura toward the group of Iyarians. A second later five of them fell dead. Next, Derus lashed out, a sword in each hand, and killed three more. Tartesol flashed here and there, stabbing three others in the back. That left one standing, alone among the dead. He did not falter or show fear, even though his death was imminent. There was no retreat, and no way to fight us off. I walked toward him.

"You should have left my family alone." Before he could respond, I drove my sword through him, and he fell to the ground. "Let's move."

We headed back up the flights of stairs until we reached floor fourteen. I cracked the door and peered through. There, in front of a large wooden door, was a small battalion of Iyarians, clearly ready for an attack.

"Can you draw them away?" I asked Leraska.

"Easily enough," he replied.

"I need only a few minutes. I'm going up a floor, and I'll come back in from the other side. Once Robert is safe, I will rejoin the fight," I said.

"Hopefully, the fight will be over by then, and we can go home heroes." Leraska smiled, which made me uneasy. When Cahirians smiled, it was just creepy.

"Forseth, steer clear of the battle unless absolutely necessary," I ordered.

They knew what to do, and I took off up to the next floor. Bursting through the door, I saw two lonely guards in front of me. I spun my sword in a wide arc, killing both of them and then took off across the long floor. Finally reaching the far side, I watched as the two Iyarian guards looked at me inquisitively, probably trying to figure out why I was wearing such a ridiculous getup. Before they could realize I knew they were there, they were dead.

Back down to the floor below, I crept into the hallway. The sounds of battle could be heard from the far end, and my way was clear. I kept to the shadows and finally arrived at the large wooden door. Pushing it open, I saw a man with his face on his desk. He was clearly sleeping. A small plaque on his desk said "CEO Mr. Robert Wistel," which confirmed my suspicion. Just beside him stood a single angel, speaking in his ear.

"Step away from him." I pointed my sword at the angel, but he ignored me and simply spoke faster, in a language I could not understand. "I *said* step away from him."

He finally looked up at me, yellow eyes burning hot. It was then that I noticed this one was different from the rest. Although he had a sword, it was smaller and seemed intended only for dire situations. This Iyarian was not meant for battle—not that that would save him.

"You do not understand," he said, reaching for his sword.

"Do not speak to me with your foul lies," I spat at him.

"You do not understand," he said again. "*I* am helping him."

"Helping him?" I sneered. "I know the kind of *help* you would bring to him, and believe me, no one deserves what you creatures do to them."

For a moment it seemed as though he would fight, but then he released his sword and looked upward.

"If you wish to make an end of this, then come and ..." Before he could finish, I drove my sword through his chest. As he fell the glow around him dissipated. I looked to Robert one last time to make sure he was all right, then headed out to rejoin the battle. But as I opened the door, I realized the battle was won. My seven ... wait ... six troops stood before me.

"Where is Forseth?" I shouted.

"He foolishly joined the battle, saving my life, but at the cost of his own," Leraska spoke.

Frustration washed over me, but there was nothing to be done about it now. Forseth was lost, but Robert was saved. The cost of one, paid for by another.

"Let's move out," I ordered the troops, and we headed down to the main lobby. I hoped this Robert was as important as Mr. Curry said he was; and if he was, then a glorious victory deserved a glorious celebration.

Chapter 27

Eyes of Terror

We left the Wistel Building and walked down the street. Leraska led the way to the closest portal. Now that I knew that I was the only visible one among us, it was easier to lurk through the city. Although most New Yorkers would ignore oddities, the police might not appreciate me walking around wielding a sword. So I still kept generally to the shadows.

We rounded a corner and walked up a dimly lit, graffiti-lined street, when a piercing noise broke the hum of the city: in a nearby alleyway, a scream. My eyes hunted the source of the sound, and again a scream erupted from the alley just across the street. With a few hand motions, I sent my troops in all different directions, so we could surround the alleyway. I headed straight in and immediately saw four angels, three warriors surrounding one like the angel who spoke to Robert Wistel. He was speaking into the ear of a man in a dark trench coat who stood over a girl around my own age. She was lying in a trash heap and shivering in fear, for it was not cold out.

With a single hand signal, I set my troops to attack, while I took out the speaker. I tore off running, bursting through the warriors and tackling the speaker in the middle. He was about to speak to me, when suddenly he stopped. As if maybe he knew it was a lost cause. His eyes went to the trench coat man, and I looked as well. He started to lower himself down on the girl; she screamed and tried to get away, but he was too strong. In a rage I drove the spike of my boot into the jaw of the angel and then stood.

With the other warriors occupied, I went after Mr. Trench Coat. Grabbing him by the throat, I lifted him off the ground and slammed him against the wall. He struggled for a moment, but then our eyes connected, and his widened in fear like I had never seen. I enjoyed the fact that he knew his time was up. My hands squeezed hard, and sweat poured from his forehead, while blood started to pour from his throat. Suddenly something blunt struck me in the back of the head, and I crumpled to the ground. Beside me I saw the trench coat man hit the ground too, but he quickly got up and ran down the alleyway. I rose to my feet, ready to chase him, but my feet could not find their footing, and he vanished into the darkness of the alley.

Realizing that someone had struck me, I turned and scanned the alleyway; no one was there. So I fumbled into the street, and there in the distance was ... well, it couldn't be. He was dead. I killed him. I watched him die. It was too late to give chase now, so I turned to make sure the girl was safe. Although she was frightened, she seemed unharmed. I reached out my hand and offered her help to her feet, but she looked at me not unlike the trench coat man had. I understood that look from him—I had been about to kill him—but why her? Her eyes were wide, as if she were looking at a monster. I took a step back, and she took the opportunity to run. As she did, something fell from her hand. Kneeling down I picked up a bracelet, a silver chain with two doves surrounding the name Charlotte.

"Sir!" Leraska called from behind me.

"She is safe." I stood and turned but immediately my heart sank. There were only five standing before me. "Where is Restas?"

"She was attacked from behind, sir," Leraska spoke coldly. "She didn't make it."

"You must stick together," I snapped. "You know better than to leave another's back unprotected." I was fuming mad; this was basic training. "I should not have to tell you this. You are supposed to be the best, so start acting like it!"

They stood in shame, except Serstis. He was cold, calculating, and dangerous, and he seemed not to care who died, as long as he lived. A good warrior, but a dangerous one as well, for you never truly knew whom he would kill to keep himself alive.

"At least Charlotte escaped," I muttered. "Then again, so did her attacker."

"We can hunt him down if you like, sir," Leraska offered with a grin.

"No, we have other priorities to attend to." I took a step forward and stumbled. Feeling the back of my head, I noticed it was bleeding very badly.

"Sir, you need medical attention," Leraska pointed out.

"Clearly, but we can attend to that back at base. Let's move out," I ordered.

"Sir, let us take respite, and I will look at that and stitch it up," Leraska pleaded with me. "Losing Restas and Forseth is one thing, but losing you would be the death of us all."

"Fine," I conceded. "Zanos and Tartesol, find us some food and meet in the abandoned building across the road. The rest of you, come with me, and we'll make sure the building is safe."

Zanos and Tartesol slipped off into the darkness, and the rest of us moved toward the abandoned building. Once inside I sent Serstis and Derus to clear the building while Leraska stitched up the back of my head. It was a few hours before Zanos and Tartesol got back; they explained that they ran into a band of sentries. They were able to escape, but it took them longer to make their way back. Once we had eaten, Leraska recommended we sleep for a few hours and leave before first light. Better to be rested and ready than tired and ending up dead.

All of them fell asleep rather quickly, but for me sleep refused to come. I wasn't sure if that was because the adrenaline was just not wearing off, or because I kept thinking of the way Charlotte looked at me. *Why was she so afraid*? I was helping her, and that seemed clear. But her eyes seemed to haunt me, and sleep refused to be my refuge. I sat awake as the hours slipped past, until soon the sun's first light approached, and it was time to go. I woke the troops, and we readied ourselves to head out.

Chapter 28

Haunted House

Leraska led us through the streets as the sun was rising. We traveled at a quickened pace, not wanting to be in the city when it burst into full life and the sun revealed me to the world. Although the rest could walk freely, it was best to retreat the city quickly. Finally we arrived at another abandoned building and broke through the wooden slats. Leraska led us down into the basement, where a single wooden door stood out from the rest of the building. The door was very old-fashioned, of solid wood with an arched top. It sat against the brick wall but clearly didn't lead through it.

"Just walk through, and we're home free." Leraska smiled. I did. Opening the door and feeling the sweet sense of victory, I walked through. There was a moment of blackness, then brilliant, hot light hit my face. I cleared the door and tried to get my bearings. Obviously, we were not in the hall of doors. Once my pupils adjusted, I could see we were standing in a cornfield. The corn was only about knee high. One by one the rest of my team appeared in the field out of thin air.

"Where are we?" I snarled at Leraska.

Looking around, Leraska spat on the ground. "The portal must have malfunctioned. We are about forty miles west of the city."

"What do you mean, *malfunctioned*?"

"I'm not sure; the portals have never messed up before." Leraska growled too, but not at me, simply at the circumstances. "Follow me, there is another portal not far from here."

We walked on through the cornfield until we reached an old gravel road. The sun beating down on us seemed very unfriendly. It was a hot day, and black armor was not comfortable in the sun. Cornfield after cornfield passed, until finally we came upon a very creepy house. It was of Victorian style and had clearly not been lived in for many years; the paint was chipping away, and the windows were boarded up. At the far end was a circular tower that rose just above the rest of the house. The lawn was filled with weeds, half dead and clearly unmowed. Willow trees are usually very nice, but as a background to this place they seemed menacing, even violent. I was about to quicken my step, when Leraska stopped and looked hard at the house. I had the sinking feeling that this was where the portal was. It was clear that whoever might have lived here, or possibly still did, did not want any visitors. There were hundreds of razor blades attached to the fence, which completed the feeling of weirdness.

Sick of waiting outside and observing the strange house, I kicked the broken gate off its hinges. I slowly walked forward, making sure there were no other fun things that might go boom or snap. The path seemed clear, and once I got to the porch I gingerly stepped on its rotting wood. It wouldn't take much weight, and I turned to the rest to let them know to hold off and enter one at a time, but they all filed onto the porch. I cringed, thinking the porch would give way, but when it didn't I looked down and saw that none of them added any weight to the porch.

A curious situation indeed. I turning the crystal doorknob, and all of us cautiously entered the house. Instantly, I felt attacked by something. Although nothing actually hit me, I could feel a great weight crushing me from all sides. It was as if the air itself was overly compressed in the house. Everything about this place gave me a bad feeling, but there was no time for foolish fears: we had a portal to find.

"Spread out, make sure the main floor is clear." I scanned the rooms and saw beams of light filter in through the boarded-up windows, illuminating the floating dust motes. Most everything was covered in a disgusting layer of thick dust. And the inside of the house was even more creepy than the outside. Pictures hung on the walls, pictures of creatures and monsters, disturbing images of people being slain or eaten. Everything inside me wanted to leave this place immediately.

"Where is the portal, Leraska?" I demanded.

"The tower, second floor, farthest room."

"Lead the way; let's get out of here," I ordered.

He did just that, and up the creaking stairs we went, and down the hall, until we got to the farthest door. I opened it slowly; the air inside felt even thicker. The room was clearly something out of a horror film. Animal skins hung on the walls, and blood spattered the once flowery wallpaper, now in torn ribbons. Strange ornaments hung from the ceiling, all of which made me uneasy, and none of which I recognized. In the center of the room, a large pentagram had been painted on the floor with something red, about which I had my guesses but refused to linger on. On each of the five points of the design was a candle, and apparently we were not alone. All five candles were lit. Centered in the pentagram was a wooden pedestal, maybe knee high, and on it was a large, old-fashioned book. I walked slowly into the room and into the center of the pentagram to examine the book, but as I tried to focus on the writing, it seemed to blur and shift. Soon I started to feel queasy. I stumbled away from the book. Closing my eyes and rubbing them, I tried to get my bearings. When my vision cleared I saw her.

In the corner was a girl of maybe fourteen or fifteen, but the way she was curled up made her look far younger. I walked over and knelt before her. I saw that her arms were full of neat little scars. To my horror she was carrying a little razor in her hand. She had no attacker: she was both victim and accused. For a moment we simply stared at each other. At first she made no reaction, then a small smile crept across her face. But in an instant it turned to fear, and she sharply drew back and tried to slide further into the darkness. I looked behind me and saw no one there. When I looked back, the girl was standing, and her eyes had become glazed over, as though she were in a trance. She no longer held the razor in her hand, and then I saw why her trance had begun: I discovered her true assailant. An Iyarian was whispering in her ear. I was about to attack it, when the little girl pulled a curved blade from her belt. I would not strike if it meant harm would come to her.

The angel's voice suddenly quickened, speaking rapidly into her ears. She walked into the pentagram, and the angel stopped outside of it but did not stop speaking to her. The little girl looked from the knife, to the book, to the door we had entered, and back to the knife again. Her head looked this way and that, until finally I had had enough. I bolted across the room, and as if the world had slowed around me, I saw the Iyarian turn his head to see me, the girl dropped the knife into her arm cutting her own arm open, and I drove my fist into the angel's forehead. He fell to the floor, and his light went out.

A sudden ruckus stole my attention, as a swarm of angels swept into the room. My troops held them and pushed them back, but three slipped through. One was smaller and weaponless, and two were clearly warriors. The smaller of the three knelt outside the pentagram and immediately started whispering in a strange language. The other two blocked my path to him. Rage fueled me as I watched the blood drip from the little girl's arm, as tears rolled down her face. Without pause I grabbed the first warrior and pulled him down, while lifting my spiked knee into his abdomen. Then I threw him to the ground, blood pouring from his wound. The second came at me, but I deflected his sword with my glove. Again he swung and this time I grabbed the blade. Squeezing hard, I spun the point of his sword around and stabbed him with it. Finally the speaker looked up at me, and before he could speak again, my sword silenced him. I sheathed my weapon and pushed the hair out of my face.

Sweat pouring down my brow, I knelt beside the girl. The crimson-covered blade was in her hands, and tears stained the floor below her. Gently I took the knife away from her and tossed it away. Looking into her eyes I could see so much pain, so much sorrow, and for a moment there was a great connection, but it ceased as quickly as it began. My lungs seemed to fill with cement. My vision blurred and blackness overtook me. I don't even remember hitting the dusty, bloody, tear-stained floor.

I don't know how long I was there, or how long the blackness held me before light returned to my eyes. But once I had come to, I pushed myself off the floor, shaking free all remnants of the strange feeling that had overwhelmed me. First I looked for the girl, who was nowhere to be seen, then I spun around to realize once again that I was short one of my team.

"Let me guess," I said bitterly, "Serstis was lost." I was surprised that it was he; I figured he would have been the last to go, tossing everyone else as shields for himself.

"Yes, sir ..." Leraska's head dipped in shame. "We tried to rescue him, but it was too late; we were ambushed from behind, and their numbers were too great. Serstis was lost in the mob."

As before, I was furious. How was it that at every turn I lost one of my team? Especially considering these were supposed to be the best. What kind of leader did this make me? How many would I lose in a *war*? Was I even meant to do this? Frustration overwhelmed me, but I knew this was not my fault. I was not here to babysit them; they were the best and should be able to take care of themselves. The fact that they were letting one another die was not my doing, but their lax discipline.

"I cannot do this on my own. I need you to be standing behind me. I need you to be ready. I need you disciplined and prepared. We are fighting an enemy who does not care in the slightest bit for any one of us, or any man, any woman." I pointed to the blood stain on the floor. "Or child." I shook my head, wiping the image of the girl and her blood-stained knife out of my head. "Remember, this is why we are here! If we cannot work together, if we cannot have each other's backs, then we are just wasting our time and talent." I paused for a moment. "Get it together."

"Sir!" they said in unison.

"Where is the portal?" I asked, and none of them could look me in the eye. That answered my question; for some reason, I did not care what, the portal was gone, not working, or something else even more ridiculous. I turned on my heel and kicked the large, old-fashioned book, sending it flying across the room, and also sending a sick vibration through my entire body. I ignored it. "*Where is the next portal?*"

"I can take you to it," Leraska spoke and turned to leave the room. The others followed and I let them distance themselves from me. I wished to be alone with my thoughts. I had had enough of this. I had completed my mission. I had done what was asked. Why could I not get back to base? And as much as I enjoyed killing the Iyarians, I knew that there were too many for me to kill alone. This wild goose chase was wasting time and talent and good warriors who could be used for more effective strikes. As I approached the door, I noticed something that stood out in sharp contrast to the dark interior of the room. On the wall in bright paper, with a fresh bouquet of wild flowers hung above it, was a name: Rachel Armstrong.

Chapter 29

Voices

It was already late afternoon by the time we left the creepy house. We walked for what seemed like eternity along the lonely gravel road. We stopped here and there to find some food, but other than that, we pushed on. As night fell and the moon rose in the sky, I could see small skirmishes in the fields. Iyarians and Cahirians battled. Part of me wished to join, but we had a mission, and that mission was to get back to base. I could not afford to lose another of my group.

"Tell me, Joshua, what help are you really bringing?" A strange voice caught me off guard, and I drew my sword, spinning around to see who was there. There was no one. Leraska and the rest were ahead of me. I brushed it off. I just needed sleep.

"I wonder what you would find if you visited the ones you have helped thus far?" The voice was too real to be my imagination, but there was no one there to be speaking it.

"Who are you?" I whispered, not wanting the others to hear me talking to myself.

"The real question here, Joshua, is who are *you*?" A shiver went through me, and somehow I knew I was alone again. I quickened my pace to catch up with the others.

"Are we nearly there?" I asked, ready to be back at base.

"It's just over the next hill ..." Leraska looked at me and seemed to be able to tell something was wrong. "Everything all right, Josh?"

"Fine," I lied. "Let's move."

With that we picked up the pace to a steady run. Up and over the hill we went, and just down the road stood an old farmhouse, with a few lights on inside, and a large red barn. Morning was not far off, but the sun's light had yet to reveal itself. We swept into the field for cover, as what looked like wheat had grown decently tall. We rushed through the field, and for a moment I felt like a child. It was fun, and I felt as if I had done this once before, many years ago. A smile crept across my face, but I brushed it away, pushing the memory down. I did not have time for memories like that; I had a mission, and a goal. Neither of those things included joyous fun. As we approached the edge of the field, I raised my hand to signal the troops to stop. On the front porch of the house were two Iyarians.

"We must be silent as thieves," I whispered and pointed to the guards. We slunk across the lawn and around the back of the barn. Before we entered I looked up and saw the name "Wolfe" above the door. That name seemed so familiar, but where had I heard it before?

"Josh!" Leraska interrupted my thoughts, and I knew we needed to move.

We slid through the back doors just as the light of the sun began to illuminate the horizon. "Keep quiet. The farmer may already be here. If not, he will be soon."

Leraska led the way, cautious to check around every corner. I took up the rear, clearly not trusting anyone else to do so. Finally we reached some freestanding stairs, and we headed to the loft above. There was a short hallway, and then we entered the massive room where all the hay was stored.

"Leraska, find the door. Derus, stand guard here." I pointed to the entrance. "Tartesol, Zanos, make sure no one else is up here."

There was a moment where everyone was doing something, a moment of peace, but again that peace was short-lived.

"Josh!" came Leraska's sharp whisper. I strode over to him.

"What now?"

"Look." He backed away and there in the hay was a man, face down, a large gash in his back. He was clearly dead.

"What of the portal?" I asked Leraska, feeling bad for the man, but knowing there was nothing I could do.

"Shhh," Derus hushed us, and then I heard it. A voice coming toward the loft. No, two voices. My eyes frantically searched for an exit, a hiding place, anything. I was not in the mood to be caught with a dead body. Then I saw it. I pointed and we all ran.

Chapter 30

Restitution Denied

Leraska, Tartesol, Zanos, and Derus snapped their wings and bolted straight in the air. I, on the other hand, didn't have that luxury. As I dashed across the floor, I could see the shadows approach the room through the doorway. I leapt to the ladder just beside it and climbed rung after rung with breakneck speed. Just as I reached the large barn beam that crossed the vast expanse, the door below opened with creaking protest. First a middle-aged woman came in, next a man, clad in plaid and clearly the farmer. My stomach sank as I watched six angels walk in after them: five warriors, and one speaker whispering in the man's ear. The man's hand reached around, and I saw attached to the back of his belt a large knife. He fingered it and I realized the woman had only moments to live.

"Susan?" he called to her.

"Yes, Chuck," she replied.

My heart pounded; I was amazed it hadn't given away our position. I had to get down there, and fast. Looking across the beam, I saw a rope wound up on top of it. What purpose it held I was not sure—maybe a rope swing, maybe something for moving hay bales. But today it was my epic way to the floor. I ran across the beam, leaping over my team one at a time, until I got to the rope. Grabbing the one end, I continued to sprint, until I was nearing its end. Then I leapt over the side. The rope grew taut, and I swung toward the thick of the Iyarians. Slamming hard into three of the warriors, it was like bowling: all five went flying. I slid across the floor and drew my sword at the same time, watching it ignite. I grew nervous as I saw the excessive amount of very flammable loose hay strewn about. Finally stopping, I turned to face my adversaries, and I smiled as they collected themselves. The speaker was still whispering in Chuck's ear. Something wasn't right, though. Chuck held the knife loosely in his hands, as if presenting it to Susan. Tears rolled down her cheeks. The unsheathing of swords drew my attention back to the fight in front of me. Five Iyarians, swords covered in white flame. I raised my hand and snapped my fingers. Immediately four Cahirians dropped from above and began to battle with the five Iyarians.

I tried to break through the fighting to go after the speaker, but one of the warriors snagged my arm. I spun and nearly fell but was able to get my footing before the angel bore down on me. He could have killed me in that moment, but instead he snatched me up by the scruff and pulled me close to him. Face-to-face his eyes drilled into mine. Why would he not take advantage of my position? He could end me right there, easily, but instead he just stared into me, as if trying to tell me something, speaking volumes with a single look. Then his eyes shot open wide, and his glow diminished, his grip loosened. There stood Leraska. His eyes were ablaze, but I realized in that moment that that wasn't the only fire. The hay had ignited and was reflected in his eyes.

I looked over to Chuck and Susan and saw that I was too late. Susan was already on the floor, still and cold. Chuck held the bloody knife and was weeping over her. Still the Iyarian whispered in his ear. Rage and indignation overtook me, and I strode over to the angel. He knelt beside Chuck, in perfect position. I kicked him hard in the chest, lifting him clean off the ground as he tumbled into the hay beyond. Taking my sword and not wasting any time, I drove it through him, ridding the world of one more "guardian angel." I turned to grab Chuck but realized the entire barn was engulfed in flames. The building did not have much time before it collapsed. Derus grabbed me by the shoulders and shoved me toward the far wall, pushing me through it. I watched him turn back. Leraska and Zanos caught me before I hit the ground. They set me on the ground, and the four of us, including Tartesol, watched the barn for Derus and Chuck. But there was a loud crash as the floor collapsed, and the walls soon caved in around them.

I screamed at the sky. Not only did I fail Susan, by not being fast enough, but I was unable to save Chuck, and once again another of my team was lost to me. I stood and watched as the barn was completely consumed by flames. Soon the whole thing caved in on itself, sending forth a great fireball.

"He should have left me!" I cried. "I could have gotten Chuck to safety just fine, and we would all be here, safe and sound!"

"He made a call!" Leraska snapped. "You are more important than Chuck, and you are more important than us!"

"I would have been fine!"

"Then go back in and get their burning corpses if it makes you feel better!" Leraska towered over me. "Our job is to protect you! At any and all costs! Do you not understand? Are you unaware of how important you are?"

"Talented, yes, but no more important than anyone else."

"You have no idea, do you?" Leraska asked sternly.

"What are you talking about?" I asked, frustrated.

"You're not just someone who can defeat the king. You're not just angry and bent on revenge." He looked deep into my eyes. "You're the *only* one! You are unique. No Iyarian, no Cahirian, no human has the power to destroy the king of the Iyarians."

"What do you mean?" I pushed for more.

"I cannot explain more, because I don't know. But you, for some reason, are the one who will find a way. Not only to destroy his armies, but to finally take down the king as well. He could take on a thousand armies and walk away unscathed, but somehow, for some reason, you will find his weakness, and you will bring him to his knees." Leraska spoke not to encourage me, but to make me understand.

"But how?" By the sound of this guy, he was indestructible.

"No one knows, but when the time comes, you will." Leraska's eyes burned into me.

"Not sure if I quite feel up to the job anymore."

"Trust me, when the time comes, when you finally face him in battle, nothing will be able to stand in your way." Leraska put his hand on my shoulder, then looked to the sun rising low in the sky. "It's time we were off."

Leraska led the way, and this time we left the roads and headed toward the forest behind the barn. Out of the corner of my eye, I saw someone running into the field, but when I looked to see more clearly, there was nothing there. I couldn't help but think of Chuck and Susan. Why had he not stabbed her right away? Why his tears once he had? And why was she not afraid? Something was not adding up; something was missing.

"About that you are correct, Joshua." A shiver ripped up my spine as I heard the voice once again. I looked to the remaining three members of my team, but none of them seemed to be paying attention.

Who are you? I thought.

"Things are not what they seem, Joshua." Another shiver, and I knew I was alone again.

In the distance I heard the sirens of emergency vehicles racing down the gravel road. Soon they would find the barn burned to rubble, and the charred remains of Chuck, Susan, and the mysterious stabbed man in the hay. That was not my concern, though; my only concern now was getting back to base, and keeping the three remaining members of my team alive.

Chapter 31

The Multitude

We kept a steady pace through field and forest alike. Wherever this last doorway was, it was nowhere close by. Soon the sun was setting once more, and the moon and stars were the only lights in the sky. The night seemed better for travel, as the sun seemed hot enough to cook us. I welcomed the coolness of night but still wanted to be finished with our journey. I looked to Leraska, as if to ask him how much farther we had to go. He smiled and I knew we must be close. I motioned for us to pick up the pace, and we began to run through the woods.

Keeping my eyes on our surroundings, I nearly ran into Leraska when he stopped suddenly. I halted quickly and motioned for the others to do the same, and then motioned them to get low. I crept up to where Leraska was and saw what he was looking at. His eyes seemed afraid, or maybe just nervous. Before us lay a large clearing in the woods, in the center of which was a dying bonfire. All around the fire were a great number of people; they hummed and chanted as if they were all wrapped in a trance. The sight was disturbing, but it got even more disturbing when many of them drew small blades and began to slash at their own skins. Blood poured forth onto the ground. I looked over to see

Zanos smiling; he noticed me looking and quickly wiped the smile away. I would deal with him later. In front of the fire stood a small altar with two ravens on it, necks broken and lying across each other. The group of people was made up of men, women, and even some younger teens. Their incantation seemed to lull my mind, as if I were quickly becoming a part of their strange ritual. I shook it off and blocked out the noise.

Then in the sky a light appeared, and a legion of angels descended on the area. They landed at the edges of the clearing and tried to walk in toward the group, but some strange force seemed to hold them at bay. There were many warriors and many speakers alike. The speakers began to speak furiously, and Leraska tried to stand, but I put my hand on his shoulder and pulled him back down.

"Wait," I whispered, unwilling to lose any other of my team. *What on earth is going on?* I asked myself. Leraska's eyes seemed to dart back and forth; he seemed overly nervous, which was very unlike him. Suddenly the invisible bubble seemed to break, and the Iyarians rushed in to surround the people. Immediately they started to whisper, and I saw what I did not expect. First, a young girl looked at her arms and started to cry. Then an older man dropped the blade he held. The group's eyes seemed to clear as they looked around in shock and tears, as if realizing what had happened. A young boy seemed to smile, not a cryptic smile but one of peace. He looked truly happy.

Leraska reached for his sword, and I put mine to his throat. "Reach for your sword again without my order, and it'll be the last thing you ever do," I warned him. He was acting all sorts of strange now, almost frantic. And he was about to reply but wisely bit his tongue. As I looked back I watched a woman with long black hair walk to the fire; although two speakers spoke to her, she did not seem to notice. A thick black aura that flowed

around her seemed to keep them back. It reminded me slightly of the way Serstis's aura had flowed around him. Everything seemed so wrong. What was going on here? She took a blade, sliced both of her hands, and then dropped her hands in the fire. Although I could not see clearly enough to be sure, it looked as though her skin did not burn. She began to hum the mantra once again, and her voice flowed farther and more powerfully than it should have. It was then that I realized she wasn't a woman at all, but someone much younger.

The bonfire seemed to erupt, and once the flames stilled, a man, wearing a black cloak that hid his face, seemed to stand in midair above the flames.

"You are being deceived." His voice boomed through the clearing, and every Iyarian went silent. "All around you are agents of deception, speaking to your left and to your right. With cunning they whisper lies into your very soul! Do not listen!" he shouted. "How long have I watched over you?" His tone was fatherly. "I have protected you. Guided you. Loved you." He paused for a moment, as if to let the words sink in. "Do not allow the enemy in! Do not trust their slippery words."

"You have led us with certainty and power!" a man shouted from the group.

"Push out the voices!" the raven-haired girl shouted, still facing the fire.

With the woman's cry, the Iyarians pushed forward, but the crowd seemed to sink back into their earlier state. Their eyes glazed over, and the mantra sounded again. With a sudden blast the angels were sent flying in all directions. Many of them crashed into trees and crumpled to the ground. And with that boom the cloaked man above the fire vanished. The crowd chanted with a renewed intensity; blood seemed to coat the ground below them. My stomach turned as I watched what was happening.

"We must go," Leraska finally spoke.

"Lead the way," I said, but not a second later I heard a scream behind me. I turned in time to see a flaming Iyarian blade leave the chest of Tartesol. I swung my sword and dispatched the Iyarian, but not before he could call out to his companions. "Back to back!" I shouted.

Leraska got behind me and drew his sword, but Zanos was cut down before he could take two steps. Within a flash we were surrounded by easily thirty Iyarian warriors, although they did not advance but merely kept their swords trained on us.

"Hold your ground, Leraska," I ordered.

"A wise order," came a voice from among the Iyarians, deep and strong, and with a body to match. An Iyarian like I had never seen before stepped forward. Lasnek had been the largest Cahirian I had ever seen, and no Iyarian had ever come close to him, but this one was easily his height. He wasn't fat like Lasnek, and he seemed even taller, because, unlike the rest of the Iyarians, he had six wings instead of just two. His presence alone made my knees weak. Something about his face was familiar. For some reason I recognized him, though I could not place it. He drew his sword, and its uniqueness matched him. The blade seemed to be made of pure crystal, and instead of igniting, it merely glowed brightly from the inside out. It was the size of a claymore, but in the Iyarian's hands it seemed a perfectly sized long sword.

"Iyarian scum," I spat.

"Iyarian?" He looked a little confused. "Haven't heard that one in a while." He laughed. "I've grown quite accustomed to 'angel', or in my case, 'archangel.'" He chuckled to himself. "'Iyarian' always makes me feel like an alien, and it always creeps people out."

"Seems fitting."

"Name's Michael." He smiled, ignoring my comment. "And you would be?"

"My name is Josh." I nodded toward Leraska. "This is Leraska, and those two," I said, pointing my sword at my fallen comrades, "are Zanos and Tartesol."

"What would have you traveling with such ..." He paused to think. " ... company like this?"

"They are my team, and we are here to wipe your foul kind off the face of the earth," I seethed, pointing my sword at his face.

"Interesting predicament you find yourself in then, isn't it?" Michael asked with a smirk.

"Depends on your point of view," I retorted.

"What do you mean?"

"I have about thirty of you here, ready to taste my sword." I smiled. "And I'll kill every one of you."

"Well then, Josh, you had best ready yourself to fight."

I slammed my sword into his. His relaxed and arrogant composure was his downfall. His grip on the majestic blade was loose, and I knocked it clear of his hand.

Before I could press my attack against the great archangel, I was swarmed, and Leraska and I fought for our very lives. Back to back, we sliced the enemy to pieces. But the numbers around us diminished even faster than we were killing them. The cowards were fleeing! Moments later we were alone again. Only about twenty Iyarians lay on the ground, and none of them included Michael. His crystal sword was gone as well, a treasure I would have liked to collect. Leraska and I took a moment to breathe and rest. My stomach was pained, and my ribs felt as if they might explode. I was pumped full of adrenaline, but my body was exhausted.

A full day's travel followed by battling fifteen-to-one odds was not conducive to rest. I turned to see Leraska, but my attention was drawn to the clearing beyond. The bonfire was now no more than coals, and the people were gone. I walked out into the clearing and scanned the area, hoping something would tell me what had gone down here. A groan came from near the bed of coals; walking over to it, I saw a young man breathing hard as he lay on the ground. A puddle of blood was forming around him, and it would not be long before he was gone.

"Sir, we must go," Leraska warned me.

"One moment," I replied and knelt beside the young man. "What happened to you?"

"I-I don't know." He coughed.

"What were you doing here?"

"I was invited. It seemed f-fun at first, b-but then everything changed." He started coughing again, and I knew he only had moments left. "Everyone just went crazy. They held me down. T-tied me up." Tears streamed down his face. "I don't want to die."

My heart sank. I knew his wounds were too deep, that he was going to die, and there was nothing I could do about it.

"I was warned ..." he gasped. "Should have listened ..." His breathing became overly labored. "Please ..." His body started to shake; then it stopped and he reached up and grabbed my face. "Don't serve them!" His whisper was harsh in my ear.

"Serve who?" I asked, but the boy slid to the ground, limp, silent, cold, dead.

"Josh, the portal is working; we must go!" Leraska's words were firm, and I knew he was right. With one last look back, I saw the boy; he deserved better than this. He seemed so full of good, and now he was nothing more than a corpse.

"And whom did he serve, Joshua?" The voice! It was there and gone in the same instant I stepped through the portal.

The cold damp feeling filled me with comfort as I stepped into the hall of doors. Leraska eyed me to make sure I was okay; I dismissed him with a flick of my hand. I wanted to be alone with my thoughts. What was going on? The more I thought about all I had seen, the more confused I became. What had happened in that forest? The Iyarians seemed to be helping, but sometimes that was the greatest form of deception. Frustrated, I walked on toward the hall of the Eternity Door. I walked along the edges, eyeing the pictures, reminding myself of the life we fought for. Freedom. Joy. Love. Life. These were the deepest sides of the battle. Footsteps in the distance caught my attention. I slipped behind a pillar and waited for whoever it was to pass.

"Charlie, follow me," Mr. Curry's soft voice beckoned.

"Where are we going?" It was the voice of the boy who had died mere moments ago. But now his voice was healthy and strong.

"You'll see soon enough," Mr. Curry said just as they came into view. I watched as Mr. Curry put his arm around the boy and walked toward the Eternity Door. I sneaked around the other side of the pillar, hoping to get a glimpse of what lay beyond the great gold and silver door. Mr. Curry unlocked the door and opened it, but he opened the door that was closer to my side, and it blocked my view. Once they both slipped through to the other side, the door closed behind them. Where had they gone? And what lay beyond those doors? I knew better than to go where I'd been told not to. I turned on my heels and headed back to my quarters, where my thoughts swirled and screamed at me. Again, no sleep would come to me; as tired as my body was, it seemed to refuse sleep. So my tortured thoughts haunted me until morning broke.

Chapter 32

The Prophecy

As morning arrived I realized sleep would not come for me; I would be cursed to walk the earth never knowing sweet rest again. I sat on the edge of my bed, my gloved hand pressing against my forehead. Images flashed past me: the eyes of the girl in the alleyway, the man standing above the fire, Charlie in his dying moments, little Rachel Armstrong with the knife to her skin. Death and pain permeated my thoughts; I could not be free of them. Try as I might to get away, they had become a part of me. Finally I stood and walked toward the door of my quarters, but out of the corner of my eye I saw a man I did not recognize. Standing in the mirror, looking back at me, was a stranger, still clad in the black armor, which I seemed to forget was on me. The skin on my face was grey and taut, pulled tight across too much bone. My eyes were sunken and hollow, and, worst of all, the pupils of my eyes seemed to engulf the whole of my once-hazel circles. Who had I become? What had I become? What had I left behind in order to seek my vengeance? This vengeance seemed to bring only more confusion and pain.

I slammed my fists down on the dresser, cracking its wooden top. My eyes followed the strange writing on its surface, as the letters began to glow a deep red. It was as if they might burst into flame, but I had seen this once before, long ago. I drew my sword, which was already glowing white-hot. Images flashed through my mind, thousands of indiscernible images. Finally I tossed the sword onto the dresser and allowed the strange writings the battle they had waited for. The red and white lights wrapped around each other, swirling this way and that. Fury overwhelmed me. What was happening? What was going on? Haslo might know, but I was sure he was too busy doing something more important to show up. Harlstril would have some form of wisdom for me, but, alas, he was gone as well, vanished into the great abyss. I was alone; it was only me now. No friends, no future. Just my anger and vengeance to keep me moving.

Finished with my self-pity, I stormed back to my sword. Leraska would know of our next mission. He would know what to do. I grabbed the sword, and a sudden vibration thrilled through me, to my core. The sword fired into pure white flames for just a moment before everything went black and I hit the floor.

When I awoke I was no longer in my room. I recognized this feeling: I was dreaming. I sat upon a cloud, miles above the earth. All around me were Iyarians, and not one wore armor, not one bore a sword or any other form of weapon; they simply sang. Their voices rang out in a beautiful accord. As much as I hated them, I could not help but be drawn into the beautiful song. Peace seemed to flow over me, my thoughts and frustrations washing away, clearing my mind of all that had happened. But that moment soon ended. Confusion rushed over me, anger filled my mind once more, and I pushed out the angels' voices. I would not be taken in by such trickery; I would not be overwhelmed by musicians. I blocked out the song, unable to stop hearing them but able not to comply with their demands. I reminded myself of all the harm they had brought, of all the pain they had dealt. They were evil beings, bent on control and manipulation. I would not allow them to sway me.

"What you see is not always as it seems, is it, Joshua?" a voice boomed through the clouds. I spun around to see where it came from, but there was no source. The angels grew silent and flew away, but not out of fear; it just seemed their mission was a failure.

"Who are you?" I asked the emptiness.

"That is of little importance right now. What matters is that you know the truth." The voice shook me.

"I *have* heard the truth!" I retorted.

"That you have," came the unexpected reply.

"What?"

"A long time ago, your parents told you," the voice rang out. And for a moment I was immersed in memories. I could see my parents reading to me; I watched a thousand dinnertime conversations take place in the blink of an eye. My parents had taught me all about life and truth, choices and consequences. As all this ran through my mind, another voice broke through.

"Josh, you are better than this." The voice was clear and calculating. It was unmistakably that of Mr. Curry. "Do not listen to these lies, these deceptions."

"But ..." What this unknown voice said seemed so right, so true.

"He seeks to control you. Do not allow this." Mr. Curry's words brought back memories of what I'd seen on my mission.

"Joshua, listen to me ..." The booming voice tried to claim my attention.

"No," I hissed in anger, realizing just who had invaded my dreams.

"Joshua, please." The Great King spoke, without the slightest trace of begging, but with a firmness like no other.

"Tell me, *Almighty One*," I spoke with sarcasm, "if you are so *loving*, why send your forces to murder my family?"

"Joshua ..." The king of the Iyarians tried to answer.

"My name is Josh," I spat.

"Your name is Joshua," came his stern reply.

"Do not tell me who I am!" I yelled to the emptiness.

"Joshua, I have known you, every piece of you, since before you were even a thought."

"*Shut your mouth*!" I screamed.

"Josh, you do not need to listen to him. You know who you are." Mr. Curry came to my defense.

"Joshua, listen to me ..."

"*No*! *You* listen to *me*, and you listen well! I am coming for you, and any Iyarian who stands in my way I'll tear to pieces. Nothing and no one will stand in my way. And once I'm done clearing a path, consider your reign over."

"Joshua, there are *two* things you need to know." I tried to lash out and cut him off again, but my mouth was silenced. I would not speak this time. "Know this: there will come a day when you and I will speak again, and your perspective will be much different than it is right now."

"As for you ..." His voice seemed to turn on Mr. Curry. "You may be The Lie, but don't ever forget the truth."

"The *truth* may not be what you believe it to be," began Mr. Curry. He paused and seemed to suffer through the last bit. "*Almighty One*."

"Joshua, the second thing you must know is simple." The king seemed to ignore Mr. Curry's words. "No matter what path you take, this will never change: Joshua ... I love you."

His final words seemed to shake my very existence. They consumed my body, flooded me and filled me. None of my defenses stood a chance. My eyes snapped open, and I found myself on the floor of my quarters, my sword lying still and unlit on the floor beside me. Fury tried to push out those final words, but the best I could do was repress them. I stood and sheathed my sword, furious that I could be attacked here, in my own quarters, a place I had always considered safe. I put my fist through the mirror in front of me, not wishing to see my sunken face. Glass shattered across the floor, and I stormed out of my room. I would find Mr. Curry, I would get the next mission, and I would do as I had promised. I was a man of my word, after all.

I stormed down the hallway; anyone in my way cleared out for fear of my wrath. At Mr. Curry's door, I barged in without knocking, only to find Mr. Curry face down on his desk. Steam rolled off of him. I ran over and examined him; he looked as though he had been beaten badly. Thinking quickly, I hit the page button.

"A doctor to Mr. Curry's ... The Curator's office immediately!" I shouted into the microphone.

When I found his assailant, they would suffer greatly. Doctors showed up within the minute, and they took Mr. Curry away on a gurney and promised me they would take good care of him. I slumped down in Mr. Curry's chair and stared into the nothingness, thinking, *Can this day get any worse? Honestly*!

"He's going to be all right." The voice brought me back to reality. "He is very strong."

"Leraska!" I saw him standing in the doorway. "What happened to him?"

"Your mind was taken by the king of the Iyarians." Leraska smiled. "The Curator went to rescue you, but apparently you didn't need much rescuing. Either way, a task like that often proves fatal to those who attempt it."

"But I was unharmed." I paused, thinking back. "Annoyed, but unharmed."

"A feat I have always believed impossible." Leraska entered the room. "Until now."

"Why me?" I asked.

"Josh, do you want to know how we know you are the one?" Leraska asked.

"Might be of some use."

Leraska stood and walked over to the bookshelf. He ran his fingers along the books until finally he found the one he was looking for. Taking it from the shelf, he dropped it on the desk. It was a thick, heavy, old-fashioned book. A great deal of dust had settled on its pages. Leraska opened it and flipped through the pages, until he came to what he wanted. He spun the book and slid it in front of me.

"This is where you come from, Josh. You hold the key that will end this war forever. For two millennia we have waited and watched for you." Leraska smiled. "Now you come, carrying victory in your wake."

The title at the top of the page was, "The One, The End, The Ruler." With eager eyes I began to read.

> *There is a child who will bring about the end of all things; the One you fight against will be brought to his knees. The dark one who was cast down will rise above and crush the One who cast out. The child will fight alongside the dark one. The choice will belong to that child alone. He shall bring about the end. Do not waver in your hunt, for to miss him would be of dire consequences. You shall find him as a small boy, not sure of himself, not sure of anything. He will be easily directed. His dreams will bring about a hatred for the One you fight against and his legions, which are far greater than any other. You will know this child by one thing. He shall stand upon a hill and scream for the one he*

knows not. You must take him and kill the one he screams for. This will be the first step in his training. Once he is ready, let him read the prophecy written here; he will then know what to do and will start the path to bring about the end of all things.

Passion overwhelmed me, bringing a determination that purged any last shred of hesitation. I heard my promises echo in my head. I would bring about the downfall of all things! Nothing was going to stop me now.

"Leraska!" I said firmly.

"Yes." His voice was full of anticipation.

"Gather the troops." I looked up and into his eyes. "We're going to war."

Chapter 33

Contingency Plan

Twelve eyes stared up at me, from the twelve members of the Council, as they sat in their twelve chairs. The farthest chair was vacant, as Mr. Curry was still not ready to leave the hospital. Leraska stood beside me now; he had indeed become my right-hand man, and there he would stay. We had spent the whole last day and night poring over maps and tactics, planning for this battle, the battle that would begin our road to victory.

"This is where our battle will take place." I pointed to the map upon the wall. "The Valley of Uthura." A murmur of disapproval rumbled through the Council. Leraska had warned me they would be difficult to convince. No Cahirian army, no matter the size, had ever taken the valley stronghold. Finally, one of the members of the Council stood and spoke.

"Sir, you will never win this battle. No one can take the valley." He breathed deep. "It is a slaughter pit."

"This time will be different," I returned, unshaken by his doubt.

"Even Harlstril could not take the valley." Another stood and voiced his doubt. "You are a fool to try."

"Speak that way again, and I will remove your blaspheming tongue!" Leraska spat, drawing his sword. Although Leraska was not one of the Council, no one dared defy him. I had learned of his legendary heroics, and stories told of him facing down armies by himself.

"Leraska, please." I did not wish to force the Council into battle. They needed to see that this could be won, or they would sow doubt in the minds of their troops. "For years, battles have been fought and lost in that valley. Of this I am not unaware." I looked out over the doubtful group. "But there are two reasons we will win this battle. One, our enemy in that place has grown proud and complacent. They assume victory, and their pride will be their downfall." I smiled as the group chuckled to themselves, imagining the possibility of victory.

"But the second reason is of even greater importance. The valley has not been used to its greatest advantages. And because the enemy assumes victory, they have never sought to improve what has worked in the past. They are predictable." I slid a map across the table. "I am aware that the fight leads us uphill. But there is more to the valley than its floor. I am aware that even Harlstril could not take the valley, but Harlstril could not beat me in any war scenario either." I struck the table with my hand, gathering everyone's full attention. "I am not Harlstril, I am not the generals of times past, I am not one of the Council. I am better!" Their faces showed their offense at my statement. "I am the one prophesied! I am the one you have been waiting for! I am the one who will lead you into victory!" I paused to breathe and allow what I had said to sink in. "The only way to meet the Iyarian king in battle is through the Valley of Uthura! You know this! I know this! Any other battle is just a waste of time!"

I looked each one of them in the eye. They were not fully convinced, but somewhere deep down they thought it possible, and that was enough. It was enough to inspire their troops. We spent the next hour going over the plans, how we would utilize every aspect of the Valley against its owners. Once afternoon came, we were ready. The generals left to ready their troops for battle, many of which were already deployed to begin the construction of siege weapons. There was only one aspect of the battle I was confused about.

"What are Shiloh Snakes?" I asked Leraska, and a smile crept across his face.

"Would you like to see one?" he asked. I nodded and we left the room. He took me through a few corridors before entering a room with a single glass window, about four feet high but twelve feet wide. Below lay a massive, cube-like room, about the size of a football field and as tall as a six-story building. The ground was all dirt except for a small patch of thick green grass near the middle.

"I see nothing."

"Wait a moment." Then a door opened at the far left of the large room. A bull walked in and snorted, kicking dirt this way and that.

"That is a bull ..." I was confused.

"Patience." Leraska smiled.

The bull looked around and must have caught a glimpse of the thick green grass in the middle. It lazily walked toward the grass, but soon the ground began to shake. The bull bellowed and snorted violently, pointed his horns at nothingness and kicked up dirt. A moment later the dirt all around the bull erupted, and a long, dark tube, thick as an old oak tree, burst out and swallowed the bull whole. A moment later the thick black tube was burying itself underground again, and the last thing I saw was the shiny silver tip of its tail.

"Wh-whoa," I stammered.

"Would you like to see it closer?" Leraska asked.

"How close are we talking here?"

"Follow me." Leraska spun around and left the room. We walked down a hallway to an old, rickety elevator. Once we were both in, Leraska closed the doors and pushed one of the two buttons in the elevator, and we descended. Down and down we went for what seemed like thirty floors. Finally the elevator stopped with a clang, and Leraska opened the door. This time we walked into a large room, maybe forty by forty by forty feet. And the farthest wall was solid glass. Behind it lay a large, open cavern. There was nothing in it at the time, but soon the ground started to shake, and not a minute later the great beast came into view.

It wasn't quite black, but of the deepest brown could be before turning to black. Its entire body was covered in thousands of bonelike scales, each easily the size of my hand. They protruded from the creature and seemed to move as it did. This must have been how the creature burrowed through the ground. Its mouth was not like a normal snake's; this mouth was full of thousands of sharp points. Its eyes seemed deeply intelligent; this was no mere killing machine. It stared at me as if to ask, "Why you? Why should I serve you?" The creature was easily over thirty feet long, and at its tail was a most curious thing. It was tipped with what looked like razor-like metal fins. A mighty weapon indeed.

"How do you get that on the creature?" I asked Leraska.

"That is no piece of armor; it grows naturally upon the beast." Leraska smiled. "The Shiloh Snakes have long been our allies, but we do not ever go near them. They are highly intelligent but very hungry all the time; we call them during war, because they may feast upon the enemy and not upon us."

"Charming."

"It is best that when they are called, our armies retreat until they are finished; then we move in once more," Leraska warned.

"What is their downside? Every weapon has its downside."

"They cannot tolerate the sun. To call them up while the sun is still up would kill them in an instant." Leraska patted me on the back. "Happy now?"

"Oh yes, indeed," I replied and we headed back up to the main floor.

As long as everything went according to plan, our army would sustain minimal casualties, and our enemy's stronghold would at long last be broken. Leraska headed off to rest, while I headed back to my room to wait until morning. For that was when we would go to battle.

I did not expect to sleep, for I had not been granted any as of late, excluding of course being knocked unconscious by strange forces. As I sat upon the bed, though, a heaviness came over me; my eyelids crept closed, and sleep swept over me. I found myself in a beautifully decorated room. Gold. Silver. Ivory. There were two chairs carved with rich ivory and upholstered in plush fabrics interwoven with silver. A table was symmetrically placed between them. Its top was shaped like a bowl and filled with the clearest water. I found myself sitting in the closer chair, while the other stood empty. I touched the water, and it spun to life like a whirlpool. The water lifted to form a waterspout. Tiny lightning bolts thundered from the sides of it. Thousands heralded their fury, as the entire twister swirled with thunderous energy. A single flash blinded the entire room and from inside its white-hot light I saw for a split second a lone figure violently fighting. I expected to wake up at this point. I had had this dream once before, but the light faded, and I found myself staring once again at a dish filled with perfectly clear water.

"A curious thing, that water dish." A voice I recognized spoke. I looked up to see Haldel sitting across from me.

"You're dead!"

"Hmm, I guess I am." Haldel smiled, and I tried to stand and throw myself at him but could not. "Do not move, Joshua."

I tried to scream at him that my name was Josh, but my lips refused to obey me.

"Do not speak, *Joshua.* I have come to deliver a message to you. My words are not meant to anger you, but to advise. Joshua, you are ignorant of the fact that you have much more to offer." He paused. "The lie you have succumbed to has stolen your potential and blinded you to what you are genuinely looking for. You are unaware that this sense of 'leading,' this plan, is not what you believe it to be. You have fallen prey to the lie that I warned you about." He did not break eye contact once, and as much as I tried, I could not look away from him. Rage fueled me. I tried with all my might to move, but I could not budge, not even in the slightest.

"Joshua, you do not need to continue along the path you have chosen. The choice is yours. You have a chance to make a real difference." He paused. "Your version of truth lacks a pivotal foundation. You do not have all the facts." I could feel my body beginning to shake from the strain of trying to move. If I could only break free, I would tear him limb from limb. But I could not move, so I screamed at him with my eyes, willing him to see every ounce of hatred I felt for him. He simply looked back at me and breathed a deep sigh.

"Joshua, I am leaving you now, but *you* must make the choice. I leave it in your hands."

"*My name is Josh*!" I screamed but found myself, embarrassingly, in my quarters, screaming at the ceiling. Rage burst inside me. I threw myself out of bed, more than ready to reach the battlefield. I looked at my face in the shattered mirror, the broken pieces of my death-ridden face. Soon I would be free of this torment, soon I would be free of this pain, and soon I would reclaim my life. Today was the day; it was time. My time. My time to end this.

Chapter 34

The Great Battle

I breathed deep the smell of wildflowers and spring filling the air. The valley was beautiful. There were few trees, but the ground was lush with flowers and tall grasses. It was a pity to destroy such a work of art, for by the end of this day the ground would be stained with the blood of the enemy.

Their pride was even greater than I had assumed. At the far end of the valley, our destination, were foot soldiers, many foot soldiers, but nothing more. They felt their advantages were so great that they could easily vanquish us with foot soldiers alone. A foolish and rash decision, and as I looked upon my own amassed army, I smiled.

There were seven thousand foot soldiers, which nearly filled the valley floor from cliff to cliff, leaving only enough room for a thousand horsemen against the left cliff and a thousand against the right. Behind the foot soldiers were two thousand archers; the archers alone could win this battle for us, but I had more. I was not in the mood for losing, or even coming close to losing. Directly behind the archers were seven catapults, and behind those were seven more towers, pressed together to create a wall, keeping hidden one more surprise. Two thousand foot soldiers lay in wait, hidden from view, just in case of emergencies.

This would be my first advance, but the moment the sun had set, we would pull back hard, and the horn to call forth our vicious Shiloh Snakes would be sounded, summoning our winning strike. In a few moments most of their army would be destroyed, and then a second horn would be sounded, and two thousand night-men, the best archers in the Cahirian army, on the western ridge and the two thousand on the eastern ridge would come out from cover and rain down flaming death upon the last Iyarian troops.

I took one last deep breath of the beautiful valley before we destroyed it. I smiled to myself, because my plan was flawless; we were ready for any surprise, and nothing was going to stop us now. The horses anxiously pawed the ground, snorting and neighing as if all too ready for battle, but the Cahirians' eyes did not speak the same. Every warrior knew all too well what this valley brought. They knew it had ever brought only death and destruction. They knew it was not a winnable battle, and even the most ambitious generals had lost in this valley. That would make this day all the more great. I climbed upon a large rock to look over the valley and all of my troops.

"*Men*!" I called to them, and everyone's eyes focused on me. "Men! You fear this place because it has proven to be a curse to you, but this day the curse will be revoked." A low clamor rose. "Today your enemy prepares for an easy win, an arrogant victory. Do you see them? They stand in their pride, fewer in number yet filled with arrogance. They believe the victories of the past will continue into the future." I paused for a moment, making sure the whole of my army was focused. "*But today we change that*!" I shouted and received an enthusiastic cheer. "This day ends the stain of time and creates a new page in history.

Today is the day of *their* curse. *They* will lie crushed by your hand. *They* will be the ones brought to ruin this day." The army rose in a unified war cry, but still it was not enough. "Today is the day we show the enemy we will not back down. We will not be defeated. We will stand strong and fight to the end." Their cheer rose and it felt as though the air vibrated around me. "Stand tall, men. Be proud. And do not back down. No more running. No more hiding. It is *their* time to run. It is *their* time to hide. It is *their* time to *die*!" I screamed, and the army rose in such a battle cry, so loud, I could feel the earth shake. Their eyes thirsted for battle and victory. And it was enough!

Suddenly, the sound of a shofar blasted through the valley. I turned to the Iyarian masses. They began to march toward us. In perfect unison they marched, the setting sun reflecting from them. It was a magnificent army, disciplined beyond measure, but it would not be enough. A second sounding of the shofar resounded from the cliff walls, and the army began to run.

"*Ready*!" I called out to the men, not wishing them to waste any energy on fanciful shows of power. Then a third shofar blast shot through the valley, and the warriors stopped abruptly; the whole of their mass knelt down and dipped their heads. A curious battle tactic, indeed. But then I watched as a single warrior rose from the army and walked forward into the open space between armies. As the warrior did this, I realized that she was no warrior. Barefoot she walked out into the openness. Her beauty was intoxicating. Her white robes flowed in the gentle breeze, as did her glowing hair. She stopped midway between her army and ours. Then she began to sing in the language of the Iyarians. The sound was incredible, calming and peaceful. Then a second woman emerged from the army, and a third, and then hundreds stepped forward. Their voices combined into one powerful melody. It seemed to reverberate within me. My grip on my sword loosened, and that was when I realized that something was about to go horribly wrong.

All my troops on the front line were beginning to relax, yet their eyes seemed to grow wild and angry. It was as if they might turn on one another at any moment. Suddenly I caught a black flame out of the corner of my eye. I ducked to the right and spun around, trying to draw my sword, but Leraska had already dispatched the crazed Cahirian. Leraska's eyes were wide, and I knew I would lose him any moment, along with the rest of my foot soldiers. I wasn't sure how, but the music was turning the Cahirians against one another. Spinning quickly, I faced the archers.

"Take them out! Kill the singers!" I screamed, and they loosed a volley of arrows; black as night they soared over us. The Iyarian women did not budge but were quickly struck down by the thousands of arrows. A few remaining continued to sing, but a second volley of arrows finished them off. As I looked across the battlefield and saw the women slain on the ground, my stomach turned. Nothing about it seemed okay, let alone glorious. And yet it was a necessary part of war, a war I would not lose.

"Forward, march!" I called to the army, and the masses behind me obeyed. In unison the Iyarian foot soldiers rose and began their march toward us. We quickened our pace to a jog, as did they. Then we ran. I signaled the horsemen to press forward, pounding into the edges of the foot soldiers, and the Iyarians began to run. Nearing the middle, I signaled two of my men, who ran just in front of the front line. I might not have wings, but I sure could find a way to fly. When the front lines of both armies were near each other, the two men dropped down and clasped their arms together. I ran hard and fast, breaking the front line, and leapt into the basket made by their hands. With a quick snap, they sent me flying over the front line of the enemy. For a moment the Iyarians watched me sail through the air, sword drawn and flaming black.

I came crashing into the midst of the army and immediately started my own personal massacre. Arrows flew overhead, as the archers had been instructed to continually fire upon the back of the Iyarian army, cutting them down and keeping the arrows clear of the front line. No Iyarian could stand against me, and soon there was a twenty-foot swath around me. I looked up to the sun and saw it was nearly below the horizon. Soon this army would be decimated.

But that was when I heard it. Only Leraska, a sentry on one of the towers, and I had horns that could call the Shiloh Snakes, but I heard the sound of the horn bellow through the valley. I turned and saw Leraska's face; he was horrified. Not only would the Shiloh Snakes be killed, but the slaughter of Iyarian and Cahirian would be equally devastating. I looked to the tower but realized the sound had not come from that direction. I turned to the source of the sound and saw him standing there. Alone. Dignified. But no, that was impossible. He couldn't be. I mean ... I hadn't seen him in ... how long? My thoughts clashed inside me as I looked to the lone figure standing there. That familiar dark and silver hair. My eyes were unwilling to believe, and I stood stunned, looking at a man who looked very much like Harlstril. My confusion mounted, yet so did the trembling of the earth beneath me. I ran hard and fast to the eastern cliff. Hopefully, I would be safe there.

"*Retreat*!" I called out, but it was too late. The Shiloh Snakes burst out of the ground, killing everything in their path, but within moments they turned to dust, scales and flesh vanishing before my eyes. I watched as our greatest weapon vanished in a thick cloud of dust. A feeling of defeat swept over me, but then I remembered the battle was not over.

"*Attack*!" I screamed to the foot soldiers. "*Fire*!" I called to the archers and catapults. A barrage slammed into the enemy, and I reentered the battle. In only a few minutes, the sun would be gone.

As soon as the sun set, I blew my second horn, calling the night-men to emerge and rain death upon the valley. Arrows lit with flame from above and came crashing down; my army cheered, as victory was within our grasp. But once again I soon realized it would not be that easy. Light began to emanate from the east and west cliffs.

"*Watch out*!" I screamed to the night-men, but it was too late. Iyarians burst out and attacked. How could they have known? In all the attacks upon the valley, the Iyarians had never thought to use the cliffs to their advantage! I would not have my own advantage turned on me, though. I turned to the towers and signaled the men to head up on the cliffs. The two thousand reserve troops split in two and went up to the cliff tops. I watched as the night went on and numbers on both sides fell, evenly dropping, until finally I heard a great crash from behind me. The last of my towers fell onto the last of my catapults.

"Shoot him!" I called to the last archer standing, and he aimed his bow at the enemy's catapult operator above, picking him off the top of the cliff. An Iyarian swooped in and cleaved my archer, but only moments before I drove my sword through him. Leraska had been lost only an hour earlier, saving my life. And now I stood alone on my battlefield of victory.

I dropped to my knees. We had taken the valley, but at what cost? I had lost thousands of warriors, all of the generals were dead, and I alone was left. Footsteps took me from my thoughts. I jumped to my feet and pointed my sword toward the approaching steps. Rage again filled me, unquenchable rage; the black flame on my sword seemed to burst into greater life. The battle was not won just yet, but this death would make it feel like a true victory. I did not know how it was possible, but for someone who has died a thousand times, what was once more?

"Last chance, Joshua." Haldel offered his hand to me. "I can show you the truth."

"My name," I snapped, "is Josh!"

Chapter 35

A Fight, a Friend, a Story

He would die! He would die for the trail of pain he had caused. My muscles tensed. Our eyes locked. The fog began to rise around us in the wreckage of the battlefield. Haldel's piercing eyes tried to penetrate my soul, but he would be disappointed; I would not be manipulated by those eyes anymore. I had sworn to myself that I would win this battle, and win it I would. There was no backing down. Not even death would stop me. There was no "trying," no "doing my best"; there was Haldel, and there was me. And I would *not* lose. This time, on this night, I would do as I had said I would.

Haldel and I battled as if the very fate of time and space hung upon the outcome of this fight—and who knows? Maybe it did. But our skill was matched and our wills were equal. We fought with swords, we fought with words, but in the end fate weighed on my side. With the help of the sun, I disarmed Haldel, and he was finally at my mercy. With his body pressed hard against the rock face, I raised my fist. Only a moment left before his death, a few seconds, and it would all be over. I would finally end the years of pain! All those years of pain would come to an end right *now*!

Time slowed. The world around seemed to cease to exist. My brain started to whirl, thoughts passing through at a million miles a second.

All those years of pain? Did I even know what that meant anymore? Did I even know ...? It was that moment that shattered my reality. The torment. The flashes. That single moment changed everything. It felt like reliving my entire life in an instant. And then it stopped, and there I was, standing in the valley, Haldel in my grasp, my heart racing, deeply confused.

"Do what you have come to do." Haldel spoke with no fear in his voice. I let my fist go.

"*Nooooo!*" The scream drew my attention, and my fist drove into the rock face behind Haldel. I spun around to see where the voice had come from, but immediately I knew the answer. I recalled the night Lasnek had stolen me away. I recalled the foolish moment when I had stood and cried out for Haldel's life. I had saved his life that night, and now I was here to end it. But why, why was I doing this?

A flash of my parents, and I remembered: his kind had murdered my parents, but something wasn't right, something didn't fit. I had seen it clearly, but deep within I did not believe it to be true. My mind seemed to war with itself, tearing me this way and that.

I recalled the night Charlie died, the gathering around the bonfire. I remembered the sinister smile on Zanos's face. If the Cahirians were so good, why smile at such horror? Nothing seemed to make sense, nothing seemed to fit. An Iyarian murdered my parents; a Cahirian enjoyed the pain of others. What was I supposed to believe? Where was I supposed to stand? My grip on Haldel slowly loosened, and I stepped back, tears streaming down my face. I collapsed to the ground, wishing I could just know what to do, where to stand, whom to believe.

Someone was lying, everyone was lying. But how was I to know? Suddenly I felt Haldel's hand on my shoulder, and I brusquely shrugged it off.

"Do not touch me!" He quickly removed his hand.

"Are you ready to see the truth?" Haldel asked kindly.

"I do not trust your words."

"I know," Haldel replied sadly.

"Then how can you tell me the truth?" I looked up into his eyes. "I would not believe it, even if it were."

"I will not tell you. I will *show* you." Haldel's eyes shed a single tear, and it rolled slowly down his cheek. "I will let your eyes see what is true and real, and then I will leave the choice in your hands."

"What must I do?" I asked, watching as the tear hung on the edge of his jaw, ready to fall.

"Just don't move." Haldel smiled, and the tear fell gracefully to the ground, shimmering in the sunlight. The tear struck the ground, and I knew in that moment that this was no normal tear. A swirl of light emanated from where it landed; the light swirled wider and wider until it had created a circle wide enough to surround Haldel and me. The light brightened and for a moment I was blinded, but when my vision returned, we were no longer in the valley but in a room I well recognized. I stood and looked around at the great pillars that towered above me, the pictures on the walls. I recalled all the happy moments there that made me smile; after such death and pain, something happy was welcome. Finally my eyes rested upon the magnificent Eternity Door, those two towering gold and silver doors shining in all their majestic glory. The word *Eternity*, or *Teralla*, written in the dialect of the Cahirians, still spanned them both. A familiar place, a safe place, somewhere I knew and recognized. A sense of ease overtook me.

I turned and stood face-to-face with Haldel, and I realized then that I would finally see beyond those great and glorious doors. I breathed deeply and readied myself. Nearly seven years I had waited for the moment I could walk through those doors. And finally I would know what lay beyond them.

Chapter 36

The Horror of the Truth

"Do you remember The Curator?"

"Mr. Curry," I corrected him. Haldel smiled in acquiescence.

"Indeed. Do you remember when 'Mr. Curry' told you never to go through the Eternity Door?"

"Yes. I have always wanted to know what lies beyond it."

"Well, today you will see the world beyond those majestic doors." Haldel did not smile as he spoke; nor did his tone convey anything glorious about the doors. "I warn you: what your eyes will behold beyond those doors, you will never forget. It will haunt you till the day you die."

"I must know," I replied.

"First, I want you to see something else." Haldel walked and I followed. We approached a picture on the wall, a picture of a couple walking hand in hand in the park. The woman was laughing, and their life seemed perfect. "Would you like to see the story of this picture, or just the still moment of happiness?"

"Show me," I replied, and immediately the picture came to life. The couple walked along the path, laughing and flirting and having fun, but then a Cahirian crept up behind the man and whispered something in his ear. A smile inched across the man's face. Not a kind smile, but something darker. He spun the woman around and gripped her tightly. After a moment of shock, she laughed, thinking this was a new game. The man pressed her against a tree and moved to kiss her, but the woman shook her head. The man moved in anyway, pressing his face against hers. This was no kiss of love; he was stealing what was not granted him. Slowly the man's hand slid up her side, and the woman's eyes widened. The picture froze in that moment.

"What happened?" I looked at Haldel.

"Happiness is a moment, a moment to be enjoyed. It is a blessing, a gift to be given, never stolen. Life is full of happy moments, but what we can see is often temporary. What is hidden in dark places often echoes into eternity."

Haldel halted before another picture: a group of teenagers laughing and playing on a boardwalk above a sandy beach.

"Would you like to see what happened with this group?" Haldel asked.

"Not really." I was being honest. The still picture made me feel good, but I suspected that the full progression would be less pleasant. Nevertheless, I knew that deep down I had to know. "But I will anyway."

The picture came to life, and the group tossed a football around. The girls laughed and cheered the boys on; the boys showed off. But then a small Cahirian slipped into the group. He seemed no bigger that a cat, and he leapt from shoulder to shoulder, whispering in ears.

A small boy walked into the picture. His glasses were perched crookedly on his nose. His clothing wasn't all that odd, but it seemed older and faded, probably hand-me-downs or items from a secondhand store. The boy called to the group and raised his hands, ready to catch the ball, wanting to join the fun, probably wanting to fit in. But one of the jocks stepped out from the group and, with one quick shove, sent the boy flying off the boardwalk into the sand. He quickly stood, trying to laugh it off, but the pain was apparent in his face. The guys and girls pointed and laughed. Slowly the little boy turned and walked away.

One of the girls stepped out and yelled at the rest of the group, her emerald eyes glaring. The group laughed and walked away, but the girl jogged off in the direction of the boy. With that the picture froze, and Haldel looked at me.

"Do not call them what you are about to call them," Haldel scolded my very thoughts. "They all have their own stories, and there are always deeper hurts in those who cause pain. Although that is never an excuse."

With that Haldel walked to the next picture. It was of a boy staring at himself in a mirror. His eyes seemed full of joy and goodness. I realized that it was the boy from the boardwalk, with his worn clothes. I sighed in relief that he was okay. He had stood strong despite the cruel attitudes of his peers.

Without my permission, the picture came to life. As the boy smiled into the mirror, another face took his place. A Cahirian face filled the mirror, only for a moment, and then was gone. The boy's eyes filled with tears. He walked across the room and climbed onto a chair. Slowly the boy slipped a noose around his neck and took a deep breath, tears streaming down his face. The picture froze.

"What happened to him?" I asked.

"The unveiling of truth is not always what we hope." Haldel avoided a direct answer, as he walked to the final picture. As we stepped in front of it, I looked into the emerald eyes of the girl on the boardwalk. Something about the girl was strangely familiar, but I could not place it.

"This is the last picture. Are you ready?" Haldel asked.

"I do not want to see it." I wasn't sure I could bear much more.

"That is good." Haldel smiled slightly. "Anyone who wants to see these stories is not a very good person."

I nodded, agreeing to watch what I must. The picture began to move. An older man walked into the hall and pointed up the stairs. The girl smiled and headed up them quickly. She skipped down the hallway and threw open the door at the end but immediately screamed and fell to her knees crying. In the shadows of the room, a motionless figure could be seen, hanging from a noose. A man rushed past her into the room and tried to get the boy free, but I had seen death enough times to know it was too late.

Then a Cahirian walked up behind the girl. Kneeling beside her he began to whisper. Her face turned cold and bitter. She opened her eyes and spoke a single icy sentence, and immediately the Cahirian stepped back. Rage filled his face as he stormed away, before the picture froze again.

"Each of these 'happy' moments was a pivotal moment. Each one, a moment of choice. A choice that would send ripples into eternity, that would change the course of lives. Simple choices are made every day, and yet there are consequences that are eternal." Haldel's voice was without humor. He spoke the truth, and deep within me I believed him.

"What now?" I asked.

"It is time." Haldel's voice was pained. "Joshua, you have known life in only one realm. Although you have seen things most mortals could never imagine, you still have not seen the life that exists after death. You were told you fought for the freedom of mankind, but you were not told the consequences of the freedom." Haldel paused for a moment.

"Mr. Curry was not altogether wrong. In every good lie there is much truth. You were indeed fighting for mankind's freedom, but you were not freeing slaves. In fact, in all honesty, you were creating them. A servant chooses willingly to be a servant. He offers his life to someone of his own accord, whereas a slave is taken involuntarily and often is unaware of what is truly going on until it is too late. The easiest way to create a slave is to offer a person great freedom." Haldel's eyes burned into mine. "Free a person from servanthood, and make him or her a slave." He paused a took a deep breath. "Now you will see where those you've 'helped' are headed."

I did not reply; I simply followed him to the glorious gold and silver Eternity Door. Haldel ran his hand over the lock, and I heard a loud click. With a flick of his wrist the door swung slowly open, and all I could see was blackness, like a thick liquid veil. Haldel placed his hand on my shoulder. This time I did not fight him. Slowly we stepped through the black veil.

Immediately my eyes shut, for the sheer heat threatened to burn them, but slowly I opened them again. The heat was nearly unbearable, but worse than the heat was the smell. Burning flesh, excrement, vomit, and other smells, unlike any I had ever smelled. Worse than the stench was the darkness. There was no light other than the ominous red glow of fires scattered about. Dark enough to be depressing, light enough to see everyone's depression. And that was far beyond any other pain I could imagine. To see the pain of an uncountable number of people turned my stomach. I wanted to run, but I could not.

Haldel kept his hand on my shoulder and ushered me forward. My heart sank as I saw what I should have suspected would be here. Kneeling on the ground about twenty feet in front of me was Charlie, the young boy I had seen die. Surrounding him were three Cahirians, torturing him and laughing at his pain and cries for mercy. I stepped forward, ready to slay them all, when my vision went blurry and I fell backward.

I came to on the floor on the other side of the Eternity Door, back in the hall of pictures. I could still smell the horrors on my clothing. Rage filled me as I remembered Charlie. It was not fair. It was not right. He was a good kid.

"Why him?" I screamed at Haldel. "What did he do? Nothing. He did *nothing*. I was there when he died; he didn't even what to be in that place. Why should he suffer?"

"Every choice, no matter how small, yields eternal consequences." Haldel's eyes filled with tears. "I am sorry, Joshua, but the choices he made sealed his fate."

"But that is not fair!"

"Not fair?" Haldel asked, and I could tell he wanted to say more but held his tongue. "There is more you must see."

"No," I replied, knowing I couldn't handle anything else.

"Do not be afraid. The worst is over." We walked again toward the Eternity Door but this time stopped well before it. Haldel motioned to the picture on the left. Suddenly the picture was much more sinister. A man and a woman walked, hand in hand, toward the open Eternity Door.

"These two had no idea what they were heading into. They walked blind and ignorant of the truth. This remains one of Mr. Curry's favorite pictures, for if deception can blind humanity, they will walk blindly into the darkness."

Then he pointed to the picture on the right. It was a beautiful garden with a great tree in the middle. The fruit on the tree was of various colors and shapes. It looked delicious. Even the picture made my mouth water.

"And this is his favorite. For this was the first victory. The fruit of this tree holds the knowledge of all things. It was this tree that gave humanity the ability to choose. The tree itself was not evil in any way. But free will was humanity's greatest gift and greatest weakness. And here, at this tree, Mr. Curry had his victory, turning humanity against itself. This is where it all began for your kind."

"What of my parents?" I asked coldly. I was convinced that Mr. Curry and the Cahirians were not what they had claimed, but that still did not absolve the angels, for one of them had murdered my parents.

"I cannot answer that question." Haldel's voice seemed honest. "I do not know what happened with your parents. I am sorry they died. I am sorry they died in the way they did. But I will tell you this: things are not what they seem." He paused and smiled a little. "But that is for you to discover, and when you are ready, you will know the truth."

"So what happens now?" I asked, confused as to where to go or what to do.

"There is one last thing you must see, and then the journey is yours," Haldel said and walked back to where we had first arrived in the room. Once we were there again, the light grew and swirled around us. A moment later, we stood once again on the valley floor.

Chapter 37

The Betrayer

"Joshua." Haldel placed his hand on my shoulder.

"Josh," I corrected him. Not in anger, just a simple correction.

"No." His stern eyes burned into mine. "Your name is Joshua, it has always been Joshua, and it bears greatness. 'Josh' is weak and fake and removed from the name your parents bestowed upon you. 'Josh' is a lie, a deception meant only to confuse your identity." Haldel paused and smiled. "You, Joshua, are none of these things, and one day you will understand why you are not Josh, but indeed Joshua Williams."

I didn't like being called Joshua, but after a mini-motivational speech like that, who could deny him? I wasn't entirely convinced, but he reminded me of Harlstril, and as much pain as the latter's lack of presence had brought me, he was always like a father to me.

"Haldel?" I asked.

"Yes?"

"Why did the Cahirian back away from the green-eyed girl? What did she say?"

"I am not sure what she said; it could have been many things, but that girl is a fighter. Her picture might hang in the Eternity

Room, but I believe that ..." He thought for a moment. "That egg was counted before it hatched?" I smiled, realizing he wasn't sure if he was using the saying right. "She is tough, but not tough enough. She was winning the battle but since meeting you has been failing and falling at every turn."

"Me?" I asked, confused. She looked familiar, yes, but I couldn't place her.

"Do you not remember the castle?" Haldel looked confused. "The green-eyed girl, her uncle, and Retrasla the beast? Any of those ringing any bells?"

"Well, of course, but ..." I paused. "But it can't be. I mean, they were ... they were just scenarios, tests. They were ... fake?" By the time I was finished, I knew it wasn't true.

"It figures as much," Haldel confirmed my suspicion. "Joshua, each and every one of the 'scenarios' was very real. Each and every one of them has affected the people you met."

I thought back to the battle with the Hiltezion. I had slain Haldel; clearly that one could not have been real, or Haldel wouldn't be here speaking to me right now.

"What about when I 'killed' you?" I asked.

"Ah yes, a sad day that was indeed," Haldel replied, and I could see the hurt in his eyes. "How I became the strange monster I cannot tell you; that is a mystery beyond me."

"Sorry," I replied, feeling a little bad. "But how are you here, then?"

"Unlike you, we Iyarians and Cahirians do not actually die. We can be vanquished, but we come back quite quickly." He paused and seemed to read my next question. "Yes, Joshua, I have died a thousand times trying to rescue you."

There was nothing I could say to that. I still did not entirely trust him, but I felt deep down that he was good.

"The time will come for you to find the girl, but right now there is a more pressing matter."

"But how will I find her?" I asked. "I know nothing about her."

"In time. Do not worry yourself with how. The more pressing matter right now is the deception that is still going on."

"What else?" I asked, getting frustrated with all this information.

"When was the last time you saw Haslo?" This question burned me. Rage came to the surface at his accusation.

"What do you mean?" I seethed.

"Please. Just answer the question," Haldel replied calmly.

"I don't know."

"Think," he demanded. "It is important."

I reluctantly thought back over the last week and a bit, finally coming to the day I was inducted. I looked down at my armor, realizing it was only just before I'd received it that he had slipped away.

"Remove it," Haldel said.

"What?"

"Remove the armor." Haldel's voice was stern.

"Why?"

"Trust me," he replied in a soft voice.

"I do not." I was sad that this was still true.

"Then give me just a moment of your trust," he pleaded. "I have been honest with you thus far."

Slowly, keeping my eyes on Haldel, I released the clamps on the armor. They unclipped easily, and I began to pull the armor apart. And it slammed shut. I was suddenly angry. I might not trust Haldel, but I sure wasn't about to keep wearing armor that had a mind of its own. I grabbed the armor and tore it open. It fought hard and seemed to clamp to my skin. The more I pulled it, the more it seemed to tear my skin apart.

"Do not give in, Joshua!" Haldel encouraged me.

I heaved the armor, and it heaved back. I'm sure it looked humorous, but it sure didn't feel that way. Finally I ripped the armor free and tossed it away. It quickly snapped shut and reclamped itself. Before they could fight back, I tore the gloves and boots off and tossed them aside. The moment all my armor was removed, I felt a great weight overwhelm me. My limbs were weak, and I fell to my knees. My breathing was labored, and my eyelids tried to shut. Then, as if all of this weren't enough, my armor began to rattle and shake. The largest part rolled over, breastplate facing the sky. Then the gloves and boots slid into place, as if there were an invisible body putting them on. Things only got weirder from there. The invisible body became very visible. Getting to his feet, Haslo looked down at me.

"You have been deceived, Josh," Haslo stated.

"No, Joshua. You have done the right thing," Haldel encouraged me.

"No, Josh. He has tricked you, with smoke and mirrors." Haslo pointed at Haldel. "He has stolen your very strength."

"Haldel?" I questioned.

"Joshua, your *strength* has not been removed. Haslo lived within you, fueling your body, ridding you of a need for sleep, and your body suffered for it. Death became imprinted on your face, but already I see life filling your skin once more. The 'strength' that has been taken from you will soon be replaced by the true strength that already lies within you. And that will be unlike anything you have ever experienced." Haldel did not seem to be trying to tempt me, but I wanted to hear Haslo's reply.

"Haslo?" I looked at him and waited. For a moment he simply stared at me. Finally, a look of distaste came over his face.

"Weak, Josh," he mocked. "Clearly, you will see only what you want to see. And if that is so, then I guess I'll just need to remove you." He drew his sword the color of night, and black flames burst from the blade.

I did not expect that from him. Haslo had been my friend; we had always been friends. I realized then that everything I knew had been a lie, and that my closest friend in the world was about to kill me. But I would not die on my knees. I saw my sword lying on the ground just behind Haslo. If I could reach it, I stood a chance. My body shook, and my limbs felt like Jell-O, but I rose anyway, a new resolve burning within me. Haslo glared into my eyes.

"Ready to die, Josh?"

"My name ..." I breathed deep. "Is Joshua!" The fire of my identity blazed through me; I held my chin high and proud. "I have beaten you many times before you became my source of power. I stand here unafraid. So bring it!" With that I rushed forward, but my limbs were unfamiliar and sluggish. I faked to the left around Haslo as he swung. Narrowly missing his blade, I rolled and tried to reach my blade, but before I could, Haslo stood with it in his hands.

"Beautiful craftsmanship," Haslo mocked, but a memory sprang up in my mind of how Lasnek had once tried to take Haldel's blade. Immediately my sword burned incandescent and scorched through Haslo's gloves. He screamed and dropped the blade, but before it touched the ground, the hilt was in my hands, and I stood to meet him. Our swords connected, and the clatter rang out in the still valley. For a moment my determination seemed like it might be enough, but seconds later my body weakened again, and Haslo pushed me back, slamming my sword again and again, until my back was against the cliff wall and I crumpled to the ground. He could have killed me there, but he took a moment to gloat in his victory, arrogantly flipping his sword back and forth as he spoke.

"Now you will die, just like your mother died, weak, on her knees, and weeping." My heart started to race. "She didn't even fight. Just weak ..." I felt my teeth clench, as he spoke against those I loved. He smiled as he watched the pain twist my face. "Just like your father, who couldn't even protect your mother." The ivory handle of my sword began to bite into my hand; I felt as though I might crush it at any moment. "Your mother was weak." My face started to burn. "Your father was weak." The corners of my eyes tightened. "And just like them ... you will die, on your knees, weak, helpless, and useless!"

Haslo eyed me, taking in my final moments of pain, but what he did not know was that something had sparked to life inside me. What he did not see was the strength of my love for my parents. What he did not expect was the new form of power that caused me to snap to my feet. The feeling was overwhelming. I had never felt anything like it before. It was almost like the power anger had fed me, but it was pure, filled with life and truth. Balance and control came to me, heat shot through my arm, and for a moment my sword was engulfed in black flames; but then a heat far beyond that forced its way up my arm, and in that instant the black flame was forced off the tip, and white flames enveloped the entire blade. My strength was restored, filling every part of me with its warmth. Haslo's eyes widened in fear, but only for only a moment, before his pride took over and he smiled arrogantly back at me.

"My mother was strong," I shouted at him, "just like my father." I glared at Haslo. "And just as they did, I know true strength." Then I smiled at him. "You will never possess the strength they had; you will never even imagine it. My parents died proud and strong, where you will die ashamed, with only your hatred to comfort you!" I let the thought settle with him before I spoke again. "Prepare to die, Haslo."

"You are a fool, Josh." He backed up and tossed his sword to the side, but this was not a sign of surrender, for immediately his body began to morph and grow. Every part of his body bubbled and grew; the armor he now wore became a part of his body, and the spikes along the back grew to great length. Curled horns grew out of the sides of his head, and a tail shot out from his lower back. When it all finally stopped, Haslo stood thirty feet tall, and his newfound wings spanned sixty feet fully outstretched. I knew this creature; I knew this creature all too well.

A low laugh rolled out of its stomach, and fear took me over. I could not defeat this creature. I had tried once before and failed. For this was the beast in the caves of the Chunya. Suddenly everything made sense. Haslo had never been captured by the creature, for he *was* the creature. The spike that had pierced the creature's back? Haslo's injury had conveniently matched it. Dersolo's screams had come when he realized a truth I could not. Despair overwhelmed me. I was beaten and would leave this world with a mile-long laundry list of wrongdoings. I would join Charlie soon enough.

"*No!*" I spoke aloud to make sure I understood. I might die here today, I might join Charlie within the hour, but I would not give up so easily. "I will die fighting!"

I raised my sword, for the last time. I looked into the eyes of Haslo, those burning, angry eyes. I readied myself and ran forward, chin raised high as I entered the fight. But everything went black as I was broadsided by the massive silver spade at the end of Haslo's tail.

Chapter 38

The Destiny

My eyes slowly opened. Everything around me seemed so bright. I had not expected to wake up to something like this. Where were the fire, the smell, the fear, and the darkness? Maybe Mr. Curry was about to walk in and escort me to my eternity.

"You are safe, Joshua," came the unexpected voice of Haldel.

"How?" I asked.

"Haslo will be quite angry with me, but it was not your time to die," he replied.

"Thanks?" I replied, unsure of how to take his comment. I sat up slowly, pushing the soft, white blankets off of me and feeling the pain throughout my body. I was probably one giant bruise from Haslo's tail. Even through the pain, something felt good and right. I felt alive, free.

"You are most welcome." Haldel smiled. "There are matters of great importance that you must attend to before you go slipping into the next life. For now, your goal is to repair the damage you have caused." My eyes fell as I began to go over all my actions. Although I still was not sure exactly what kind of damage I had caused, I had a sinking feeling I would start to know soon enough.

"And what about *them*?" I thought of the Cahirians. "Won't they want revenge for my betrayal?"

"Oh yes," he replied, instilling no confidence in me. "But, Joshua, I have a gift for you, a gift that will help you along your way. I have waited many years to give you this." He produced a long, thin, white-and-silver box and pulled out *my sword*.

"Um." I felt a little confused.

"Actually, this is *my* dagger, and you have merely been holding it for me, but it is far more than just a dagger."

"Yeah, it's a growing dagger."

"Humorous." Haldel smiled.

He placed the sword in my hands, and it started to glow and shake. I gripped it hard with both hands but soon could not hold onto it. Setting the sword on the bed, I watched as bands of pure white light spiraled around it. Soon it began to shrink and morph. The ivory hilt turned into a royal-blue ribbon, and the blade became the spine of a book, which quickly filled with pages. Then the light dimmed. Before me was a thick book, with a shiny silver cover and a blue ribbon. On the front of the book were the same seven words that had been on the blade of the sword.

"What does it say?" I asked, fingering the strange letters.

"It is a representation of who you are," Haldel replied.

"And that means?" I pressed.

"When you discover who you are, the words will become apparent to you."

"And the book?" I opened it and leafed through. "What is it about?"

"It's a history of the world. Full of guidance and tips that you may find very helpful. You would be wise to study this as you have studied the art of war." He smiled and put his hand on my shoulder. “For now, I leave you with one final piece of advice. All you will need to do is put your left foot in front of your right, and you’ll know what to do.”

The End

About the Author

Jonathon Wilkins has been a writer since he was thirteen years old. He is the youngest of five and the son of a firefighter and a stay-at-home mom. *War Child* is his first full-length novel. He has lived in a bus, a car, and random strangers' homes, and he currently lives in a small house in the country in central Ontario.

CPSIA information can be obtained at www.ICGtesting.com
Printed in the USA
BVOW05s0737200715

409357BV00001B/6/P

9 781458 215338